For Asher and Nolan

&

Alana, Madelyn, and Jillian

&

Oliver and Calvin

With thanks to Eli Bishko for naming Ma Yaklin's dog.

Dearest Reader,

If flowers aren't your thing and you've never heard of a peony, never fear! Sloane and Amelia find themselves in the same situation. Neither one of them cares much about the flower competition they find themselves entangled in. For them, it's nothing but a bunch of nonsense that keeps getting in the way of the real mysteries: Who kidnapped Bootleggin' Ma Yaklin's dog, Eli, almost a hundred years ago? And what happened to two million dollars that went missing around the same time? To untangle those mysteries, however, they'll have to push their way past that nonsense created by the adults around them. To help you keep everyone straight, both past and present, here is a guide to all you will encounter:

Present Workers, Guests, Four-Legged Friends, and Suspects of Tangle Glen

Hayden Boening-Bradley..president of the Ohio
Peony Enthusiasts Club

Shakespeare Wikander...............................manager of Tangle Glen
and a budding magician

Zahra Abu-Absi....................................head chef at Tangle Glen

Sergeant Pepper Arroyo........................gardener at Tangle Glen

Sherwood Lindsay...................................owner of Tangle Glen

Chiave..........................Sherwood Lindsay's super-snorfing dog

Baker..a fancy grower of peonies

Kuneman.............................an even fancier grower of peonies

1932 Bootleggers and Four-Legged Friends

Anderson Lindsay.........................bootlegger and grandfather
to Sherwood Lindsay

Jacqueline "Ma" Yaklin..................a bootlegger of the 1920s and '30s

Two Thumbs Lundquist..............a bootlegger and rival of Ma Yaklin's

Eli...Ma Yaklin's bloodhound

Elizabeth..................................Anderson Lindsay's bloodhound

Prologue
A Vacation Gone Wrong

Rain spattered thirteen-year-old Sloane Osburn's face as she climbed through the attic window. The wooden frame still felt soft from last night's downpour. The clouds had taken a break for a while, but now they were rested and ready to go again, right when Sloane needed clear, calm weather to keep from plummeting to her death. Sloane slid carefully on her bottom down the wet, sloping roof of the three-story mansion and toward a probably spattery death below.

Definitely toward a bone-cracking, skull-splitting drop to the ground.

I knew it, Sloane thought glumly as she dug her nails into the cracks between the slate shingles. *I knew it.*

She'd known no good would come of spending a long weekend away from home.

Even if it meant getting to stay in a hundred-year-old mansion that had once belonged to a bootlegging gangster.

And solving a mystery that would bring more subscribers to the YouTube channel she shared with her friend Amelia.

No, Sloane had known that spending a night anywhere other than her bed back in Wauseon would lead to bad luck somehow.

1

Sleepovers always had that effect on her, stealing important parts of her life. As if a thief lurked in the night, waiting for Sloane to turn her back so it could pounce and snatch away whatever was most precious to her.

She'd been worried that meant her dad.

Turns out, it meant her life.

"Careful! Careful!" Amelia called from the oval-shaped attic window out of which Sloane had just escaped.

"That's not helping, Amelia!" Sloane clenched her teeth as the wind smacked her long black ponytail into her eyes, blinding her. Then it playfully changed directions and pushed at her back as though this was all a fun game.

At least the roof's broken, mossy shingles snagged her shorts, slowing her downward slide.

A bit.

A very little bit.

Hopefully enough of a bit.

"Sloane!" Amelia squeaked in terror, gripping the splintered frame around the attic window. "Sloane, don't die!"

Sloane's shorts tore free from the old, crumbling slate tiles. Instantly, she picked up speed on the slick rooftop, causing her to race faster and faster toward the abyss beyond the rain gutter. Just as she thought she was going to have to send Amelia a note from the afterlife saying, *Whoops! Sorry!* her right foot hit the gutter's metal trough and sunk down into the soggy mess of old leaves still stuck there from last autumn.

Whew! Sloane's left foot joined her right foot in the gunk. Her knees bent, allowing her bottom to come to a gentle stop. Before

Sloane could sigh in relief, she made the mistake of looking down.

It was a long way to the ground.

Three stories, to be exact.

Long enough to make her very, *very* grateful for the rain gutter. Even if it was now filling her shoes up with water.

Soggy socks and ruined shoes were still better than ending up as a soggy, ruined mess yourself.

Sloane turned back around to find Amelia still peering anxiously out the window, her red curls bushing out around a 1920s-style flapper headband made of sequins and feathers. Calling up to her friend, Sloane said, "I survived!"

"Oh, good!" Amelia's very freckled face relaxed.

Then, that face disappeared with a shriek as Amelia was yanked backward, into the attic.

"Amelia!" Sloane cried, twisting around to try to crawl back up the slick shingles to help her friend. "Amelia, don't you dare die, either!"

Barking covered whatever Amelia might have yelled back. Inside the murky gloom of the attic, Amelia and her attacker merged together into a misshapen beast with too many elbows and twirling backs—as well as the teeth and tail of a very frightened bloodhound.

"OW!" someone screamed. Whether it was Amelia or their pursuer, Sloane didn't know.

She just knew that she'd been right.

"AMELIA!" she shrieked again.

But her friend didn't answer her.

Instead, a dog jumped out of the window.

To hurtle straight toward Sloane.

With enough speed to knock them both over the side of the building onto the patio stones three stories below.

When they did, Sloane's shoes wouldn't be the only soggy mess.

1

Earlier That Week...

Technically, Sloane's Granny Kitty and Granny Pearl were to blame for the chain of events that left their granddaughter sliding toward her doom.

It was the first day of summer vacation and the grannies had agreed to help Sloane and Amelia with the YouTube movie they were making for their newly formed detective agency, Osburn and Miller-Poe Detective Agency. Building on their recent success in finding the Hoäl Jewels that had disappeared from town over 125 years ago, their detective agency focused on long-forgotten crimes.

Sort of like cold-case files for robbers rather than murderers.

As they researched their cases, Sloane and Amelia also put together documentary films about their investigations. Their YouTube channel now had close to a thousand subscribers, thanks to the publicity they'd gotten a few weeks earlier from finding the Long-Lost Hoäl Jewels (or possibly the Cursed Hoäl Jewels, depending on Amelia's mood). However, that was down from slightly *over* a thousand subscribers just a week ago.

Possibly because Sloane and Amelia weren't having very much success in solving their latest case: The Mysterious Incident of the Robbed Bank.

A bank robbery might sound interesting, but this one happened back in 1952. So, there weren't very many people around who could tell them anything about it. Belinda Gomez, their favorite librarian at the Wauseon Public Library, was on vacation in the Poconos with her dog, Bunny. The board of the Fulton County Historical Society was mildly miffed at Sloane and Amelia for causing them a great deal of extra paperwork. While they weren't *technically* banned from the museum, both girls felt it wise to let things cool down a bit before they asked anyone there for help.

That left Sloane and Amelia with the internet.

Which was very helpful when you wanted to watch funny videos. But less helpful when you needed to research a seventy-year-old cold case.

As a result, Osburn and Miller-Poe Detective Agency hadn't managed to do a whole lot of successful investigating.

Which gave them even less to film.

With the result that their YouTube subscribers were dropping like flies.

Since they didn't have anything else to show, Amelia had decided to film some reenactments of the 1952 bank robbery. Only, the bank wouldn't let them inside. (Possibly because Amelia enthusiastically mentioned blowing up the bank vault just like the robbers had.) Then they tried using the post office since it looked a bit like an old-timey bank, but the postal workers had chased them away too. (Probably because Amelia had once again brought up the possibility of dynamite.)

Now they were left with filming what it *might* have looked like *if* the bank robbers had escaped by train. (There was absolutely no evidence that the bank robbers had done so. However, the Wauseon Train Depot was open to the public and looked satisfyingly old-timey too. Sometimes, you just had to make the best of what you had.)

Sloane's two grannies stood on the old wooden train platform beneath the hot June sun. In spite of the heat, they both wore heavy wool overcoats, heels, purses, and wide-brimmed, veiled hats.

"Aaaaand . . . action!" Amelia cried, snapping together a black-and-white film clapboard in front of her phone, clipped to a tripod.

As Amelia hopped up into her director's chair to squint at the screen on her phone, Sloane marched forward. She wore an old-fashioned belted raincoat with its collar turned up to half cover her face. The other half of her face was mostly hidden by a fedora pulled low so that Sloane could barely peer out from underneath it.

Carrying a battered leather briefcase, she walked past Granny Kitty and Granny Pearl. Looking as suspicious as she possibly could (which wasn't very), Sloane headed toward the depot's long brick-and-stone building with its sloping roof. She went up to the ticket counter and pretended to pay for a ticket. Fake ticket clutched in her hand, she joined her grannies to wait for a train that had come and gone more than seventy years ago. Making Sloane very late.

"CUT!" Amelia shrieked.

With a gasp, both Granny Kitty and Granny Pearl shrugged off their coats and hats. Beneath, they wore very bright, very flowered tracksuits and gold fanny packs. Out of these, they pulled handheld fans, which they turned on their sweaty necks and foreheads.

"Goodness!" Granny Kitty panted. "When you asked for our help, Sloane-y, I had no idea that it would involve so much sweating!"

Sloane took off her own coat and hat to reveal normal shorts and shirt. Since her costume hadn't been as hot, she turned her own fan on her grannies to help them cool down. "Thanks, Granny Kitty. Thanks, Granny Pearl. Amelia and I really appreciate it."

Sticking a fan down the back of her shirt, Granny Kitty perked up. "Oh, well! It will all be worth it if we help you get more subscribers. How's the film looking, Amelia?"

"Um. Uh. Er . . . well . . ." Amelia replied, making faces at her camera screen. She wore a striped shirt, a white scarf around her neck, and a black beret on top of her very bushy red curls. A pair of pointy black sunglasses covered her eyes and a few of the many freckles on her face. (According to Amelia, this was how important film directors dressed.)

Joining her, Sloane and her grannies watched the video.

It showed a person walking.

And then standing.

Next to two other people.

That was it. That was as exciting as it got.

Oh, sure, Amelia had added a very dramatic film noir filter to the video. And yes, the costumes all looked very stylish.

But . . . it was still essentially a video of some dork walking past two other, older dorks.

"Do you really think this will get you more of that clickbait or whatever?" Granny Kitty asked skeptically.

"Maybe?" Optimistically, Amelia played it again. Maybe it would improve the second time they watched it.

It did not.

Slumping, Amelia sighed and swiped the hat off her hair too.

"Probably not," she admitted, yanking the sunglasses from her head and the scarf from around her neck. She thrust them toward Sloane. "Here, take these, Sloane! I don't deserve them! Only geniuses can wear such things! And I—I am clearly no genius!"

Amelia ended this statement with a hiccupping sob.

The grannies immediately switched into full-on granny mode. Setting down their fans, they patted Amelia's head, pinched her cheeks, and assured her that she was absolutely brilliant. Quite possibly the most brilliant movie director to have ever lived, in fact.

"Even that Hitchcock fellow you like so well made some real stinkers," Granny Pearl said, pulling a slightly melted candy bar from her fanny pack and handing it to Amelia.

Amelia went rigid, wailing, "You think this one is a real stinker too?"

She snatched the gooey candy bar out of its wrapper and stuffed it into her mouth for comfort.

Granny Kitty, Granny Pearl, and Sloane all looked at one another.

Because, yeah. What they had was pretty much a great big stinker.

"The problem," Granny Kitty said as Amelia sniffled, "is that your case isn't very interesting."

"We've been listening to the two of you research all week, and there's just no, well . . . *zip* to it." Granny Pearl took Amelia's hat, scarf, and sunglasses from Sloane's hands. "What the two of you need is a better case. Something with a bit of style."

"Oh, Pearl! What an excellent idea!" Granny Kitty agreed, plucking the scarf from Granny Pearl's hands and winding it around Amelia's neck again. "But wherever would they find such a case?"

"I'm glad you asked!" Granny Pearl smushed the beret back down onto Amelia's fiery mane of hair. "Did you know that two million dollars went missing from a bootlegger's home down in Toledo back in 1932?"

"Two million dollars!" Granny Kitty said with a very fake gasp as Sloane narrowed her eyes suspiciously. "From a bootlegger's home! Oh, my! Aren't the 1920s and '30s trendy right now, Pearl?"

"They most certainly are, Kitty!" Granny Pearl slid the pointy sunglasses onto Amelia's nose. "Exactly the sort of thing to win subscribers!"

Sloane narrowed her eyes and crossed her arms.

"Uh, grannies," she began to say, only to be cut off by Amelia.

"Do you really think so?" she demanded. *"Do you?"*

"Oh, absolutely!" Granny Kitty slapped the black-and-white clapboard into Amelia's hands. "'The Mystery of Bootleggin' Ma

Yaklin's Missing Millions' is guaranteed to win back all of those lost subscribers. And a few thousand more, besides, I should think!"

Amelia hopped down out of her director's chair, tossing the clapboard to the side and sweeping her sunglasses right off her face. "Sloane! Sloane, what do you think? A female gangster! A lost fortune! Glamorous clothing! I think your grannies might be right!"

Though her friend tugged enthusiastically at her arm, hopping up and down as she did so, Sloane was slightly less convinced. Sure, it sounded good . . .

But her grannies were up to something.

She was sure of it.

(Sloane wasn't just being suspicious. Her grannies were pretty much *always* up to something.)

Still, they had a point.

"Okay, but . . . didn't you say these millions went missing in Toledo?" Sloane asked doubtfully. "I mean, that's like a forty-five-minute drive from here. How are we supposed to get down there and back? Are you guys going to drive us?"

"You just let us worry about that," Granny Pearl said sweetly, pinching Sloane's face.

Sloane crossed her arms, more suspicious than ever. "Grannies, what are you plan—"

Amelia interrupted her. Taking Sloane by the elbow, she hissed, "Who cares what they're planning! They're helping us, right? We've *got* to get a better case than this one, Sloane."

"Yeeeeessss, buuuuut . . ." Sloane dragged out the words, trying to figure out how to explain her suspicions to Amelia without being rude to her grannies.

The thing of it was, her grannies' solutions to problems weren't always exactly, strictly . . . legal.

Along with Sloane's great-granny, Nanna Tia, Granny Kitty and Granny Pearl ran an illegal bingo game out of Nanna Tia's living room. First, it had been to help pay for cancer treatments for Sloane's mom. Then, after Maisy Osburn passed away, they'd just kept at it as a way to deal with their grief.

Sloane understood that. Having something to do was always better than being left alone with your thoughts when you were sad.

But she also wasn't sure that whatever her grannies were suggesting wouldn't get her and Amelia arrested.

Before Sloane could figure out how to explain all of this, Granny Pearl said, "Say, Amelia. Isn't that your parents, come to take you to Miller-Poe Death Match Night or whatever it is you all do together?"

"Miller-Poe Tennis Night," Amelia groaned as a sleek black van flew over the railroad tracks down on Fulton Street, leaving tire marks scorched into the asphalt. Then it careened around the corner and onto Depot Street. A flock of panicked turtle doves took off from where they had been pecking at some potato chips they'd found in the street. The birds landed on top of the old nineteenth-century buildings that still made up Wauseon's downtown.

In a cloud of burning rubber, the Miller-Poe van screeched to a halt by the depot. Amanda Miller, Amelia's mom, leaned on the horn as she rolled down the window and yelled, "Amelia! Time to go! Is that what you're wearing? Why aren't you dressed for tennis?"

One of the van's back doors zipped open so Amelia's half sister and half brother, Ashley Miller and Aiden Poe, could lean out to stare at Amelia. Both Ashley and Aiden were much older than Amelia, being students at the University of Toledo. They were home for the summer, which meant that Amelia had even more bossy, competitive people in her life than she had with just her parents during the school year.

"Yeah, Amelia," Ashley barked in a voice as loud as her mother's. "Nobody wears clothes like that to tennis."

Pushing past his stepsister, Aiden leaned eagerly out the van. "What you need to do, Amelia, is—"

"Nothing!" Amanda Miller cut in. "Aiden, she needs to do nothing!"

Everyone in the Miller-Poe van sucked in their breath and clamped their mouths shut. The effort of it pushed out their cheeks, neck and jaw muscles straining. Clearly, they were all fighting to keep various bossy, judgmental comments to themselves.

They had bossed Amelia around her entire life, never once listening to what she had to say or bothering to really get to know her. When Amelia had finally scrounged up the courage to point this out to them a few weeks ago, they had all been mortified.

Because they really did love Amelia. And wanted what was best for her.

It was just really hard for the rest of the Miller-Poes to admit they didn't know what was best for absolutely everyone. Or know everything about everything at all times.

Now, at least they were trying. But . . .

Well. Take right now. Every last one of the Miller-Poes was either gaping at Amelia in her striped shirt, scarf, and beret or else giving her the side-eye while trying *not* to gape at her.

Either way, Amelia could still feel the weight of all those held-back judgmental, bossy thoughts floating around in their heads.

Sloane gave Amelia a reassuring squeeze on the shoulder as Amelia's dad, Alexander "the Judge" Poe hopped out of the black van to help load all the costumes and props into the back. As he did so, Granny Kitty and Granny Pearl suddenly acted like they were in the middle of a conversation.

"Yes," Granny Kitty said, "it *is* a shame that Timothy Neikirk— *you* know Timothy Neikirk, Pearl? Tia's boyfriend? *Anyhow,* it's such a shame that he won't be able to be a judge at this year's Annual Ohio Peony Enthusiasts Competition!"

(Obviously, Granny Pearl knew that Timothy Neikirk was Nanna Tia's boyfriend. However, Amelia's father most definitely did not.)

"Yes, yes," Granny Pearl clucked. "He was such a fine judge. Really, the very best of judges. I can't imagine anyone else being a better judge than him. Wherever will the Ohio Peony Enthusiasts Club every find anyone who knows anything about judging at such a late date? It would take an incredible judge, indeed."

Alexander "the Judge" Poe stuck his head out from the back of the van. He still clutched the cardboard box of costumes in his hands.

"What's this about being a judge?" he cried. "Am I to understand that someone needs a judge?"

The Judge was, well, an actual judge. At the tall brick courthouse just down the street. He'd sat on the bench for years, and like all the competitive Miller-Poes, he prided himself on being the very best judge there ever was.

Granny Kitty and Granny Pearl knew this. So, Granny Kitty slyly said, "Oh, they don't just need 'a' judge. No, 'a' judge will never do. They need an amazing judge. An exceptional judge. Whoever accepts the job for the weekend will have to be the very best judge."

"That's me!" the Judge shouted, shoving the cardboard box into Amelia's startled arms. She drooped under the sudden weight, and Sloane had to jump forward and help her as Amelia's dad ran back around the car to Granny Kitty and Granny Pearl. "I'm the best! I'm the top-ranked judge in Fulton County! Not a single ruling overturned in the past five years! I'd go so far as to say I'm the best judge in all of Northwest Ohio! Possibly all of Ohio! Did you know I was voted as having the 'Most Distinguished Gavel-Pounding' as voted by *Lawyer Quarterly*? And that's a national magazine!"

Without waiting for the two of them to answer, the Judge demonstrated his gavel-pounding motion with an imaginary gavel.

"Oh, my. That *is* impressive," Granny Pearl agreed, going all wide-eyed. Sloane squinted at her from the back of the van as she and Amelia managed to shove the enormous box into the cargo hold and slam the door shut. Batting her eyelashes at the Judge, Granny Pearl turned to her coconspirator. "What do you think, Kitty?"

Having hooked their fish, Granny Kitty proceeded to reel him in.

"Oh, we're sure you're a wonderful *legal* judge," Granny Kitty said doubtfully. "But you see, what Timothy Neikirk needs is someone who knows how to be more than one type of judge. Someone who understands competitions. Someone with a sharp mind and keen instincts—"

"That's me! That's me!" The Judge practically jumped up and down as he insisted on it.

Leaning out the driver's-side window, Amanda Miller cut in to support her husband. "No one has a sharper mind or keener instincts than a Miller-Poe!"

From the backseat, Aiden and Ashley helped out too. "Yes! We're all the sharpest and the keenest!"

Amelia bet that neither of them knew what "keen" meant. It didn't matter, though. Miller-Poes had to be the best at everything. And for once, she didn't care. Amelia gripped Sloane's arm excitedly. She didn't know what a peony competition was—or even what a peony was—but she was sure it had to do with Bootleggin' Ma Yaklin and her long-lost two million dollars.

As all the Miller-Poes continued to shout about how the Judge was the best judge there was and that he should definitely be the one picked to replace Timothy Neikirk, Granny Kitty and Granny Pearl exchanged a satisfied look.

They just had one final question. "Ah, but can you reschedule your cases? You see, this weekend's competition is a two-and-a-half-day event. It's quite the commitment. I just don't know that you'd be able to pull it off."

The Judge puffed up his chest. Even when not wearing his judge's robes, he somehow gave the impression of wearing them.

As though he were bigger and more solid than most people. As if he could step out in front of a speeding truck and stop it simply by holding up one hand, superhero style.

(It's the sort of authority one gets when pretty much everyone at a job has to do exactly as you tell them to do.)

"Mrs. Osburn and Mrs. Dobbs, I assure you that I can rearrange my schedule quite easily! Tell your friend Timothy Neikirk that he can count on me to be the best possible judge he could have chosen." Amelia's father whipped out his phone and started jabbing at his screen. "I'm adding it to my calendar now."

"Excellent. I'll let the people at the Ohio Peony Enthusiasts Club know to expect you." In an instant, Granny Kitty brought out her own phone and tapped at it swiftly. "All done! They'll be expecting you at Tangle Glen down in Toledo on Friday afternoon."

"Wait. What?" The Judge jerked his head up from his phone as behind him, Amelia and Sloane jumped up and down silently and punched the air. "*Where?* Isn't the competition here in Wauseon?"

"Nope!" Granny Pearl clasped her hands together and smiled sweetly. Like a harmless little old lady. "It's at Tangle Glen down on the Maumee River in Toledo. You know, the former mansion of notorious 1920s and '30s gangster Ma Yaklin?"

"But—but—but—" The Judge's mouth hung open, shoulders drooping and phone limp in his hands. "How will everyone I know in Wauseon see what a perfect judge I am?"

"We'll make sure that they know." Granny Kitty patted his arm soothingly as she led him back to the passenger seat of the van.

Amanda Miller had her phone out too. She had her blond

hair pulled back into a tight, sharp ponytail. Everything about Amanda Miller was tight and sharp. If her husband gave the impression of being a boulder, she came across as a knife. "Don't worry, dear. It looks like Tangle Glen is quite the luxurious inn these days. It will make for a lovely long weekend together with the family. We'll all learn how to play—er, what did you call it? Peony? Is that a type of pickleball?"

"No, it's a type of Frisbee!" Aiden called from the back, determined to show off what he knew. "I play it all the time on the quad down at the university."

"Is not!" Ashley argued, convinced she was actually the smart one. "It's a very particular type of cornhole, and I'll have you know that I'm very good at it!"

"Why, peonies aren't any kind of sport, you sillies!" Granny Kitty tittered, all sweetness and innocence as she shoved the Judge into the van.

"Nope!" Granny Pearl agreed innocently, slamming shut the door. "They're flowers!"

"Flowers?" All the Miller-Poes except for Amelia gasped together in horror.

"Yes. Big, poofy flowers like pom-poms. They smell heavenly and come in all sorts of colors."

The Miller-Poes didn't seem to be either comforted or encouraged by those details. Together, they wailed, "We don't know anything about flowers!"

However, while the rest of her family slumped in their seats, confused and horrified at the thought of spending a weekend not being able to pretend that they were the smartest, best people in the room, Amelia celebrated with Sloane.

"They did it!" Amelia cried, hugging Sloane. "Your grannies did it! They're the best! They got us a case that has everything! Bootlegging! Missing money! A gorgeous mansion! And the costumes, Sloane! We'll get to spend the weekend in 1920s flapper dresses! *And* we'll get to have a sleepover together! I've never had a sleepover before, and I've always wanted to try one. This is going to be so much fun."

Still chattering happily, Amelia climbed into the Miller-Poe family van. Normally, on tennis night, everyone else was talking and boasting while she just sat there, silent and miserable.

Today, those roles had most definitely reversed.

As the van limped away with far less energy than it had arrived, Sloane watched it go with a sinking feeling tugging at her stomach.

Sleepover?

Somehow, it hadn't occurred to Sloane until Amelia said it that she'd have to sleep away from home. All the excitement she'd been feeling shriveled up inside, leaving Sloane to press one hand against her stomach while the other reached up to tug at her ponytail in despair.

In just a few short seconds, everything had gone from being perfect to all wrong, all messed up.

She didn't want to sleep anywhere other than her own home.

She *couldn't* sleep anywhere other than her own home.

This case wasn't the mystery she and Amelia needed to promote their YouTube channel.

It was doom.

Sloane's only consolation as she followed her grannies across the railroad tracks was that at least this time, she and Amelia weren't being set up the way they had been with the last mystery they solved. At least this time, no one would try to attack them.

Unbeknownst to Sloane, she was very wrong about both of these points.

She and Amelia were, in fact, being set up.

And they would be attacked before they solved the Mystery of Bootleggin' Ma Yaklin's Missing Millions.

It just wouldn't be the same people responsible for both.

2

Bootleggin' Ma Yaklin

Even as a little kid, Sloane had never liked sleepovers. Oh, she loved them until it was time to sleep. Then she hated them. Sloane had never been able to sleep on someone else's mattress or floor. Neither ever fit against her back or sides the way her comfortable, familiar mattress did. She didn't like how the blankets were never quite warm enough or cool enough or soft enough the way her blankets were.

She didn't like the unknown sounds every house made at night, as though the floors and walls and plumbing were snoring softly in their sleep. Sure, Sloane's house made those sounds too—made even more of them, given that it was a big, old, half-fixed-up Victorian—but those didn't bother her. She knew every creak, groan, click, and bump her house was likely to make and knew that it didn't mean that there was anything horrible creeping about, looking for someone to pounce on and devour.

You couldn't really count on that in anyone else's house.

At least, not at two in the morning.

At two in the morning, it always seemed like *anything* could happen.

Then one day about three years ago, it did.

Not something pouncing on Sloane at two in the morning. It didn't happen until she'd gotten home after a slumber party at her future volleyball teammate Mackenzie "Mac Attack" Snyder's house. Sloane hadn't slept at all, tossing and turning in her sleeping bag as the tree branches and the streetlights from outside made horrifying shadow puppets on the wall. The only thing she'd wanted in the whole wide world was to be safe and snuggly in her own bed with her parents breathing peacefully across the hall and the old house itself curled up comfortably around her like a dog around a puppy.

That desperate, anxious need to get home as quickly as she could had caused Sloane to pack up her bag as soon as the sun rose and walk home without even calling her parents for a ride.

Which was just as well.

Because her mom had taken a bad turn in the night, and they were at the emergency room.

Sloane's worst fear had been confirmed when she walked into the house, only to find it empty and cold. It was as though the sleepover had snatched away every shred of safety and security Sloane had ever wrapped around herself.

Sleep somewhere other than her own room, and who knew what she might come back to find?

Or, more accurately, what might she lose?

Her parents came back from the emergency room that day. They already knew that Maisy Osburn had cancer, but until that day, everyone thought she was going to beat it. They'd even found ways to joke about it, with Sloane's mom saying that she needed to get her hands on the Doctor's sonic screwdriver from *Doctor Who* since that seemed to be able to fix just about anything.

After that day, the confident, happy sense that they were going to beat the cancer together was gone.

From there, it was a slow slide over the next year until Sloane could never again lay in her bed at night, listening to her parents' breathing across the hall when she needed to feel comforted because she was feeling very small in a very large universe.

Now, it was just David Osburn over there. And Sloane got a sense that he tossed and turned as much as she did, missing his wife.

Obviously, Sloane knew that none of that was because she'd stayed the night at Mackenzie's house.

But knowing something and *feeling* something are two different things.

"I don't know what I'm going to do without you for two and a half days, kiddo," Sloane's dad said as he helped her pack her bag and Chromebook case. They were in Sloane's room on the second floor of the pink-and-green Victorian house. It sat at the south end of Wauseon, not that far from the courthouse where the Judge listened to cases. Sloane's room had a long window seat overlooking South Park, one of the town's oldest green spaces. It had lots of trees, a playground, and a huge gazebo.

All of it was familiar and comfortable, and Sloane gazed at it miserably.

Maybe if she memorized every detail and took them with her, she'd be able to make sure that everything was exactly the same when she came back.

"If you don't want me to go, I could always stay home," Sloane pointed out as casually as she could, twisting the tip of her ponytail round and round her fingertip.

"Nah, I'll be fine." David Osburn grinned, sitting down next to Sloane's concrete goose, Cordelia. His eyes crinkled when he smiled, and he had more gray in his hair than before Maisy Osburn passed away. Still, he was comfortably "Dad"—the same dad Sloane had always known. "You go have fun with your friend Amelia. I know you don't like being away from home, but it'll be good practice if we go with Cynthia and her kids camping down in Hocking Hills."

Ugh. Cynthia. Seife.

Her dad's new girlfriend and her two kids, Skye and Brighton.

Who were all fine! Really, they were. Or, at least, Cynthia was fine. Sloane hadn't actually met her two trolls. Er, kids.

It was just . . . well, it took a little getting used to, this idea of her dad being with anyone who wasn't her mom. It wasn't bad, just different, and Sloane hadn't entirely gotten used to the idea of it yet.

Meanwhile, her dad and Cynthia wanted them to all go spend a long weekend down in southern Ohio, hiking and cooking s'mores over a bonfire. Mentioning it again now, her dad couldn't quite keep the hope out of his voice.

The hope that Sloane liked Cynthia as much as he did.

That she was as far down the path of moving forward with their lives as he was.

Sloane sat down too, slinging an arm around Cordelia the concrete goose. She'd recently purchased it with her birthday money. That wasn't how she'd planned on spending her birthday money, but she'd needed to bribe a shop owner into giving her information about the last case she and Amelia had worked on. Dressing up concrete garden geese was sort of a thing in the Midwest. Sloane had always thought it was super weird—until she'd gotten one of her own.

Now she had Cordelia dressed up in a *Doctor Who* costume. Specifically, a Fourth Doctor costume, as that had been her mom's favorite Doctor. That included a long striped scarf, which Sloane twisted around her fingertip instead of tugging at her ponytail the way she usually did when she was feeling nervous.

Her dad's smile wavered. "You do still think you might want to go camping with Cynthia, Brighton, and Skye, right?"

No. Definitely not. Sloane hadn't even met Cynthia's little gargoyles. Why would she want to be stuck in the middle of nowhere with them? It would probably end up being like a horror movie. Only, instead of being menaced by an ax murderer, Sloane would be running from a couple of annoying brats.

(She didn't know that they were either annoying or brats. But she also didn't know that they weren't. It seemed better not to take any chances.)

"Um, sure!" She gave her dad a limp smile. "Why don't we see how this goes first?"

Her dad gave her a hug. "That's my Slayer Sloane. Always thinking things through."

"Slayer Sloane" was a nickname Sloane had earned from her teammates on the volleyball court. Right now, Sloane didn't feel like a slayer. But she did feel like someone who could think through what was going to happen next, though.

Right now, the gears were whirling in her head, making her realize that a camping trip was really just an outside sleepover. If her dad was comfortable doing a joint family sleepover *outside*, what was to stop him from having one *inside*?

In their own house.

While Sloane was gone.

What if she returned from Tangle Glen to find that her home wasn't *her* home anymore?

That her family wasn't her family any longer.

That they'd both now belonged to Cynthia and her kids?

Panic spiraled upward from Sloane's stomach to grip her throat as tightly as she was clutching Cordelia the concrete goose.

Fortunately, her dad didn't notice, his attention caught by the Miller-Poe family van as it squealed into view from the window, looping around South Park to screech to a halt in front of the Osburn house. David Osburn flinched, taken aback by how aggressively it was being driven. As he and Sloane stood up, he asked, "You always wear your seat belt, right?"

"Of course, Dad." Prying her fingers free of Cordelia's neck, Sloane wiped her suddenly sweaty palms against her jeans. She took both her clothing bag and her Chromebook case from him. "They teach us physics in school. 'Fragile human' times 'fast-forward motion' plus 'sudden stop' equals 'gooey mess.' Although . . . you know, if you're really worried about it, maybe I shouldn't go with Amelia and her family."

It was a last-ditch effort to stay here without seeming like a cowardly coward.

For one brief moment, hope fluttered in Sloane's stomach.

Then her dad laughed and gave her a hug. "No, I don't want to ruin your fun, Slayer. You go have a good time with your friend Amelia."

Her shoulders slumping, Sloane leaned into the hug.

It was going to be fine.

Everything was going to be fine.

Whoever was driving the Miller-Poe family van laid on the horn. Like a referee's whistle, starting the game. Time for Slayer Sloane to come out and play her best for the team. So, she tightened her arms fiercely around her dad to make sure he'd still be here when she got back. Then she gave him a kiss, and bounded down the zigzagging, crooked steps of their house, out across the crooked porch, and into the very back row of the Miller-Poe van. As Aiden pushed the door shut, she took one last look at her dad and her house.

At least if Cynthia moved in while she was away, she'd still have her grannies.

They might be semi-criminals, but they were hers, and that would never change.

(Unless, of course, Timothy Neikirk made them go into hiding. Sloane had found out that Timothy Neikirk very much loved being a judge at the Annual Ohio Peony Enthusiasts Competition and was furious that Granny Kitty and Granny Pearl had told the Peony Enthusiasts committee that he couldn't attend and the Judge would be taking his place. Nanna Tia managed to calm her boyfriend down and soothe his disappointment. But every time he looked at either one of the grannies, he was clearly thinking about shoving his cane up one or both of their nostrils. Possibly at the same time.)

"Hi, Sloane!" Ashley Miller chirped as Sloane got into the car. "Glad to see *you're* wearing something normal!"

Sloane was wearing a shirt and shorts, "normal" clothing for an eighty-degree day in early June. Amelia, on the other hand, was wearing a knee-length black dress covered by a cape-style checked coat, and a bell-shaped hat with a thick ribbon around it. She also had an old, slightly cracked magnifying glass on a thick gold necklace-style chain.

Amelia flamed bright red. Hotly, she said, "I am dressed very 'normally' for a girl detective of the 1920s. If we were surrounded by 1920s girl detectives, all of you would look very weird!"

"Yeah, but we aren't," Aiden pointed out, sharing a snicker with Ashley.

"Aiden, Ashley! Stop teasing your sister," Amanda Miller ordered. But in the rearview mirror, Amelia could see her mom give her outfit the side-eye and a little shake of the head. Her dad had recoiled in horror when he saw it earlier too, though he hadn't said anything because his wife had whapped him on the arm before he could.

Yeah, they were all bossing her around less.

But they were still judging her every bit as much.

Having people wince and turn away from you really wasn't a huge improvement over them telling you what you should be doing. Either way, they made Amelia feel like there was something wrong with her.

Like she was a defective Miller-Poe.

They'd ordered up a daughter/sister exactly like them, only to get some weirdo.

One they couldn't return.

Sure, they'd agreed to stop complaining about it.

But that didn't mean they thought she was any less defective.

"I think your outfit looks great." Sloane smiled encouragingly at her friend. "I didn't know that girls wore sneakers back in the 1920s."

She nodded at Amelia's shoes as the van took off at breakneck pace. They were black and comfy-looking, not tight and heeled the way Sloane had seen in all the pictures of flappers they'd looked at over the past couple of days.

"Oh, they didn't," Amelia explained as she and Sloane opened up their Chromebooks so they could go over the case. "I tried flapper shoes, but they hurt my feet. But if sneakers had been around in the 1920s and '30s, girl detectives would totally have worn them."

Outside the van window, the houses of Wauseon quickly gave way to fields, woods, barns, and farmhouses. Puffy white clouds scampered across the blue sky; while cattails and purple wildflowers filled the ditches on either side of the road. Birds swooped down from overhead, and an occasional pheasant or wild turkey stuck its head out from between the rows of soybeans to see what was going on.

As they traveled, Sloane and Amelia tried to discuss the case of Bootleggin' Ma Yaklin's missing millions, but Sloane kept getting distracted by the other Miller-Poes. Having realized they knew nothing about peonies, they'd spent the last several days turning themselves into experts.

Which meant they also wanted to show off that knowledge.

And prove how much smarter they were than the other Miller-Poes.

"What are the peony forms?" Ashley demanded loudly right as Sloane turned her Chromebook to show Amelia what she'd typed up about the case.

The Judge tried to answer, but Aiden got in first. "There are six forms!"

"Ah!" Ashley crowed triumphantly. "I didn't ask how many forms there are. I asked what they were!"

"Single form! Japanese form! Anemone form!" the Judge shouted from the front of the car. Then he paused, having forgotten the other ones.

Aiden cut back in. "Bomb form! Double form! And—er—um—ahem!"

"Semi-double form!" Amanda Poe finished. "I win!"

Declaring "I win!" around a Miller-Poe was like waving a red flag in front of a bull. A new round of peony-based competition broke out. This one about roots.

"You get used to it," Amelia advised Sloane. "Just concentrate on the case, and eventually, you can tune them out. At this point in my life, unless they're talking directly to me, it's just sort of background noise."

Taking a deep breath, Sloane did as her friend advised and concentrated on the information they had put together into a Google Doc. This was everything they had discovered from internet sleuthing with the help of Belinda Gomez, one of the librarians at the Wauseon Public Library. She hadn't been able to help them quite as much as they hoped, because her German Shepherd, Bunny, had eaten a printer cartridge and the librarian had to rush him to the vet on her motorcycle.

(Bunny was fine, though his tummy was definitely upset. Something Sloane could definitely relate to.)

Hopefully, going through things with Amelia would help calm all the sickly squeezing and knotting going on in her stomach, too.)

The case Granny Kitty and Granny Pearl had found them had once been a really big deal, just like the case of the long-lost Hoäl jewels. And just like *that* case, everyone had forgotten all about the missing millions over time. The inn they were heading to for the Annual Ohio Peony Enthusiasts Competition was called Tangle Glen, and it was a mansion that had once belonged to Jacqueline "Ma" Yaklin, one of Toledo's most notorious gangsters of the late 1920s and early 1930s. She'd been the head of a gang named after her called the Jacks.

Being a fan of old movies, including those from the 1920s and 1930s, Amelia had already known what a bootlegger was, though Sloane had not. It turned out that in 1920, alcohol was made illegal in the United States because people at the time thought this was a marvelous idea and voted to ban it. However, as soon as they did just that, lots of those same people then also decided it would be an equally marvelous idea to go ahead and drink it anyhow.

That was adults for you. They never could make up their minds about what they want.

So, Ma Yaklin and the Jacks saw an opportunity to make money by becoming bootleggers, people who sold illegal goods. Ma turned out to be really good at it, too. She made enough money to build a mansion on a cliff overlooking the Maumee River. She'd even added a tunnel from the house to the river so her gang could smuggle their goods by boat.

Then another gangster named Two Thumbs Lundquist brought his crew of bootleggers called the Digits Gang down from Detroit. The two gangs fought each other for territory, having speeding gun battles in which they would shoot at each other from cars while driving down the brick-lined streets of the city, much to the awe and excitement of the people of Toledo.

Until the feds arrested Ma in 1932 for doing something called tax evasion, which sounded very boring. Everyone expected Ma to hire some fancy, big-shot, fast-talking lawyer to get the charges dropped.

Instead, she had to go with a free public defender.

Because Ma Yaklin was suddenly broke.

Sure, she owned a mansion—Tangle Glen. Sure, she owned several fancy sports cars, including something called a "roadster" that made Amelia swoon (or at least, pretend to). Yeah, she had lots of fancy clothes and jewels to wear and horses to ride.

What she didn't have was cash.

Ma Yaklin cleaned out her bank accounts right before she was arrested. She'd taken out just over two million dollars, so there should have been plenty of money for that fancy, big-shot, fast-talking lawyer.

Except there wasn't.

What had happened to it, Ma wouldn't say. Then, she *couldn't* say—because she died of pneumonia in prison while waiting for her trial. Tangle Glen and all of her belongings were auctioned off to pay for that tax-evasion problem. (Whatever it was, it seemed to be expensive.)

Ma Yaklin and the Jacks were gone, but what had become of her money?

Had she gambled it away? Maybe, but someone would have noticed. Had Two Thumbs Lundquist and the Digits Gang taken it? Also maybe, but bootleggers weren't exactly humble people. Someone would have bragged about it. Probably Two Thumbs himself. Could it be at the bottom of the Maumee River, which ran behind Tangle Glen and was used by the Jacks to smuggle their goods? Sure, it was possible, but the Maumee wasn't particularly deep. Some walleye fisherman would have hooked it a long time ago.

No, the most likely explanation was that Ma Yaklin's money was still hidden somewhere inside Tangle Glen itself.

Along with the secret of why she wouldn't use it to free herself.

"If we can solve this mystery, we'll be famous," Amelia said happily as fields and woods gave way to metroparks, freeways, and suburbs. "It's just what our YouTube channel needs. And it's given me an idea, Sloane. We could ask our subscribers to suggest old cases for us to solve. We could travel all over Ohio, Michigan, and Indiana, investigating crimes!"

Sloane's stomach clenched into a hard knot of panic at the thought. She could be homesick and have nighttime panic attacks in three different states! First, she'd come home to find her dad married to Cynthia Seife. Then, they'd probably have a new kid together. And finally, she'd come home to find a FOR SALE sign stuck in the yard, her house and entire life sold away while she was gone.

Okay, probably not.

But . . . not *definitely* not.

"Sounds great," Sloane said, her mouth suddenly very dry. When Amelia looked at her strangely, Sloane tried to pull herself together. Weakly, she managed to say, "I mean, it should be easy this time! No one is using us to solve the mystery for them. No one is tracking our every move or trying to get to the money before us. After almost getting fed to the coyotes when we found the Hoäl jewels, this is gonna be the easiest thing ever. I mean, 'not getting fed to coyotes' alone will make this easier."

(Sloane was wrong about most of this. However, she did get the part about the coyotes right.)

Amelia, meanwhile, noticed the strangeness in her friend's voice but didn't say anything.

Because they had just reached Tangle Glen.

3

TANGLE GLEN

The mansion rose up over a long stretch of grassy lawn. Three stories tall, its graceful white columns held the roof high above the porch. Some sort of thick vine twisted round and round those columns. Bunches of purple flowers rather like grapes dangled from those vines to make bright flashes of color against the boring bricks of the house. Elaborate gardens with fountains and more brick walls stretched out on either side of Tangle Glen. A wood wrapped itself protectively around it all, blocking out the view of the Maumee River beyond. Somewhere on the other side of all those trees were neighborhoods and streets, but it was hard to believe, looking at them. Other than Tangle Glen and the grassy sweep of yard leading up to it, trees surrounded them.

Sloane and Amelia snapped their Chromebooks shut and pressed their faces against the car window.

A gravel drive looped around the front of the mansion. Amanda Poe yanked the car to a halt in a spray of loose stones. The Miller-Poes tumbled out of the van like Vikings having just pushed their longboats ashore, weapons raised and horned helmets atop their heads. Obviously, the Miller-Poes had neither weapons nor helmets, but they still managed to give the same impression of a crowd of tall, muscular people having arrived to storm the gates and pillage a community.

"What's a petal guard?" Amanda Miller demanded, flinging a bag at the Judge as she began to unpack the trunk.

"It runs offense for the rest of the petals!" The Judge tossed the bag to his stepdaughter.

"Wrong!" Ashley shrieked, slinging the bag over her back like a sack of plunder. "It's the outer petals that protect the inner petals."

Aiden came to his dad's defense as he caught his own bag. "That's essentially the same thing!"

Still squabbling, the Miller-Poes stampeded across the tall, shaded porch and in through Tangle Glen's double doors.

Once they'd gone and it was safe, Sloane and Amelia slid out too.

As Sloane got their bags out of the back of the van, Amelia snapped her phone onto a selfie stick, adjusted her bell-shaped hat (called a "cloche," as she had informed Sloane) and breathlessly declared for her camera, "And so, the adventure begins!"

Still filming, Sloane and Amelia carried their bags into the entry hall.

Sloane looked around and whistled. "Swanky."

A grand stairway swept up the left side of the entrance hall. Reaching the wall, it turned gracefully to the right to create a wide balcony before continuing its way up to the second level. A glittering chandelier drooped down from the ceiling high, high above. Sunlight danced in from the floor-to-ceiling windows on the back wall to spin through the chandelier's crystal prisms and throw little rainbows up into the air like confetti. A fireplace sat between the windows, though of course it wasn't being used this time of year. Leather chairs and velvet couches were scattered about the entrance hall in case anyone got tired crossing it and needed to sit down for a while to rest.

An enormous vase of peonies sat on a marble table directly underneath the chandelier. They filled the entry hall with the most amazing smell. Light and sweet, like you'd fallen into a meadow of wildflowers on the most perfect day of summer.

By now, both Sloane and everyone in the Miller-Poe family could recognize the big pom-pom-like flowers as peonies. However, neither Sloane nor Amelia had ever seen so many different colors and shapes. There had to be almost a hundred different blossoms in a vase so big it was practically the size of a barrel.

"This . . ." Amelia sighed. "*This* is exactly the sort of glamour our channel needs. I want to get our first video uploaded to YouTube tonight so our subscribers can follow along with our investigation."

The rest of the Miller-Poes were talking to a man in an elegant green suit. He was tall, had a very rigid back, and long, rigid arms and legs. In spite of his stiffness, he had a way of leaning forward that reminded both Sloane and Amelia of a grasshopper. The dark green suit only made him look more like an insect. As did the round glasses he wore, which made his already-bulging eyes seem even bigger and rounder than was humanly possible.

He didn't seem very impressed by the rest of the Miller-Poes.

"This isn't a *boxing* match," the grasshopper gasped, snapping a silk handkerchief out of his pocket with which to wipe his fingers, as though they were kicking up so much dust brawling that he was getting contact-dirt just being near them. "My name is Hayden Boening-Bradley the fifth. I'm the president of the Ohio Peony Enthusiasts Club, and I demand to know who you people are and what you're doing here. This entire inn is reserved the next several days for our Annual Ohio Peony Enthusiasts Competition. Perhaps there's a barn somewhere out in the countryside where you can stay."

"I'm a judge!" The Judge gasped.

"Not just any judge," Amanda Miller corrected. "He's *the* judge."

"Well, one of them, anyhow," Ashley cut in.

Determined to be part of the conversation, Aiden added, "He's here to replace Timothy Neikirk."

Mr. Boening-Bradley's lip curled back in disgust as he pulled three sets of keys out of his pocket. "*Really?* When Timothy Neikirk promised me an actual judge for our committee, I assumed I would be getting a man of class and breeding."

"And that's exactly what you got," the Judge said smugly, while the rest of the Miller-Poes preened, clearly impressed with themselves.

Then Aiden snatched a key out of Mr. Boening-Bradley's hand and shouted, "First one to our rooms!"

Challenge accepted, the Miller-Poes grabbed the two

remaining sets of keys and pounded up the wide staircase that zigzagged around the entry hall, leaving behind a stunned Mr. Boening-Bradley. His mustache quivered with outrage, which looked not unlike the antennae on a bug if that bug was also outraged.

Turning around, he complained to Sloane and Amelia, "This is what comes of holding a respectable, dignified event like a peony contest in the—the—the *den* of a bootlegger! A—a—rumrunning hooligan! At a time when women were expected to be well-behaved, upright citizens, that Yaklin woman was little better than a pirate!" Finally seeming to realize he was speaking to two kids, he suddenly went stiff with outrage. "What are you doing in here? This isn't a playground. Go away. Shoo! Shoo!"

He actually waved his hands at them like they were chickens.

(Given that chickens eat grasshoppers, maybe his dislike was understandable.)

"We're with the Judge and his family," Sloane said in a small voice, afraid that might make matters worse.

Amelia seemed to worry about the same thing, so she added, "We're also girl detectives with a YouTube channel and almost a thousand subscribers."

She waved her selfie stick at him to prove it.

"I don't know what any of that means," Mr. Boening-Bradley sneered dismissively. With that, he stormed out of the entry hall, legs moving in the same, slightly jerky fashion of a grasshopper bounding through the grass.

Watching him go, Sloane said, "Maybe don't include all of that in the video."

Amelia, however, had already moved on to other matters. She'd spotted a large, silver-framed picture over on the front desk at the back of the entry hall. "Hey, Sloane, look! It's a picture of Bootleggin' Ma Yaklin."

Together, they went over to it. Of course, they'd seen other pictures of Jacqueline Yaklin online, but they hadn't exactly been great. Most of them were blurry, grainy reproductions of old newspaper pictures. The only clear picture had been on a very short and pretty unhelpful Wikipedia page that showed Ma in handcuffs on her way to court. She'd understandably looked messy, unhappy, and in shock.

This picture showed a powerful and in-control woman maybe a little bit older than Amelia's mom. She had dark hair tucked under a tight-fitting hat and wore dark lipstick. It was an up-close photograph, but they could see an elegant coat with a thick velvet collar. Ma cuddled a dog to her chest, and it wasn't any dainty little teacup-sized dog, either. Instead, it was an enormous bloodhound with long, droopy ears and heavy jowls dangling from its jaws.

There was a placard next to the picture; Sloane read it aloud while Amelia adjusted her cloche, trying to angle it like Ma Yaklin's. "'Jacqueline Yaklin was a successful businesswoman who won the 1932 Annual Ohio Peony Enthusiasts Competition with a delicate herbaceous peony in distinguished tones of oyster shell and dusty pink. Alas, the exact breed has been lost and is much sought-after by fans of historical breeds. Pictured with her is Jacqueline's dog, Eli, a prize-winning bloodhound whose keen nose could sniff out a peony even through a lead-lined box.' Hm. That seems like an odd competition."

Amelia had other thoughts on what they'd just read.

"'Successful businesswoman,' huh? Guess that sounds better than 'criminal bootlegger.'" She chuckled. "I wonder what happened to Eli the prize-winning bloodhound after his successful businesswoman owner got sent to prison."

"Probably ate all of those prize-winning peonies. That's why the breed went extinct. Come on, Amelia. Let's go find our room, and then we'd better get started. Two and a half days isn't much time to solve a ninety-year-old mystery."

"Yeah, but this mystery is, like, forty years younger than the last mystery we solved," Amelia pointed out, encouraging as they carried their bags toward the stairway that zigzagged around the entryway and up to the second floor. "And we solved that one in a week."

Hmm. Sloane supposed her friend had a point. Maybe they'd be able to solve this one by tonight, and she could go home.

They found their room on the second floor, across from Amelia's parents' room and just down the hall from the room Aiden and Ashley were sharing. Reaching it, Sloane pushed open the door.

"Wow," Sloane and Amelia said together.

Large windows let in lots of emerald-and-gold light from the open lawn and woods surrounding Tangle Glen. A crystal chandelier hung from a ceiling frothy with swirly decorations. A huge wardrobe straight out of Narnia stood on one wall, while two beds with headboards that reached all the way up to the ceiling stuck out from the opposite wall. Delicate silver wallpaper covered the walls themselves, while a rug so expensive that Sloane was afraid to step on it was draped over the floor.

Amelia showed no such worry, tossing her armful of suit-cases off to one side and dashing over to another door.

"Look, Sloane! It's got one of those old-fashioned claw-foot tubs! I wonder if Ma Yaklin ever used it to brew up gin in it?"

(From 1920 to 1933, alcohol was illegal in the United States. Regular stores didn't sell it. That's where bootleggers stepped in. They either brought it in from Canada to sell to people or else they made it themselves. If they made it themselves, they frequently made it in bathtubs.

That's right. People drank something made *in the exact same place where they washed their feet and their butts.* If anyone ever tells you that alcohol is good or something worth trying, keep that in mind. People who don't mind drinking something made in the same place that their naked bottom had recently been scooting around in are not people to be trusted.)

Sloane joined Amelia in the bathroom doorway to peer at the tub. She made a face. "Let's hope not."

Amelia filmed their bedroom since it looked every bit as swanky as downstairs. She said it was important to add in lots of inside shots of Tangle Glen to their YouTube video. That way, their subscribers would find it easier to follow along with their investigation as she uploaded their videos to YouTube each night.

The goal was to post a video Friday and Saturday nights before revealing what had actually happened to Ma's money on Sunday night.

Assuming they could figure that out between now and then.

"I think I saw a picture gallery off the entry hall downstairs,"

Amelia said, peering into a heavy gilt mirror to adjust her checked cloak, cloche hat, and magnifying glass. "Let's find out and then see if we can find the bootlegging tunnel. There's *got* to be clues in a bootlegging tunnel."

"Let's just keep an eye out for that buggy Boening-Bradley guy. This is exactly the sort of place people get murdered in on TV shows. And he's exactly the sort of guy to do the murdering!"

"On the bright side, we're exactly the sort of super-smart detectives who solve the murders!" Amelia pointed out modestly as they headed back downstairs. "So, we're unlikely to be murdered."

Fortunately, Mr. Boening-Bradley was outside on Tangle Glen's tall, columned front porch. A couple of expensive cars were speeding along the gravel driveway, and the cranky, grasshopper-like president of the Ohio Peony Enthusiasts Club had gone out to meet them.

As Sloane and Amelia reached the heavy marble table with the enormous vase full of peonies, Sloane's phone buzzed. Taking it out of her pocket, she saw that Granny Kitty and Granny Pearl were FaceTiming her.

"Oh, don't you look like the bee's knees!" they cried in delight, taking in Amelia's 1920s girl-detective outfit.

Amelia explained to Sloane, "'The bee's knees' is a way of saying 'great.'"

"We're *so* glad we were able to help out Osburn and Miller-Poe Detective Agency," Granny Kitty continued in a super-innocent way that made Sloane frown suspiciously.

"Yes, we've recommended it to all the bingo players in Nanna

Tia's living room," Granny Pearl chirped. "Though, I have to admit that most of them are more excited that you're going to the Annual Ohio Peony Enthusiasts Competition!"

"And speaking *of* . . ." Granny Kitty twinkled as though a thought had just occurred to her. "If you get the chance to grab us one or two cuttings, we wouldn't mind a few new bushes for our yard! You know, just to say thank you to us for helping out!"

"Sure!" Amelia nodded like this would be the simplest favor in the world.

However, Sloane scrunched up her face uncertainly. "I'm not sure we can do that, grannies. I don't think they let you take any of them home with you if they don't belong to you."

Granny Pearl and Granny Kitty both let out faintly hysterical laughs. Quickly, Granny Kitty said, "Oh, ha-ha-ha! We aren't suggesting that you *steal* anything!"

"We would never suggest that!" Granny Pearl chirped. Then she glanced around shiftily and added, "It's just that darn Millie Snyder is always bragging about her peonies. You know Millie, Sloane-y. She's that Mackenzie Snyder's grandma. You should see the braggy things she's always posting on Instagram and Facebook about her garden."

Ugh. Both Sloane and Amelia made faces. Mackenzie Snyder had made the end of seventh grade very difficult on Amelia. Then, when Sloane had gotten to know Amelia and started taking her side on things, Mackenzie tried to make life very hard on Sloane as well.

That hadn't worked out so great for Mackenzie, but neither Sloane nor Amelia were fans of hers.

"Look at all of those beautiful peonies in that vase!" Granny

Kitty sighed wistfully, clasping her hands together as though she'd fallen in love. "There have to be hundreds of them! Surely no one would notice if a stem or two went missing."

Slyly, Granny Pearl added, "It would annoy Millie to no end if we got a few stems for our garden. You can start a bush from just a cutting or two, you know. Those Snyders all need to learn that they can't make fun of other people."

"Yeah!" Amelia enthused, nodding vigorously. "It's like—it's like they're cruel, arrogant lords, and the rest of us are peasants they try to grind down into the dust. And by getting you peonies for your garden, we'll be helping you overcome our oppressors!"

The grannies both blinked at this. They exchanged a confused look. Then, Granny Kitty shrugged and said, "Sure."

Pushing Amelia out of view of the camera before she could commit to any felonies and end up in prison for tax evasion or something just like Bootleggin' Ma Yaklin, Sloane said, "We'll ask Mr. Boening-Bradley if we can have a couple of the flowers. But he doesn't seem to like us very much, so don't get your hopes up."

"You're such a good granddaughter, Sloane-y! Much better than that bratty Mackenzie!"

With that, the grannies signed off, and Sloane and Amelia crossed the entry hall to the double set of glass doors that led into the picture gallery Amelia had noticed earlier. The room had a high ceiling patterned all over with stylish geometric shapes. There were more crystal chandeliers and lots of velvet and gilt-trimmed furniture scattered about. Most of the couches and chairs seemed to be arranged so you could sit down and gaze at the startlingly large number of pictures hanging on the walls.

"Are you seeing what I'm seeing?" Sloane rubbed at her eyes.

Amelia slowly lifted her magnifying glass necklace up to one eye. "Are you seeing a whole lot of paintings of dogs? Like, a ridiculous number of paintings of dogs?"

"Yup." Sloane dropped her hands from her eyes.

The paintings were all still there.

Sloane and Amelia swiveled their gaze all around the room.

"Guess Ma Yaklin liked dogs," Amelia said finally.

Or at least, one dog. It was actually the same dog repeated over and over again in all the pictures. Eli, the adorably goofy-looking bloodhound from the picture out on the front desk. There was the dog's face on top of Henry VIII's body, those ears pooling onto the stiff, lacy collar. In another painting, a very talented artist had added the dog's face to what was probably George Washington's body, given the ax in one hand and the cherry tree still standing in the background, waiting to be chopped down. A powdered wig sat above the dog's sad-yet-adorable face. The same artist had also done a version that transported the dog into Da Vinci's *Mona Lisa* and Vermeer's *Girl with a Pearl Earring*. A lot of the other paintings seemed to be canine duplicates of famous paintings, but neither Sloane nor Amelia could come up with their names. Only that they seemed to be vaguely familiar.

Ma Yaklin herself leaned against a fancy dark green roadster. Tangle Glen loomed in the background, but it was almost entirely swallowed up by the woods around it. Ma Yaklin had one heeled foot perched on the car's running board, elbow resting on her knee in a most unladylike fashion. She wore the same fitted hat and coat with the big velvet collar that she wore in the photograph out on the front desk. However, in this one, she wasn't cuddling Eli. Instead, Eli stood next to her, sniffing a pale pink-and-white peony she held casually in one hand.

A gold plate fitted to the thick, ornate picture frame read: *Et clavem intus est occultatum.*

"Do you know what that means?" Amelia asked Sloane.

Sloane shook her head. "I mean, doesn't 'occult' mean, like, witches and Ouija boards and stuff like that?"

"I think so. But I don't see anything like that in the painting." Amelia shrugged. "We could use Google to translate it."

"Maybe later." Sloane couldn't imagine that it held any big clue to where the money might be hidden. "Let's see if we can find the bootlegging tunnel first. The Tangle Glen website said it was down in the basement, but I don't think guests are normally allowed to see it."

"We must be stealthy, Sloane!" Amelia cried, immediately pressing her back against a wall like she could blend in with the paint.

"We might be stealthier if you put away your selfie stick."

"No way. Creeping about an old mansion is going to look great in the video I post tonight."

It took them a bit to find the entrance to the basement. Partly this was because Tangle Glen was large and had many rooms, and partly it was because they really did have to be stealthy. Mr. Boening-Bradley kept welcoming guests into Tangle Glen, sending them this way and that as they clutched crystal vases filled with peonies. All of them looked terribly snooty and very well dressed.

None of them seemed to like Sloane and Amelia any better than insect-like Mr. Boening-Bradley did.

Every time *he* spotted them, he curled up both his lips and nostrils as though smelling a particularly pungent fart. His bug eyes would bulge behind his glasses, and then he'd make shooing motions at them again with his hands.

Neither Sloane nor Amelia could remember if grasshoppers ate other bugs. Or people.

Either way, they agreed it was best to steer clear of the president of the Ohio Peony Enthusiasts Club.

"If we find the money, we'd better not tell him about it." Sloane grimaced. "Because I think he really would murder us for it! He'd clamp those claws of his right around us and, *SNIP!* That would be the end of it."

Finally, they found the basement door not far from what they assumed was the kitchen, given the nearby sounds of pots and pans banging and clanging about.

As basements went, it wasn't a very sinister one. The ceiling was high, the walls were painted white, and there were plenty of big windows they could escape out of if they encountered anything horrifying (which is something you can never entirely rule out in old basements). Most of the space seemed to be given over to a washer, a dryer, and shelves for kitchen stuff like dishes and tablecloths. Farther back, there were stacks of chairs, probably for when Tangle Glen hosted something big like a wedding (or a peony competition).

Pushing aside towels and squeezing past shelving, they tapped the foundation walls, searching for the tunnel.

"Do you know what a bootlegger tunnel would sound like?" Amelia asked Sloane.

Sloane shook her head. "I'm hoping we know it when we hear it."

If there was one, they didn't. Eventually, they found a door and short set of stairs down into a murkier, dirtier basement. It had a cooler, damper feel to it, rather like what they both imagined the inside of an Egyptian tomb would feel like.

There were no longer any nice big windows they could crawl out of should they discover anything horrifying in there with them.

Amelia looked at Sloane uncertainly.

Sloane looked back at her just as uncertainly. Then, screwing up her courage, Sloane summoned Slayer Sloane, Ruler of the Seventh Grade Volleyball Court...

... and marched down the short flight of steps.

Finding a light switch at the bottom, she flicked it on. Dim, staticky bulbs hissed to life. They cast a sullen light onto old wooden crates filled with dusty bottles.

"No tunnel," Sloane huffed into damp, mildewy air. "But there are lots of dusty old bottles and crates. I think they might be left from the bootlegging days!"

That caught Amelia's imagination and swept away all worries about rats, ghosts, and rat-ghosts. She hurried down the steps to join her friend. "This seems like the perfect place for Ma to have hidden her millions. Like, there could be a secret compartment here just like there was at the Hoäl house in Wauseon."

"Yeah, but if Ma had hidden her money down here, don't you think people would have found it already?" Sloane objected, though she turned her phone's flashlight on and used it to sweep the brick walls all the same. "The only reason no one found the secret compartment in the Hoäl house was because they didn't know to look for it."

"Hey, do you hear that?" Amelia asked, lowering her selfie stick so she could look around better.

Sloane followed her gaze toward an outside wall. An empty shelf leaned against it.

Yet it sounded very much like footsteps were coming toward them.

Through the stone.

"The bootlegger tunnel!" Sloane gasped, straightening up. "Amelia, *and there's someone in it!*"

"Or a ghost!" Amelia cried shrilly, her imagination running away with her as she gripped her tripod for protection. "Sloane, don't open it! It could be something coming for us!"

Before Sloane could answer, the shelving unit swung open, knocking over Sloane and Amelia.

As they fell backward into empty wooden crates, sending clouds of sawdust up into the air, they saw a long, dark tunnel open before them.

Out of which sprang Eli, Ma Yaklin's bloodhound.

They hadn't just found the bootlegger's tunnel.

They'd released a demon ghost dog out into the world.

4

Sloane and Amelia Take the Ghost Dog for a Walk

Amelia let out a shrill, hysterical shriek as she fell backward into an open crate. Her arms and legs flailed about, though whether to fend off the ghost dog or push herself farther down into the safety of the crate, it was hard to say. More graceful than her friend, Sloane was able to quickly get up out of the crate she'd fallen into. Her heart hammered and her skin crawled with cold terror—but she was determined to give the demon dog a good fight.

That fight turned out to involve a very wet slurp from an enormous tongue.

"Ewwwww!" Sloane threw her hands up to protect her face.

An excited bloodhound turned its attention to the trapped Amelia, slobbering all over her face as it licked her eyes, nose, and mouth enthusiastically. It seemed that this dog was no ghost. This dog was very much alive. Enthusiastically, wetly alive.

"Hey! Stop!" Amelia gurgled, turning her face from side to side in a vain effort to avoid both the tongue and the drool. *"Patooey! Blech! Sloane!"*

"I'm trying to help!" Sloane grabbed at the dog, but the bloodhound was so pleased to see them that it couldn't stay still. Paws scrabbled at the wooden crate, long ears flopped everywhere, and each time Sloane tried to catch the dog by the shoulders and pull it away from Amelia, she got beaten up by a fiercely wagging tale.

"Chiave! Down, girl!" a voice commanded from the tunnel.

Amelia froze and made a sound like "EEP!" clearly convinced the voice belonged to some dead bootlegger. Even Sloane went rigid with fear and then spun around, half expecting to see something ghastly float out of the darkness.

Instead, it was a thick-set, oldish man who wheezed his way out of the tunnel, which was not nearly as dark as Sloane and Amelia had thought, thanks to the ancient electric lights that swung from cords overhead. He wore a floppy hat, a well-worn shirt, and baggy shorts. The man also leaned on a gnarled walking stick. With his gray hair and broad face, he looked ridiculously like a troll—but at least a nice troll. As if Sloane and Amelia had discovered a hidden doorway to a magical land of rainbows and candy-haired people.

Chiave listened to her person and thwapped her butt down onto the stone floor. She panted happily, tail still whacking the nearby crates excitedly.

"Now, who might you be?" the troll asked them in surprise.

"Who might *you* be?" Amelia demanded in response as Sloane tugged her free from the crate. With the back of her arm, Amelia wiped at her sodden curls and face with as much dignity as she could.

"I'm Sherwood Lindsay," the man said, patting Chiave's head with a hand as gnarled as his walking stick. "And *I* own Tangle Glen."

"You own this place and you live in the basement?" Sloane

asked incredulously. "You know there are much nicer rooms upstairs, right?"

Mr. Lindsay chuckled. "I don't live down there! Chiave and I were just taking a walk along the river. The smugglers' tunnel is the fastest, easiest way back up to the house. I pulled some muscles in my back last week, and now walking is pretty painful."

With a grimace, Mr. Lindsay used his walking stick to tug himself the rest of the way into the basement. Unlike his dog, he moved slowly and carefully, lumbering like a troll. Or maybe a mushroom that had learned to walk. Chiave didn't seem to mind, though. She smiled up at her person, tongue lolling out of her mouth.

"Sorry if Chiave and I frightened you." Mr. Lindsay reached down to scratch his dog's head. "She's not even a year old, for all that she's grown into her full-size. She gets away from me pretty easily, but I wasn't expecting any of the guests to be down here!"

Pushing Chiave's nose and tongue away with as much dignity as she could, Amelia introduced herself and Sloane. "I'm Amelia Miller-Poe and this is Sloane Osburn. We're from Osburn and Miller-Poe Detective Agency, and we're here to find Bootleggin' Ma Yaklin's missing money. Please subscribe to our YouTube channel, where you can watch the videos we'll be uploading each night to show what we've discovered during the day. If you'd like, you can google our names, and you'll see that we recently solved the case of the long-lost Cursed Hoäl Treasure."

Mr. Lindsay blinked in surprise at all of this, so Sloane added, "And Amelia's dad is one of the judges at the peony competition this weekend."

"Ah." Mr. Lindsay nodded in understanding. Then a twinkle sparked in his eye. "I should never have had Shakespeare add that to our website, that bit about Ma and her missing money. You wouldn't believe how many of our guests go poking and prodding about the house, looking for that missing two million. Hate to tell you this, but my granddaddy already turned this place upside down a long time ago, trying to figure out what she did with it. No luck, though! Whatever Ma did with the money, she was too smart for him. Too smart for herself, even! She hid it in such a clever spot, she couldn't find it again, heh-heh-heh. Here, if one of you would be so kind as to help me take Chiave upstairs and outside so she can run around, I'd be happy to tell you what I know."

Sloane thought this was a fair enough trade, and besides, she liked dogs. So, she happily took the leash from Mr. Lindsay and clipped it to the back of Chiave's harness. Less of a fan of animals in general, Amelia pushed away Chiave's quivering, sniffing nose from her girl-detective costume with a grimace. Hoping to make the best of things, she switched her camera back on to record Mr. Lindsay.

"My grandparents bought Tangle Glen for a song and a dance after Ma Yaklin got arrested back in 1932," Sherwood Lindsay explained, pulling himself through the cluttered base-ment and up the stairs to the main floor by leaning heaving on his walking stick. "That means they got it for practically nothing. You see, 1932 was the worst year of the Great Depression, but Granddaddy Lindsay had a bit of money saved up because he'd done some bootlegging himself! Rumor had it that Ma Yaklin had hidden money all over the mansion in case she ever had to go on the run from either the feds or Two Thumbs and the Digits Gang. 'Course, when she did, she couldn't find it. Instead of grabbing it and taking off in her roadster, she ended up trying to run from the feds on foot. They caught her in the woods around Tangle Glen. Granddaddy figured it had to still be here somewhere in the house. His thoughts were that Ma wasn't thinking straight the night the feds came for her, and that's why she couldn't remember how to get back to the hiding spot. See, her dog, Eli, had run off, so maybe she was trying to find him in the woods. There's a bunch of pictures of Eli up in the portrait gallery over there, if you girls want to take a look. That dog was like a son to her."

They'd reached the entry hall by now. As Mr. Lindsay waved his hand toward the portrait gallery, Sloane had to brace her legs and hold on to Chiave's leash with all her strength. The bloodhound had either spotted or smelled the giant vase filled with hundreds of peonies in the middle of the room. A man in a tuxedo stood on a stepladder to add more flowers to it. Spotting Chiave, he clutched the peonies to his chest and trembled.

"We've already seen it," Amelia replied, collapsing her selfie stick and tucking it into a pocket of her checked cape coat so she could help Sloane tug on the dog's leash. Together, they managed to yank Chiave out onto the front porch. Behind them, the man in the tuxedo sagged in relief.

Mr. Lindsay joined them to collapse on a bench beneath

Tangle Glen's high, columned porch. With his floppy hat and brown clothing, he looked like a mushroom growing up out of the wood. "After Ma was arrested, the feds searched Tangle Glen for the money. Granddaddy said they thought there must be a secret compartment behind one of those paintings of Eli. Never found a blessed thing. Anyhow, Granddaddy bought the place, thinking he'd find what neither Ma nor the feds had been able to find. He never found a blessed thing, either. You want my opinion? The money is sunk on one of them islands out in the river."

He used his cane to poke in the general direction of the back of the mansion. Where the cliff swept quickly downward to the Maumee River.

Sloane and Amelia exchanged an unhappy look.

Dredging a wet, weedy, tick-infested island for buried treasure was well beyond what they could do. At least, not without a map.

"Did anyone ever find Eli?" Sloane asked, grappling with her own bloodhound as Chiave ran over to one of the peony bushes planted all along the front of Tangle Glen and promptly peed on it. Mr. Boening-Bradley had just hopped outside in his dark green suit to greet another car pulling up the gravel driveway. His mustache twitched with excitement at the sight of more peonies. Exactly like a grasshopper's antennae would.

"*What* are you doing?" He gasped in horror at Sloane, going as rigid as if someone had just tried to electrocute him. "You can't do that here!"

"It's not like I'm the one peeing!" Sloane protested.

"Please don't use that word." Mr. Boening-Bradley made a face.

Amelia tried to help. "Don't think of it as a word. Think of it as a letter!"

It didn't help. Looking very much like he wished he could drop Chiave, Sloane, and Amelia into the river, he hurried forward to this newest rich person stepping out of a fancy car. Where he sneered at Sloane and Amelia, he practically bowed and drooled all over this person.

"Odd bunch, these peony enthusiasts." Mr. Lindsay shook his head, then returned to Sloane's question. "No, Eli never showed up, and I think Ma cared more about that than being sent to prison. Right before she died of pneumonia, the only thing Ma would say about her lost millions was, 'When I lost Eli, I lost everything.' You see, without your loved ones, what does money matter?"

"Not a whole lot," Sloane admitted, throat clenching up tight. She'd give any amount of money to have her mom back.

And to make sure that her family and life at home were exactly as she left them when she got back.

That Cynthia Seife and her two kids hadn't moved in while Sloane was away.

Which, *obviously*, wouldn't happen.

Probably.

Amelia had a slightly different reaction to Mr. Lindsay's words. Passionately, she said, "Even if you have your loved ones, what does money matter if they still think you're some giant weirdo? I mean, yeah, love is great and all, but you can love someone without liking them or—or respecting them, you know? Sure, you can be grateful that you have your loved ones around, but maybe it would be nice if they'd stop looking at you in a way that lets you hear all of the negative things they're thinking even if they don't say them out loud!"

Stopping to catch her breath, Amelia realized that both Sloane and Mr. Lindsay were gaping at her, open-mouthed.

So were Mr. Boening-Bradley and a man clutching a vase filled with orange peonies, who he'd been leading into the mansion.

Her skin going hot and prickly, Amelia stuck her nose in the air and tried to look dignified. "I'm just saying, that's all."

"Uh, those are good points too." Sherwood Lindsay blinked and squashed his hat back on his head, becoming a mushroom once more. Then he hefted himself slowly, painfully to his feet. Without enthusiasm, he said, "Suppose I'd better take Chiave for her walk."

Sloane and Amelia exchanged a look as Chiave hopped up and began to frisk about once more.

The trouble with looks, though, is they can sometimes be misunderstood. Amelia's look said, *Thank goodness!* while Sloane's look said, *We should help him out,* with the result that Amelia went stiff with horror as Sloane said, "Hey, we could take her for a walk for you!"

"Uh, could we, though, Sloane?" Amelia hissed.

Mr. Lindsay didn't hear her as he scratched his chin thoughtfully. "Are you sure? My back is hurtin' something terrible, but I know my Chiave can be a handful."

More like tongue-ful, Amelia thought as Chiave spat out

a mouthful of bright pink peony blossoms and turned to give Amelia's girl-detective outfit one more wet sniff.

"We don't mind," Sloane reassured him.

Sherwood Lindsay's face brightened. (As much as a mushroom could brighten.) He leaned both hands on his walking stick as a muddy-faced Chiave smiled up at Amelia. "That'll be a big help. I could sit down in the sunroom for a while and rest my knee for a bit. I've been saying that I could really use a vacation. Maybe a nice weekend at a spa . . ."

Trailing off with a wistful sigh, Mr. Lindsay gave Chiave a fond pat on the head and lumbered back into the house.

As Sloane and Amelia dragged Chiave away from the peonies and toward a garden off to the side of the house, Amelia said grumpily, "We really need to come up with some sort of code. A way of saying 'Don't offer to walk the dog.'"

"Sorry." Sloane grinned sheepishly. "Don't you like dogs?"

"I like dogs. I don't like getting sniffed or licked by dogs! Or-or-or *snorfed* by a dog."

"What's snorfing?"

"When a dog sniffs something so enthusiastically that they actually pull whatever their sniffing into their nostrils." Amelia explained her definition of the word she'd made up, then shuddered with revulsion.

No one wants any part of themselves to end up inside something else's nostril.

As Sloane and Amelia each strained to keep their animal

under control, they pushed open a white gate and walked through a brick archway into a garden. Sloane had hoped it would lead toward somewhere they could take Chiave off the leash and play fetch with her. Instead, they found themselves in a very formal garden with geometric paths leading the way sharply through perfectly trimmed trees and orderly rows of rose bushes.

Hand on hip, Amelia took it all in and said, "It looks like the Red Queen's garden. You know, the angry, uptight one from Alice in Wonderland?"

Before Sloane could respond, Chiave broke away from her and ran over to a girl who looked like she could be a long-lost member of the Miller-Poe family. She had the same well-muscled, outdoorsy look to her that Amelia's parents and siblings had. Though her messy ponytail, freckled face, and wide grin also made her seem like she'd be more relaxing to hang out with than the Miller-Poe family.

"Hey there, girl! Settle down!" she laughed, setting down the clippers she'd been using to trim a rose from one of the bushes. Her face crinkling, she knelt to embrace Chiave. "What are you doing out here? Did you get away from your person again, you bad dog?"

"Sorry, that's our fault," Sloane explained, hurrying over to catch Chiave's leash again. "I'm Sloane Osburn and this is Amelia Miller-Poe. We're staying at Tangle Glen this weekend, and we offered to help Mr. Lindsay by playing with Chiave for a while."

"We're also girl detectives," Amelia added importantly. "Here on a very important case."

The girl looked suitably impressed, pleasing Amelia. "Wow! I didn't know there would be any kids staying here this weekend. I thought it was going to be all uptight peony competitors. Do *not* get in their way. They're intense. Oh, and I'm Sergeant Pepper Arroyo."

"You're in the military?" Amelia asked as Chiave continued to beg the sergeant for pets.

"No, my parents were huge fans of the Beatles," Sergeant Pepper explained. Trimming the thorns from the rose she'd cut, she tucked it into Chiave's collar, giving the bloodhound a stylish look.

When Amelia tried to look knowledgable while really being confused, Sloane caught on and explained, "The Beatles were a band in the 1960s. *Sergeant Pepper's Lonely Hearts Club Band* was the name of one of their albums. My grannies are fans too."

Sergeant Pepper nodded. Still grinning, she stood up and tucked another rose into her own ponytail. "I'm just glad they didn't name me after the whole thing! Anyhow, I'm the gardener at Tangle Glen. My family has been hanging out around here for ages. Grandma used to visit the mansion when she was a little girl, and she told my dad a lot about it. There's so much history along this stretch of the Maumee River, you know. Tangle Glen was built by a notorious bootlegger named—"

"Bootleggin' Ma Yaklin," Sloane and Amelia finished in unison.

"Oh." Sergeant Pepper blinked in surprise. "Well, did you know that she misplaced two—"

"—million dollars somewhere in Tangle Glen," they finished once again. To this, Amelia bragged, "That's why we're here, you know. To find that missing money."

Once again, Sergeant Pepper looked suitably impressed. "Well, good luck with that! Lots of people have tried to figure out where it went, including my grandma when she grew up! I think Mr. Lindsay's grandfather once chased her out of the peony bushes when she was a teenager, convinced the money must have been buried under one of them."

With a laugh, Sergeant Pepper returned to spreading mulch around the rosebushes. As she did so, Chiave lunged forward and swiped her wallet out of her back pocket. Before anyone could stop her, the dog took off with it, romping back to the front of Tangle Glen.

Fortunately, neither grasshopper-like Mr. Boening-Bradley nor any of the super-fancy peony enthusiasts were outside right then, because Chiave spat the wallet out into a pool of drool on the grassy front lawn. Then the bloodhound wagged her tail and grinned at Sloane, Amelia, and Sergeant Pepper as they finally caught up with her.

"Ugh! This dog!" Sergeant Pepper laughed again, not really seeming to be bothered by the fact that her wallet was now very slimy. "I was cutting back the peonies earlier, and I must have touched my wallet afterward. Chiave is peony-obsessed. Mr. Lindsay said all the dogs in her line have been that way, all the way back to when he was a little boy."

"His family breeds dogs?" Sloane asked curiously, picking up a stick and throwing it for Chiave so the dog could romp after it.

"Not really. Just one litter from each dog before they get them fixed. See, they've had a bloodhound named 'Chiave' ever since Mr. Lindsay's grandfather, Anderson Lindsay, was a bootlegger. He made a lot of money working for Jacqueline Yaklin, and he never got caught and sent to prison the way she did. So, I guess they figured always having a bloodhound named Chiave around was lucky for the family."

As she returned to the side garden and Sloane continued to throw sticks for Chiave, Amelia considered what the gardener had just told them. "Hm. It's interesting that Mr. Lindsay didn't mention that his grandfather worked for Ma Yaklin."

"Maybe he was embarrassed by it," Sloane suggested.

"He told us his grandfather was a bootlegger." Amelia scootched behind Sloane when Chiave returned, tail-wagging, to barf a peony stem at her feet.

"Blech." Sloane picked up a new stick and threw it, sending the bloodhound bounding happily after it. "Yeah, but he might have been ashamed that Ma Yaklin went to prison and he didn't. I mean, if he worked for Ma, then Mr. Lindsay's grandfather must have been guilty too."

"If he worked for her, you'd think he'd have a pretty good idea of where she'd hidden her money," Amelia said thoughtfully, tapping her chin with her finger as she looked up at the columned brick mansion looming over them. "I mean, if Anderson Lindsay worked for Ma Yaklin, then wouldn't he have known some of her hiding spots?"

"Sure, some. But I bet not all. It's not like she was going to tell everyone working for her, 'Hey, here's my money. Come and get it!'" Chiave returned with another wilted, dripping peony stem. Sloane found a new stick.

"Let's think this through. Ma Yaklin's beloved dog, Eli,

disappears from Tangle Glen." With her finger, Amelia drew a line from the mansion to the trees surrounding. "So she goes looking for him in the woods. Only . . . doesn't she already know the feds were after her? Why wouldn't she take off in her roadster to escape them and then come back to look for Eli later? After all, she can't find him if she's in prison."

Sloane shrugged as an exhausted Chiave flopped down at her feet, panting and clearly worn out. At least for the moment. "Mr. Lindsay said that everyone said she was so upset that she wasn't thinking straight."

Amelia snorted. "Please. That's the sort of thing people used to say all the time about women. 'Oh, they're all emotional. They can't think straight.' Believe me, I see it all the time when I watch movies from back in the 1920s and 1930s. Jacqueline Yaklin was a successful businesswoman and the owner of prize-winning peonies *and* the owner of a prize-winning bloodhound. You don't get that way without being super smart and super competitive. Believe me, I know. I live with a whole pack of super-smart, super-competitive people. They're annoying and treat everyone else like weirdos, even when they're not exactly 'normal' themselves. Whatever 'normal' is supposed to be! Why aren't I every bit as 'normal' as them? Who decided what 'normal' even is, anyhow? *I* don't think it's actually a thing! *I* think it's all made up. I—" Amelia caught her breath, realizing that she was ranting. Both Sloane and Chiave made sympathetic faces at her. Quickly, Amelia finished up before either one of them could say or do anything nice, because it might very well make her cry. "Anyhow, the point is: Super-competitive people aren't going to stop thinking logically just because their dog disappeared. If she knew the feds were coming, Ma Yaklin would have gotten into that roadster, driven off, and then planned a way to find Eli."

Sloane didn't answer right away. She could tell that Amelia didn't want to talk about what she'd just said about the Miller-Poe family. Her friend was sniffling and rubbing at her nose with the back of her hand like it was her allergies causing her eyes to water.

Sloane might be afraid that things would be different when she got home.

But Amelia was afraid they'd be exactly the same.

Oh, her family was trying. Clamping their mouths shut instead of bossing Amelia around.

But you could still hear all of their criticisms pounding at their clenched teeth, trying to escape out into the air.

It was like being haunted by ghosts.

Just because you couldn't see them didn't mean you couldn't feel them.

Speaking of ghosts . . .

Sloane went rigid.

"Amelia," she squeaked, her gaze fixed on one of the round windows poking out of Tangle Glen's attic.

"What?" Amelia snuffled wetly.

"Gst" was all Sloane could force out.

"What?" Confused, Amelia swung around to look upward too.

She squeaked just like Sloane had.

Movement flickered in one of the attic windows.

It was a face.

No more than a smudge of darkness where the eyes and mouth would be. A hint of a line to suggest a nose.

Then it vanished.

That face just *dissolved*. Both Sloane and Amelia could have sworn it.

"It—it was a trick of the light." Sloane gulped. "Right, Amelia? *Right?*"

Amelia couldn't answer.

She didn't know.

She just hoped that they were the only ones looking for the missing two million dollars.

Because what if Ma's ghost was looking for them, too?

5

PRIZEWINNING PEONIES AND PRIZEWINNING POOCHES

"On the bright side," Sloane said after she'd finally recovered from the shock, "a ghost is unlikely to try to tie us up and leave us for coyotes."

Now that her heart had stopped pounding, she didn't believe they'd really seen a ghost. It had probably just been . . . someone hanging out in the attic? The way people did?

"How do *you* know?" Amelia demanded shrilly, clutching her cloche hat in her hands. "How many ghosts have you run into? Maybe ghosts *do* tie people up and leave them to be eaten by coyotes! Maybe that's a pretty common thing for them to do!"

"Amelia, breathe," Sloane said encouragingly. She took her friend's hat from her, and then got Amelia to bend over and put her head between her knees.

"I'm breathing," Amelia wheezed. "I'm breathing. Which is more than I'll be doing once Ma Yaklin's ghost murders us for looking for her money. I bet she's guarding it! I bet the whole house is filled with the skeletons of people who've gone looking for it! And we'll end up as skeletons too! And my family will be all like, 'We always knew she'd come to a bad end! We used to try to fix her, but once she pointed out that there was no fixing her, we just gave up!' *That's probably what they'll chisel into my tombstone!*"

With that, Amelia collapsed onto Tangle Glen's grassy lawn, sobbing theatrically.

Several newly arrived, posh peony contestants gave her the side-eye, clutched their flower vases to their chests, and hurried inside. Mr. Boening-Bradley peered through the double doors into the mansion, turned around, and shouted out a request for a pest-removal company.

Sloane suspected that she and Amelia were the pests in need of removing.

Which was ironic, because if a pest company actually arrived, Sloane was sure that the first thing they'd do was zap Mr. Boening-Bradley with bug spray.

Instead of removing herself, she sat down next to her friend.

"You know your family loves you," she said, patting Amelia on the back.

"Loves me, maybe. But they don't like me." Amelia sniffed. "I want to be liked, too."

"They *do* like you," Sloane assured her friend, picking up the cloche hat from where it had fallen when Amelia threw herself onto the ground. She worked on pushing it back into shape after Amelia had crumpled it up. "They just think that the best thing anyone in the world could possibly be is exactly like them. Honestly, they're so weird."

Amelia let out a snorting, hiccupping laugh. Setting upright, she asked, "Do you really think so?"

"Oh yeah," Sloane agreed easily, handing her the hat. "I mean, everyone's weird. That's what makes them fun and worth getting to know. However, even if we're all on a weirdness scale, your family is definitely at the very top. Mostly because they think they're the only normal people in the universe."

Wiping her eyes, Amelia snort-laughed again. She settled her cloche back onto her head. "I guess I just thought that once they stopped bossing me around all the time, everything would be perfect. Instead, having them silently judge me is almost worse."

"Being silently judged is definitely the worst." Sloane nodded her head in agreement, tossing her ponytail over her shoulder. "Mackenzie Snyder is the master of it. I've seen her tear apart another kid's self-esteem with one sneer."

"Uh, yeah. She did that to my self-esteem," Amelia pointed out.

"No, she didn't," Sloane got to her feet and helped her friend up too. "She tried and tried, but no matter what, Mackenzie couldn't get you to change who you are. You were like Mackenzie kryptonite. The one thing she couldn't destroy. But we've got bigger problems than Mac Attack Snyder—or ghosts. I don't think that was the spirit of Ma Yaklin up in that window. I think it was someone else, looking for her missing two million dollars."

"Not again," Amelia groaned as they headed into the house.

"Yup. We've got competition," Sloane said grimly.

"Ugh. I really don't want to get sort-of kidnapped and sort-of-almost left for coyotes again. Once was fine, but doing it again will only bore our YouTube subscribers. We need new content."

Sloane had different objections to getting kidnapped by someone else looking for Ma's money too, but she just said, "Come on. Let's see if we can find our way up to that attic."

It was actually getting fairly close to dinnertime as they reentered Tangle Glen. Amanda Miller spotted Sloane and her daughter as they circled their way around the enormous vase of peonies, now more mountainous than ever. She warned the two of them that it was almost time to get dressed, since dinner was going to be a fancy affair to kick off the One Hundredth Annual Ohio Peony Enthusiasts Competition.

Sloane and Amelia solemnly promised that they were just getting ready to change.

Then, as soon as Amanda turned the corner at the top of the stairs, they darted off down the long hallway that led past the door to the basement.

When they were exploring earlier, both Sloane and Amelia had opened a door and discovered a less-grand stairway far at the end of that hallway. They were both betting that it was the servant stairway—a narrower, less-fancy stairway than the main one that zigzagged its way around Tangle Glen's front entry hall. When Jacqueline Yaklin built the house, the stairway in the entry hall would have been for herself and her fancy guests to use. Rich people back then didn't want to see the people working for them, so they had servant stairs added to their mansions.

The main stairway didn't go up to the attic.

But they were both betting the servant stairway did.

They passed the kitchen, inside of which there was a flurry of activity. Various junior chefs clanged and banged pots and pans, while servers dashed about, carrying napkins and tablecloths to the dining room. Delicious steam drifted from the room, making both Sloane and Amelia's mouths water.

"I think it was this one," Amelia said right after they passed the kitchen. She pushed open a heavy door and hurried inside. "Quick! Before anyone sees us and asks what—whoops."

Sloane had already hurried after her, only to slam into her friend when Amelia screeched to a stop.

"Wrong door." Amelia grimaced. "Wait. Why are there old pictures and newspaper clippings all over the wall?"

They'd accidentally opened the door into someone's office. There was a big wooden desk in front of a window overlooking the trees and cliff down to the Maumee River. A bunch of the photographs seemed to be old black-and-white pictures of peonies. Someone had circled different parts of them with Sharpie markers and added notes on Post-its stuck next to the photos on the wall.

There were also lots and lots of old newspaper clippings.

"Maybe Mr. Boening-Bradley is using it as an office during the competition?" Sloane suggested, before spotting a very large, new color photograph on the wall. "Only, if so, why does he have a picture of that big painting of Ma and Eli from the portrait gallery?"

Sensing there were clues to be found in this room, the girls went over to have a look. Amelia shook out her selfie stick and started taking pictures and video.

The photograph was indeed of the painting of Ma and Eli, with Ma leaning on the roadster she should have used to escape the feds and Eli posed to look like he was sniffing the peony in her hand. More Post-it notes covered the wall by this photograph. They all had notes scribbled on them like, Shirley Temple crossed with Angel Cheeks? and Sarah Bernhardt with Bowl of Cream?

"I wonder who Shirley Temple and Sarah Bernhardt are."

Sloane cocked her head from side to side and squinted. Hoping that would somehow make better sense of the notes.

"Actors," Amelia said distractedly. "But I don't know why anyone would want to give them creamy cheeks. Never mind that, though. Sloane, look! It's an article about Eli being kidnapped!"

She jabbed excitedly at one of the crumbly, yellowing newspaper clippings, drawing Sloane's attention to it. The headline screamed:

PRIZEWINNING DOG KIDNAPPED!
PRIZEWINNING PEONIES DESTROYED!
DIGITS GANG TO BLAME?

In spite of the question mark in the headline, the writer of the article didn't seem to really think there was any question about it. It was clear that everyone assumed Two Thumbs Lundquist and the Digits Gang were to blame. The gangster had pleaded his innocence, but it didn't sound like anyone believed him. The photograph the newspaper had included probably hadn't helped. In one, they showed the holes in the garden where the prizewinning peonies had been. In the other, Ma Yaklin scowled at the camera with one hand up to half block it from taking her picture. In the other, Two Thumbs smirked out from underneath a fedora.

She looked angry, and he looked guilty.

"Why tear up the peonies?" Sloane asked thoughtfully, bending closer so she could get a better look at the holes. "I mean, Eli was Ma's beloved pet, right? Like a son to her, Mr. Lindsay said. So, taking him would be about the worst thing Two Thumbs Lundquist could've done to her. Why bother with the peonies? Unless . . . maybe he thought she'd hidden her money there?"

Amelia had a different question. She pointed to the date above the headline: June 8, 1932.

"Sloane, that was a couple of days before the feds arrested Ma. So, I was right. There was no way she would've 'lost her head' and gone running through the woods, looking for Eli. She knew that Two Thumbs had him. Why go running through the woods?"

Sloane looked from the newspaper date to the picture of the torn-up peonies, and then back again. Slowly she said, "Maybe Two Thumbs Lundquist thought the money was buried beneath her peonies . . . but it was really buried somewhere out in the woods!"

"Ooh!" Amelia's face went dreamy, her eyes focusing on images only she could see. "It's a treasure hunt, then! Maybe Ma forgot where she hid the map, but it's still there! And someone else knows about it, so if we find it, we'll have to dig the money up in the dead of night! With only old-fashioned candle lanterns to see by. And—"

"Hey! What are you kids doing in there?" a voice demanded, yanking Amelia back to the present and causing both girls to whirl around in surprise.

They found themselves confronted by a youngish woman wearing a poofy white hat, checked pants, and clogs. She held a meat cleaver in her hand and mysterious, terrifying stains smeared her apron.

Amelia let out a squeak.

She really didn't want to get turned into one more stain on that apron.

"Definitely nothing suspicious!" she said in a small voice.

Sloane thought fast. "Isn't this the . . . um, bathroom?"

"Of course it isn't!" The woman crossed her arms, tucking that scary meat cleaver into the crook of her elbow.

"Oh, then I'm glad you found us before we, uh, sat down." Sloane scooted past the woman and out the door, dragging Amelia with her. Once they were both out of the room, the woman pulled out a key and locked the door, keeping Sloane and Amelia from getting back inside. "I'm Chef Zahra Abu-Absi, and I run the kitchen here at Tangle Glen. This hallway is off-limits to the guests because my staff will be going up and down it all evening long. I can't have them tripping over people as they try to get dinner out."

"And what a delicious dinner it smells like, too!" Sloane said, sucking up to Chef Zahra in case she was thinking about doing anything to them with that meat cleaver.

Amelia wrinkled her nose. "It smells like fish." Sloane elbowed her in the ribs, causing Amelia to brighten and say, "I mean, it smells like *delicious* fish! Yum! What kid doesn't love fish? Sloane, let's go get changed for dinner so we can hork down a bunch of that delicious fish!"

With that, the two of them scampered down the long hallway, toward the entryway with its big vase of flowers. Just before they rounded the corner, Sloane looked back to make sure that Chef Zahra wasn't chasing after them, possibly with a meat cleaver raised in one hand.

But no, she wasn't.

Instead, the chef opened another door—the one they should have opened to get to the servant stairs—and went inside.

Wait.

Why would Tangle Glen's head chef be going upstairs right when she was getting dinner around in the kitchen? If she needed something from upstairs, why not send one of the people who worked for her?

Could she be going up to the attic?

Could it have been *Chef Zahra* they saw in the window?

"Maybe." Amelia made a doubtful face as they zigzagged their way up the stairs to their room on the upper level. "But don't you think that was Mr. Boening-Bradley's office? I mean, a lot of that stuff seemed to be about peonies. Maybe he's planning on doing some sort of history of the competition."

"*Was* it his office, though?" Sloane asked as she unlocked the door to their room. "Maybe it was Chef Zahra's office. Maybe it's just coincidence that the headline was about peonies. Maybe one of them is trying to figure out where Ma hid her money."

"Oh! Or Mr. Boening-Bradley could be doing the same thing," Amelia suggested, flopping onto her bed. "Like, if anyone asks, he could be all like, 'Oh, I'm just researching about peonies!' But what he's really doing is trying to figure out where Ma hid her money?"

Before they could discuss the case any further, Sloane's phone vibrated in her pocket. Surprised, she pulled it out to see that her dad was FaceTiming her.

Instantly, Sloane's heart began to pound, her palms going all sweaty as her stomach scrunched down like an animal trying to hide. Oh no—why was her dad calling her already? She'd seen him only a few hours ago. Why would he be calling her unless something had gone wrong at home?

Maybe her dad had gotten hurt.

Maybe her grannies were in the hospital.

Maybe Nanna Tia was at death's door.

Maybe...

Maybe...

All sorts of horrible thoughts flashed through Sloane's head in the few seconds it took her to swipe open the call.

Expecting to see her dad's face, Sloane instead found herself peering at a little girl with a purple Popsicle shoved into her mouth. More of it smeared her face, and she had a matching purple bow in her hair. Behind the toddler, Sloane could see the house her grannies shared. Sloane recognized all the 1980s peach and teal furniture filling the split-level between the kitchen and the family room.

"Who are you?" both Sloane and the little girl asked at the same time.

"Skye Seife." Purple juice ran down her fingers as Skye sucked on her Popsicle and stared at Sloane like she was waiting for her to do something interesting. "Do you know the 'Baby Shark' song? Can you sing it to me?"

"Skye!" Cynthia Seife, Sloane's dad's girlfriend appeared behind the gremlin. She had longish hair and dimples and in general seemed like she probably would have been a nice person if she wasn't trying to steal Sloane's life away over the weekend. "How did you get ahold of that? We don't use people's phones without asking first! Oh—hi, Sloane! I hope Skye didn't bother you."

"Nope," Sloane managed to say, even though her throat had gone as dry and gritty as sandpaper.

"Sloane-y!" Granny Kitty cried off-camera. Cynthia took the

phone from Skye and swiveled it around to show the grannies' gold-and-ivory kitchen. Both Granny Kitty and Granny Pearl stood by the freezer drawer, helping a boy of about seven get a Popsicle out of the freezer. That had to be Brighton, Cynthia's son.

Oh, this was bad.

This was very, very bad. It took everything Sloane had not to start hyperventilating right then and there.

Cynthia Seife and her kids weren't just moving in on Sloane's dad.

They were taking over her grannies, too.

Hanging out at their house. Smearing their gross fingers all over the furniture so it would all be sticky when Sloane got back. Maybe the grannies would even have to buy new furniture.

Sloane would come back on Sunday night to a granny house she wouldn't even recognize.

While her grannies ignored her and played with the new, popsicle-chomping tots that Cynthia had brought them.

Sloane would be the old, boring grandchild they'd had forever.

Not the cute new ones Cynthia had gotten them.

"I . . . have to go," Sloane said weakly.

"Oh." Cynthia turned the camera back to herself. "Don't you want to talk to your dad first?"

"No. I, um, think I hear Amelia getting, uh . . . eaten by coyotes."

Amelia—who had still been crashed on her bed during all of this—helped Sloane out.

"AUGH! Help, Sloane! Help!" she shrieked, flopping about. "It's already gotten one of my toes! Quick, while I still have the other nine!"

"I'm coming, Amelia!" Sloane ended the call before Cynthia could ask any follow-up questions.

She dropped her phone like it had burned her and collapsed onto the bed next to Amelia.

"Good news," she told her friend. "Those coyotes aren't eating you anymore."

That was because they'd moved on to gnaw at Sloane's stomach.

Just like Cynthia and her kids were devouring Sloane's family while she was away.

6

Amelia Helps Avoid a Massacre

"Would you like my help splitting up your dad and Cynthia?" Amelia offered after Sloane explained why she was curled up in a ball on her friend's bed, hands pressed hard against her stomach. She'd made the mistake of looking up at the headboard on the bed.

It towered upward, practically all the way to the ceiling.

From the mattress, it looked like a tombstone rising up above a grave.

The grave of the life Sloane had known.

She'd just gotten used to life without her mom. What had she been thinking, staying away from home again? Sloane knew that she had to be there, had to take care of that life, if she wanted to keep it.

"We could turn a skunk loose on her and her kids. That would make your dad and your grannies want to stay really far away from them for a while," Amelia suggested. "I got sprayed by a skunk when I was six, and it was the most peaceful time of my entire life. No one wanted to get close enough to boss or judge me for two entire weeks." She sighed happily at the memory. "It was lovely."

Sloane uncurled enough to look at her friend clearly. "Would you really help me catch a skunk and turn it loose on them?"

"Sure," Amelia agreed easily, getting up to go root through her suitcases for a new outfit to wear. "You need me to help keep your life together, I'm there. You've got a pretty great life, so I wouldn't want to lose it either, if I were you. Plus, I might get sprayed again!"

Amelia was the only person Sloane could think of who actually got excited about the thought of getting drenched in stinky skunk juice. Though, if Sloane had four sets of competitive, critical Miller-Poe eyes on her all the time, she'd definitely need a break too.

Her phone rang. Sloane pulled it out to see her grannies were trying to FaceTime her. Sitting upright in bed, she opened the call.

"Sloane!" They peered anxiously at the camera from their peach-and-turquoise family room. If her dad and Cynthia and the kids were anywhere close by, they were staying very quiet. "Are you okay?"

"Oh, I'm fine," Sloane said unconvincingly. Amelia stopped rooting through her clothes long enough to hold up her phone and point silently at a picture of a skunk. Sloane shook her head, then asked her grannies, "So . . . Dad and Cynthia and Brighton and Skunk—I mean, Skye—are over at your house, huh?"

"Just Skye and Brighton," Granny Kitty assured her as Amelia gave them a wave and then disappeared into the bathroom to change into a new 1920s flapper dress. "David and Cynthia wanted to go listen to music out at the Red Rambler coffee shop, but Cynthia's babysitter canceled on her."

"So, Kitty and I are watching the kids tonight," Granny Pearl added. "You don't mind, do you, Sloane? I know you haven't really had a chance to meet the two of them yet."

"No, it's fine," Sloane lied unconvincingly.

Granny Kitty adjusted the glasses on her face so she could get a better look at Sloane. Who felt like her granny was using some sort of special Granny-Vision to pierce through the internet to read Sloane's mind. "You know that taking care of Skye and Brighton doesn't change how we feel about you, don't you? You'll always be our little Sloane-y, no matter what."

Sloane's stomach unclenched a little bit.

Not a lot. But a bit.

"I do," Sloane admitted.

She didn't add that knowing something and feeling it were two very different things.

Briskly, Granny Pearl turned into granny-problem-solving mode. "You know what you need? You need to do something special with us when you get back! How about if you grab us a couple of those award-winning peonies downstairs, and we'll show you how to start a new bush. We'll make a day of it. Digging holes, planting peonies, drinking lemonade, eating cookies, and taking pictures to post on Instagram to show Millie Snyder that she isn't the only one in town with a wonderful granddaughter and prizewinning flowers!"

"Grannies! I am not stealing for you!" Sloane cried, dropping her phone so that it fell against her knees.

Before she could scold Granny Kitty and Granny Pearl for trying to take advantage of her when she was feeling down, Aiden and Ashley busted into the room.

They bounced across Sloane's bed, knocking her phone to

the floor, so they could surround Amelia and bombard her with questions as she came out of the bathroom.

"Amelia, who do you think knows more about peonies? Me or Aiden?" Ashley demanded, taking Amelia by the shoulders and spinning her to face her half sister.

"Ha! She already knows it's me!" Aiden crowed, grabbing Amelia and twirling her back to him. "The *real* question is, who do you think knows more: me or Dad?"

"Please!" Seeming to think Amelia was a top, Ashley gave her another whirl. "Amelia, Aiden didn't even know what peony eyes are. Don't you think that should disqualify him from being the smartest?"

"Double-ha!" Back Amelia went toward Aiden. "Amelia, Ashley didn't know that a peony crown is where the roots meet the stem! Can you believe it? How can anyone *not* know that simple fact?"

Aiden let go of his half sister. Instead of answering, Amelia staggered a few steps and collapsed onto the bed.

"Ohhh! I think I'm gonna barf," she moaned, clamping a hand to her eyes to keep the room from spinning.

From underneath the bed, Sloane's phone spoke up as she scrounged around under the mattress, trying to find it.

"Is that Amelia's brother and sister?" Granny Pearl's voice asked.

"Yup." Finding her phone, Sloane held it up so the grannies could get a good look at Aiden and Ashley . . .

. . . who froze in surprise for a moment. Then, realizing that they had a new judge to confirm which of them was best at boring flower trivia, they began to badger Granny Kitty and Granny Pearl with questions.

"We'd, uh, better go," Granny Kitty said in alarm.

"Yes!" Granny Pearl agreed swiftly. "I think I hear Skye and Brighton, uh . . . shaving the neighbor's rottweiler. So sorry about earlier, Sloane-y! We love you!"

They made kissy-faces at the camera and then signed off.

Before Aiden and Ashley could start up round three of "I Know More Than You!" Sloane told them that she needed to change her clothes for dinner and that they needed to leave "now, please." As Aiden and Ashley crowded their way toward the door (somehow, just two of them managed to make a crowd), Ashley looked Amelia up and down as her sister got woozily to her feet.

"You're not wearing *that*, are you?" she demanded, hands on hips.

Ashley herself wore an expensive blue dress and heels, her hair pulled up in a bun. Next to her, Aiden wore a boring shirt and tie, a suit coat slung casually over one shoulder. Their parents would probably wear something similar, all of them together looking like a social media post for a fancy vacation.

Amelia, on the other hand, wore a gold dress with a matching, glittering feather headband around her forehead. More feathers graced the boa wrapped around her shoulders, and she had long black gloves on her hands and arms.

She flinched at Ashley's words but stuck her nose up in the air and said grandly, "*I* am dressed as a 1920s flapper going to a party. As this is the one hundreth anniversary of a competition started in the 1920s *and* we are staying at a mansion built by a bootlegger, *I* am the only person dressed correctly in this room."

Ashley rolled her eyes at Aiden. Who grimaced and raised his eyebrows.

Neither one of them said anything else.

They just hurried from the room like Amelia was toxic.

Amelia immediately drooped, her skin going blotchy with embarrassment. She didn't know what she expected them to say or do. What she wanted them to say was, Hey, that's a great idea! Let's all dress up too! But she knew that wasn't very likely.

Observing her friend's sadness, Sloane went over to Amelia's bags and pulled out another glittery, feathered headband. She pulled it over her own forehead, lifting her ponytail up and out of the way so it could still swing free.

Smiling at Amelia, she said, "There. Now I'm dressed correctly too."

Amelia rubbed at her face with the back of one gloved hand. "You don't have to do that."

"Hey, if you're willing to catch a skunk for me, the least I can do is dress like a flapper for you."

"Oh, I was just going to order one online."

In the end, none of Amelia's flapper dresses fit Sloane, so Sloane just went with the plain black jersey dress she'd brought. Still, the headband was enough to make her look plenty 1920s–ish. Pleased with their appearance, Amelia put her phone into her selfie stick, raised it up high, and off the two of them went to find the dining room.

Downstairs, they followed the tinkling of glass and the

murmuring of voices across the entry hall and down a different hallway than the one leading to the kitchen and servant stairs up to the attic. They finally located the dining room behind a set of wide, heavy double doors. The floor was a black-and-white checkerboard, like there should have been giant chess pieces around somewhere. Instead, round tables covered in white tablecloths filled the room, each one set with china plates and crystal glasses around stylish vases of even more peonies. Chandeliers drooped from the painted ceiling, while a wall of windows looked out over the Maumee River.

"Well, ain't this just the bee's knees!" Amelia cried, catching the attention of several snooty-looking people dressed in silk ties and dresses. Many of them wore diamonds, and a few of them even had furs draped over the backs of their chairs.

All of them stopped talking to gape at the two middle schoolers wearing eye-catching headbands. Sloane would have preferred to drop to the floor and crawl to their table to avoid all those eyes. Amelia, however, was in her element.

Because these people weren't looking at her with disapproval.

Confusion, yes. But not disapproval.

If anything, many of them smiled and nodded in approval at her outfit. They whispered to each other, but not in a smirking sort of way. In a *Hey, check this out!* sort of way.

"I just arrived in my cake basket from the hen coop to this nose-baggery," Amelia continued loudly as she sashayed across the room and toward her family's table by a low wooden stage. "I don't want to seem like an ostrich, but is there anything swell to eat?" she asked in an accent from the South (the south of where was harder to determine).

(Meanwhile, roughly translated, this all means, *Isn't this great?* *I just arrived in my limousine from the salon to this restaurant, and* *I don't want to seem like I don't know what's going on, but is there* *anything good to eat?* Amelia had spent some time googling flapper words on her phone.)

With Sloane slinking behind, less comfortable with all of this attention, Amelia made it to their table. She smiled at the Judge and said, "Gee, Dad. You sure look like a brooksy."

The Judge glanced down at his clothing as though trying to figure out what a brooksy might be and whether or not he did, in fact, have any of it on him. "Thank you?"

The rest of the Miller-Poes had gone stiff with contact embarrassment. Their smiles had the clenched, strained appearance of people trying very hard not to scream.

Flinging her feather boa around her neck so she wouldn't sit on it, Amelia sat down among her mortified family.

Meanwhile, the rest of the room applauded. A lady wearing a tiny tiara said to Mr. Boening-Bradley, "I say, Hayden! The entertainment this year is top-notch! You're so clever to think of adding a couple of flappers to give us that authentic 1920s experience. Bravo!"

Several other people added their own bravos, causing Amelia to smile smugly. Mr. Boening-Bradley had seemed like he was heading their way to kick Sloane and Amelia out of Tangle Glen with one grasshopper foot, but he immediately changed his expression.

Preening, he stroked his silk tie and said, "Thank you! I *am* clever, aren't I? So good to be appreciated."

The rest of the Miller-Poes visibly relaxed when they realized the entire room wasn't laughing at them. Still, they gave Amelia the side-eye the way one might a snake that could strike at any moment.

Well, the Judge didn't. He was staring at his tie, still trying to find this "brooksy" business Amelia had been talking about.

Both Sloane and Amelia were starving from a busy day of investigating. Servers brought them each a plate of shrimp and sauces that looked more like a sculpture than something to eat. Amelia made a face and reached for the basket of bread rolls right as someone turned down the lights, plunging the room into grayish gloom.

No sooner had the chandeliers been turned off than a spotlight was directed onto the stage next to the Miller-Poe table. At the same moment, a puff of smoke filled the stage, causing everyone at the table to cough and wave their hands in front of their faces.

When it cleared, a young man about Ashley and Aiden's age stood on the stage, holding Chiave by the leash. He had slicked-back hair and wore an old-fashioned-looking tuxedo with long black tails, a vest, shiny black shoes, and white spats. He swept a top hat from his head and bowed deeply.

"Good evening, ladies and gentlemen! I'm Shakespeare Wikander, manager of the Tangle Glen Inn, and I'd like to welcome you all to the One Hundredth Annual Ohio Peony Enthusiasts Competition!" Shakespeare Wikander announced to a smattering of limp applause. Shakespeare Wikander's smile faltered. Clearly he'd been hoping for the crowd to be impressed by his magic trick. Chiave whined and strained to get away from him—either because she was embarrassed by the grimaces people were throwing in her direction, or because she desperately wanted to go snorf the vase of peonies in the middle of the table closest to her.

Either way, Shakespeare Wikander strained to keep her under control as he announced, "I'm also an amateur magician, and Mr. Sherwood Lindsay, the owner of Tangle Glen, has been kind enough to let me entertain you tonight."

The applause was even weaker than it had been before. Long-limbed, bug-eyed Mr. Boening-Bradley glared at stocky, mushroomy Mr. Lindsay as he sat at a table at the back of the room. Still wearing his cargo shorts and fanning himself with his grubby hat while the snooty people at his table leaned away from him. He did sort of give the sense that he might have brought a huge mound of soil with him, but both Sloane and Amelia would have thought gardeners wouldn't mind that sort of thing.

"I, uh, shall now make this dog disappear!" Shakespeare's voice shook as he spoke.

Before he could do whatever trick he had planned, Chiave did her own disappearing act by yanking her leash free of his hands, romping through the room, and diving under the tablecloth at Mr. Lindsay's table.

A titter filled the room.

Up on the stage, Shakespeare Wikander broke out in a sweat. "I mean—I mean—I—uh, will make a bouquet of flowers appear!"

Smoke exploded from the floor of the stage. Under its cover, Shakespeare Wikander dove forward and grabbed a fistful of peonies from the Miller-Poe family table, as it was the closest to the stage.

He held it up triumphantly as the smoke cleared. "Ta-*da*!"

Stony silence filled the room for a moment.

Then, a woman in a blue silk dress and pearls stood up and gasped, "Those are *my* prizewinning Pink Hawaiians! How dare you use them for some tawdry little magic show!"

A woman in a satiny pink dress and diamond necklace chuckled and sneered. "No tawdrier than that garish color, Baker. If your peony beats my Coral Charms, I'll eat your pearl earrings!"

"Then open up, Kuneman!" Baker yanked the pearls out of her ears.

Kuneman snatched up a silver shrimp fork and waved it about threateningly.

Up on the stage, Shakespeare Wikander clutched his bouquet of quickly wilting flowers and looked ready to cry.

In front of a roomful of people who laughed at him.

And would probably chuckle some more while whispering behind their hands as he did so.

Well, Amelia wasn't about to let that happen.

Feeling a sudden and fierce loyalty to this person who was also suffering the pain of people treating him like he was a weirdo when all he was trying to do was be himself and make them happy, Amelia sprang to her feet.

In her loudest voice, she cried in her 1920s slang, "Stop bumping yer gums like a buncha stool pigeons! This guy here is the big cheese! He's Wikander the Wonderful Wizard, and he will now make me disappear!"

At Amelia's appearance, the entire room settled down and perked back up again. They had enjoyed her entertainment before, and with Amelia clambering up onto the stage, both Kuneman and

Baker slowly sat down elegantly, arranging the silk folds of their skirts to keep them from wrinkling.

Though they still shot daggers toward each other with their eyes. Fancy, expensive, silver daggers.

"Was Amelia scheduled to be part of this act?" Aiden whispered to his stepmom, clearly bewildered.

Before Amanda Miller could reply, Shakespeare Wikander twirled Amelia around. As he did so, he threw something down onto the ground. White smoke billowed up, enveloping them both.

Then the floor collapsed beneath Amelia's feet.

The next thing she knew, she was tumbling downward into darkness.

7

Out of a Trap and Then Back in Again

Amelia landed on a soft dirt floor, breaking her fall. Though it did stir up another cloud of dirt and dust that, combined with the smoke from above, caused Amelia to cough and sputter. Overhead, the trapdoor she'd fallen through snapped shut, blocking out the little bit of light it had allowed in. Overhead, she could hear wild applause, followed by the sounds of people talking, forks clicking against plates, and chairs scooting about.

What she couldn't do was see anything.

Amelia's heart hammered, but she told it not to be afraid. Obviously, Shakespeare Wikander had to know she was here. He should be here any second to let her out.

But again, knowing something and feeling it are two entirely different things.

When Amelia tried to move, she tripped over something squarish and wooden, landing on her hands and feet. Glasses clinked within the box, some sort of liquid sloshing inside them.

It was a hidden smuggling room, Amelia realized with a thrill of excitement that pushed its way through her fear.

There could be clues in here as to what happened to Ma Yaklin's missing two million dollars!

If she could just see them.

A door burst open in one of the walls, allowing in a rectangle of light. Amelia squinted and threw an arm up over her face to block out the sudden brightness.

"Amelia!" Sloane rushed in to help her up off the dirt floor. Shakespeare Wikander and Sergeant Pepper the gardener followed close behind.

"Did you *hear* all of that applause?" Shakespeare Wikander asked, a dreamy smile upon his face as he clasped his white-gloved hands together. "They love me—er, us! I mean, they loved us! I've never had anyone clap for me before."

He sighed happily as Sergeant Pepper helped Sloane dust off Amelia and pick cobwebs out of her hair.

"I did not," Amelia said grouchily. "I was too busy falling into this hole!"

The smile slid from Shakespeare Wikander's face. He immediately shook a string of colorful, connected handkerchiefs out of his sleeve and offered them to Amelia to wipe her face. "I'm sorry about that. I worked with Chiave all week to get her to go down through the hidden door, but I guess she didn't want to do it tonight even though I put a bunch of treats down here." He pointed toward a pile of Snausages. "I've wanted to do my magic act in that room ever since Mr. Lindsay showed me how to get into this old hiding spot from the dining room. I might be the manager of Tangle Glen, but my real dream is to become a world-famous magician."

"I told you to put a bunch of peonies down here," Sergeant Pepper told Shakespeare Wikander as Amelia handed back the rope of handkerchiefs to him. The gardener shook her head in frustration. She still had a red rose tucked into her ponytail in an attempt to be a bit fancy, but it didn't work very well. Like mushroomy Mr. Lindsay, she looked like she'd be a lot more comfortable outside. "I can't keep her out of those bushes! What a weird dog."

Sloane checked out the rickety ladder Amelia (well really, Chiave) was supposed to climb down. "Ma had a hiding space under her dining room, huh? Between this and the tunnel down to the Maumee River, I bet there are more hiding places all over this house!"

However, before either Sloane or Amelia could get too excited about that idea, both Shakespeare Wikander and Sergeant Pepper shook their heads.

"I'm afraid not," the gardener said as Sloane and Amelia poked about the room. There wasn't anything terribly exciting in it. Mostly just a bunch of old crates filled with dusty bottles and some burlap sacks. Anything mice could gnaw on, they had. If money had been hidden down here, it had long ago been turned into snuggly nests for mice families. "Originally, that was just a root cellar. You know, for storing vegetables back before people had refrigerators? So, it was pretty easy to turn it into a hiding spot when Ma decided her other bootlegging spots weren't safe anymore."

"Why did she decide those other spots weren't safe anymore?" Amelia asked.

However, before either Shakespeare or Sergeant Pepper could answer, Mr. Hayden Boening-Bradley jumped into the basement. Spotting the doorway into the root cellar, he held his silk handkerchief to his nose and came over to them. "Wikander! Arroyo! Whatever are you doing down here? That dreadful Baker woman is chasing after that even more dreadful Kuneman woman again! I need both of you to help break them up before someone's skull gets cracked open and peonies are planted inside!"

"Sorry! Sorry!" Shakespeare Wikander frantically tucked his many brightly colored handkerchiefs back into his sleeve. To Amelia, he said, "Thanks so much for your help! I didn't know we had any professional actors in the audience."

"Oh, I'm not an actor," Amelia said airily. "I'm a director and *artiste*! Also, we're both detectives with Osburn and Miller-Poe Detective Agency, and we're here to crack the case of Bootleggin' Ma Yaklin's Missing Millions. Subscribe to our YouTube channel to find out more!"

She handed him a business card, much to Mr. Boening-Bradley's annoyance. As Shakespeare and Sergeant Pepper hustled upstairs to break apart the brawl between jewel-encrusted competitors, Kuneman and Baker, Mr. Boening-Bradley turned his disapproval on the two girl detectives.

"Why don't the two of you go upstairs and watch the Teletubbies while I have Chef Abu-Absi send up some peanut butter and jelly sandwiches for you?" he sneered threateningly. "I don't want your ridiculous 'investigation' to ruin my peony competition!"

"Teletubbies?" Sloane repeated in outrage.

"And I prefer peanut butter and pickles!" Amelia cried after him as he waved his silk handkerchief dismissively at them both and returned to the dining room.

Sloane sat down on a crate and twirled the tip of her ponytail round and round her fingertip, thinking. "I think we can probably rule out this room and the bootlegger tunnel as places where the money could be hidden. Everyone seems to know about them, so I can't believe that someone wouldn't have found the money if it had been hidden behind a loose stone or something."

Amelia joined her on a crate. "I still think there *could* be hidden compartments in the mansion, but I have to admit that the Lindsay family *probably* would have found them by now. This isn't like the Hoäl Mansion, which sat empty for most of the last hundred years. I think we need to check out the attic next."

Sloane nodded her agreement. "Chef Zahra going up there right when she was in the middle of the dinner rush seems suspicious. Even if the money isn't up there, there might be clues."

"Then it's settled," Amelia agreed briskly. "We'll investigate the attic. Even though it's surely haunted and full of ghostly dolls!"

"What?" This was all news to Sloane, who let go of her ponytail so she could gape at her friend in horror. "What makes you say that?"

Amelia shrugged like it was obvious. "It's a big, creepy old house. All big, creepy old houses have ghosts and haunted dolls."

"My attic is old and it doesn't have those things!"

"That's because your parents probably removed them before you guys moved in. You know, along with the cobwebs and dust and things like that."

As if this wasn't terrifying enough, things suddenly got even worse.

Because the door into the hidden room slammed shut.

Plunging Sloane and Amelia into darkness.

Amelia let out a shrill scream and grabbed Sloane in the dark. At least, Sloane *hoped* it was Amelia grabbing her hand. After what Amelia had just said, she couldn't entirely rule out the possibility that it was either the ghost of a long-dead bootlegger or a creepy, haunted doll.

Sloane's heart hammered in her chest like it was trying to break free. "Amelia, do you have your phone on you?"

"Left it on the table when I jumped up on the stage to help Shakespeare," the darkness said in Amelia's voice. Then, it went quiet for a moment before adding, "Don't you have yours?"

"Accidentally left it on the table upstairs too," Sloane admitted, squeezing Amelia's hand tightly. "Let me see if I can find my way over to the door."

With many *oofs*, grunts, bumps, and scrapes, Sloane managed to do just that. "It's locked."

"Then we're trapped!" Dramatic Amelia had quickly replaced Frightened Amelia. "We've been kidnapped again! We are lost in the darkness, Sloane! We shall perish down here, our fates a mystery to our loved ones! Our bones will be entombed here forever... though at least our spirits shall roam the hallways of the Ma Yaklin Mansion forever!"

In spite of their dire situation, Sloane grinned. "Uh, probably not."

"Let me have this for a moment, okay?" the darkness snapped. "Sloane, who shut that door? Did you see them?"

Sloane shook her head, then realized Amelia couldn't see it in the darkness. "No, but I'm sure it didn't just fall shut. It was heavy and not very easy to move when Shakespeare opened it earlier. Amelia, I don't think we're the only ones looking for Ma Yaklin's missing two million dollars."

"Ugh. Not again," Amelia said, and heaved a sigh. "Why are

people always trying to solve the same mysteries as us? No one bothers with these things for, like, a hundred years. Then suddenly, just because we're trying to figure out what happened, they try to do it first. Typical adults."

Sloane couldn't argue with any of that. "The good news is that I don't think anyone is trying to use us this time to solve the case for them. And I think they're really only trying to scare us off, not really kidnap us. Because we can still get out through the trapdoor. How about if we try climbing up the ladder and getting out that way?"

"Fine." Amelia sighed again as Sloane *oof*ed, grunted, bumped, and scraped her way back over to her friend. (Or, again, given the complete darkness—what she hoped was her friend instead of a dreadful something.) "Let's head back up and out of the darkness to my family so I can watch them silently judge me for not eating those shrimpy things."

"Did you want to stay down here in the darkness for a little bit longer?" Sloane asked as they both felt their way toward the ladder. "Because once we get back up into the dining room, I promise to help you silently judge *them* for eating the shrimpy things."

"I thought you liked the shrimpy things too," Amelia pointed out as they climbed the ladder together.

"Yeah, but you're my friend, and anyhow, I think I might be pretty good at silently judging people. So, I'll stick to the bread with you."

"Thanks, Sloane," the darkness said quietly. "It's good to have someone on my side."

"Hey, I think anyone would want to be on the side of someone ordering a skunk off Amazon." Reaching the top of the ladder, Sloane found the trapdoor locked. However, she could easily hear people talking above them. So, she pounded her fist against the wood.

Somewhere up above them, a distant voice said, "Hey, did you hear something?"

Sloane kept pounding, and after several startled seconds, the people above finally seemed to realize what was going on. Then there was a lot of scraping of chairs and thudding of feet. Finally, Shakespeare and Sergeant Pepper opened the door and peered down at the two of them in astonishment. The red rose slipped out of the gardener's ponytail and smacked Sloane in the face as the house manager asked, "What are you two still doing down there?"

"That," Sloane gritted through her teeth as she climbed out the trapdoor, "is a great question."

Amelia emerged after her, dust-covered and cobwebby once more. "Some mook tried to send us to the hoosegow!" When everyone glanced at each other in confusion, she explained, "Someone tried to lock us up to scare us away from searching for Ma Yaklin's missing money."

By now, everyone nearby was looking at them uncertainly. Both mushroomy Mr. Lindsay and buggy Mr. Boening-Bradley were missing from the room, which Amelia thought was very suspicious. Where had the two of them been when someone shoved that door closed? Sure, the owner of Tangle Glen acted all friendly, but what if that was a ruse? And while Mr.

Boening-Bradley made it clear that he didn't like her and Sloane, what if it wasn't because he didn't like kids because they had a tendency to squash bugs and he was clearly the result of a science experiment to cross a human with a grasshopper? What if what he really didn't like was the fact that the two of them were looking for money he was hoping to find and keep himself?

However, she couldn't voice these concerns to Sloane because her mom was smiling at them both with clenched teeth, her fingers practically tearing right through the tablecloth and down into the wood underneath as she gripped the table.

"Amelia, you and Sloane are *making a scene*," Amanda Miller hissed. "Making a scene" was one of the worst things a Miller-Poe could do unless it was by winning a competition.

Ashley and Aiden slunk as low into their seats as they could possibly get, clearly hoping no one realized they were with Sloane and Amelia.

Only the Judge didn't seem embarrassed. Just confused. He looked up from a book on peonies he'd been reading. "What's happened? Who's making a scene? Why do Sloane and Amelia look like they just climbed out of a grave?"

"They disappeared for half the dinner!" Amanda Miller waved her hand at the plates of uneaten food at Sloane's and Amelia's places: oysters, lobsters, and salmon.

"Oh, well. She's back now." Considering the matter resolved, the Judge buried his nose in his peony book again as Sloane and Amelia sat down.

"I can't eat any of this anyhow." Amelia crossed her arms

grumpily, slumping down in her chair as Aiden and Ashley finally straightened up in theirs.

"Why not?" Aiden asked, reaching for the plate of lobster since his sister didn't want it. Ashley claimed the salmon.

"I'm a vegetarian."

That got the Judge's attention again. He dropped his book into his lap in shock.

Everyone gaped at Amelia.

"Since when?" Ashley gasped.

"For over a year now."

"But—but—" For the first time in his life, the Judge seemed to be struggling to find something to say. "We have steak every Friday night!"

"Yes, and haven't you noticed how I never eat any of it?" Amelia arched her eyebrows meaningfully. Then, when everyone continued to stare at her, she went hot with embarrassment and slunk even lower in her chair until her nose was practically resting on the tablecloth.

Amanda Miller was the first to recover. "Well! If you don't eat meat, then we'll get you something else to eat. We'll get you . . . what is it people who are vegetarians eat?"

"Vegetables?" Sloane offered helpfully.

"Yes!" Amanda Miller seized on this suggestion and grabbed the plate of lobster back from Aiden. She scraped the potatoes and asparagus off the side and onto Amelia's bread plate. "Fresh, yummy vegetables."

They probably had been fresh and yummy at one time.

However, Sloane and Amelia had been gone for so long, they'd become cold, damp, and wilted.

Sloane handed her friend the bread basket.

As she did so, she noticed Aiden's phone light up. A message had just come through from one of his friends, but that wasn't what caught her interest.

There was also a message from her granny Kitty.

"Why are my grannies texting you?" she asked in surprise.

"Oh, just to praise me on how much I know about peonies," he bragged around a mouthful of lobster. Ashley swallowed her bite of salmon indignantly.

"You mean, how much *I* know!" she exclaimed.

That set off another round of bickering among the Miller-Poe family.

Sloane and Amelia listened to it silently, both of them trying to figure out where Bootleggin' Ma Yaklin's missing millions could possibly be.

And how they could get to them first.

Most important of all—what would the person who had locked them in the hiding spot do, now that they knew Sloane and Amelia didn't scare easily?

Next time, would that person do more than just try to scare them?

SUSPECTS, SUSPECTS EVERYWHERE, BUT NO MONEY IN SIGHT

Still hungry after dinner was over, Sloane and Amelia went back to their room. The sun was setting, the world dissolving into golden light with shadows waiting in the corners for when it was over. Sloane always thought of this as the sad part of the day, when her mother's loss could still sneak up on her and wrap its arms tightly around her chest.

They took turns using the bathroom to take baths and get all the cobwebs and gunk out of their hair and off their skin. Cleaned and changed into pajamas, they both felt a little better even if their stomachs were still rumbling grouchily.

Amelia flopped with her tablet onto her fancy, old-fashioned bed with its heap of pillows and high headboard. She uploaded the video and pictures she'd taken and began to edit them. "So, Ma Yaklin makes a fortune as a smuggler during the 1920s and early 1930s. Not only is she the best bootlegger in town, but she also has the best peonies and the dog who's best at sniffing. I wonder if I'm related to her too, because she sure sounds like the rest of my family."

"Maybe," Sloane admitted, collapsing onto her own bed with its scary, tombstone-like headboard. She picked up a brush from the bedside table and ran it through the tangles in her hair. "But your family loves each other."

"They sure have a hard time showing it," Amelia grumbled.

"What family doesn't? The point is, the only living creature Ma really likes is her dog, Eli. She's at war with Two Thumbs Lundquist and the Digits Gang, and the feds are onto her. She knows she might need to go on the run, so she stashes a million dollars in escape money somewhere around Tangle Glen. Two Thumbs sends the Digits Gang to tear up her garden, looking for the money. They don't find it, so they dognap Eli instead. But before Two Thumbs can demand a ransom, the feds show up to arrest Ma. She tries to escape through the woods rather than hop in her roadster the way any sensible person would. Possibly because she actually buried her money out there."

"*Probably* buried it out there," Amelia corrected, adding dramatic black-and-white lighting effects to the video they'd shot.

"Possibly," Sloane argued back. "I still think there's something interesting up in the attic."

"Yeah, I already told you. Haunted, creepy dolls."

"Besides those," Sloane said, not really wanting to argue the point. "Anyhow, whether it's in the attic or the woods, Ma is a bit of a mess, saying, 'When I lost Eli, I lost everything.'" Sloane expected Amelia to cut in with some sort of dramatic take on that. But her friend was too busy putting together silent-movie-style title cards. So, Sloane continued, "No one ever sees Eli again, but let's hope the dog ended up in a happy home with someone in the Digits Gang. Meanwhile, Mr. Lindsay buys Tangle Glen for next to nothing and the family spends years trying to find the money. They find the smugglers' tunnel and hiding place but nothing else. No one else could have found it, either, because the Lindsay family would have at least noticed a giant hole in their yard or in one of their walls. Nothing else happens for a very long time. Then, Mr. Lindsay turns Tangle Glen into an event center and inn—and suddenly people are looking for the money again. Or at least, us and someone else."

"My vote is Mr. Hayden Boening-Bradley. He's the worst." Amelia added title cards to her video and then started looking up music.

"Definitely the worst," Sloane agreed easily. Having finished with her hair, she twisted it back up into a ponytail again and then pulled out her phone. "But that doesn't mean he's looking for Ma's money. Shakespeare Wikander wants to be a magician, not a house manager. I bet two million dollars would make it a lot easier to quit his job and pursue his dream."

"Then there's Chef Zahra Abu-Absi. She's definitely up to something in the attic." Amelia found a song she liked and added it to their video. "And even though I didn't like her food because it was all fish, I heard other people talking about how amazing everything was and how she should open up her own restaurant. Two million dollars would help out with that, too."

"Those bread rolls were the best I ever tasted," Sloane agreed, pulling up Instagram to see if her dad or grannies had posted anything. "But how about Mr. Sherwood Lindsay or Sergeant Pepper Arroyo? I mean, I can't think of anything they'd want the money for, but . . . who wouldn't want two million dollars if they could get their hands on it?"

Amelia nodded in agreement as she uploaded their video to YouTube and checked their subscriber numbers. "And then there's all of those snooty peony competitors. How do we know it isn't someone like that Kuneman or Baker? Even the rich want more money, sometimes."

"Let's ask your family if they saw Mr. Boening-Bradley, Shakespeare, Sergeant Pepper, and Mr. Lindsay during the time that someone locked us in that room. I don't think there's any point about asking them if they saw Chef Zahra, but maybe someone from the kitchen staff noticed if she disappeared down into the basement. I don't think we need to bother with either Baker or Kuneman unless we see them doing anything else weird or suspicious."

"Like try to fillet each other with silver cocktail forks?"

"Weirder than that."

"Okay, but not yet," Amelia pleaded, laying down her tablet. "I need a few more minutes before I can face another round of Miller-Poe lip curls."

She imitated the way all four of her family members tended to pull up their lips and nostrils when they *really* wanted to boss Amelia around and tell her how she should be doing things differently.

Sloane laughed, and Amelia went off to change her clothes again so they could check out the attic before it got too late and the haunted dolls woke up.

While Sloane waited, she pulled up the Instagram account Granny Kitty and Granny Pearl shared. Earlier in the day, Granny Kitty had posted a picture of Granny Pearl hard at work in their garden. Sloane didn't know much about gardens, but it looked pretty to her.

The flowers were bright, there was lots of shade, and a tire swing hung from an old tree. What more could you possibly want from a garden?

Apparently, a lot. Because one of their followers, @mackenziesgrandmaisthebest, had left the comment:

LOLOL—I love how casual you are about your garden! It's just like a comfy old sweatshirt!

Hmmm . . . that didn't exactly sound like a compliment.

Sloane tapped on @mackenziesgrandmaisthebest and looked at what she posted. A lot of her pictures were of her granddaughter, Mackenzie Snyder, Sloane's volleyball teammate and nemesis.

The rest were of a garden full of flowers that had been pruned within an inch of their lives. It was all straight rows and not one single bloom dared to wilt or even so much as droop. Grandma Millie Snyder must be out there with a pair of garden scissors every day, lecturing her flowers on what would happen if their petals got spots or their leaves curled up.

It looked like a garden that even the bugs didn't risk entering.

So, yeah. Comparing Sloane's grannies' garden to a comfy old sweatshirt definitely had *not* been a compliment.

Sloane casually pulled up Instagram to check her grannies' accounts.

Switching back to her grannies' Instagram account, Sloane

saw that they'd just added to their story. First, there popped up a picture of the grannies at the Imagination Kingdom playground over at Reighard Park. Then, it switched to a video of Granny Kitty showing Cynthia Seife's kids, Skye and Brighton, how to walk along the top of the fence. The story concluded with a picture of the kids helping to put ice packs on her granny's hip and knee, along with a laughing emoji and the words "Not as young as I used to be, lololol!"

Wow. It looked like the evening had been a disaster.

Except . . . had it? Sloane studied both pictures carefully.

Actually, it looked like everyone was having a lot of fun. Strained hip and knee or no strained hip and knee. They were all smiling, and a minute later, a picture appeared of all of them smiling and eating ice cream together. This caption read, *Just what the doctor ordered! Never too old for ice cream!*

Hey, eating ice cream together was *their* thing! Sloane and her grannies!

Not her grannies and Cynthia Seife's evil little gremlins.

Sloane's stomach squeezed together in distress, trying to digest this. She flopped backward onto her pillows to stare up at the headboard looming over her. It looked more than ever like a tombstone.

She swore she could almost make out words on it.

Here lies the remains of Sloane Osburn's family. Eaten alive by two sticky gremlins.

"Amelia," Sloane called out in a slightly strangled voice. "Let's keep looking for a skunk, all right?"

"Don't worry. I've been looking up tips on how to catch a wild one," Amelia assured her as she emerged from the bathroom. "You know, just in case. Knowing how to catch a skunk seems like a good life skill."

Sloane expected Amelia to return from the bathroom in her cat burglar outfit, including a cat-eye mask. Or possibly dressed in a new flapper look.

Instead, Amelia emerged with a white fedora that smushed her curls to her head. A pinstripe suit hung from her shoulders, complete with a white shirt and tie underneath. Amelia had even managed to get her hands on a pair of shiny black shoes covered with white spats.

Understandably, Amelia looked *extremely* pleased with herself.

"Ain't I the cat's pajamas?" she demanded.

"I thought you were the bee's knees."

"That was when I was a flapper. Now I'm a bootlegger. Let's go grill my siblings and make them sing like canaries."

However, when they knocked on Aiden and Ashley's door, it was clear the two of them were talking to someone on FaceTime. Someone they didn't want Sloane and Amelia to hear. There was a lot of shushing after Amelia knocked and called in through the wood door. Then the room went very silent until Ashley unlocked the door and cracked it open so they could only see one eye.

When they asked her about Mr. Boening-Bradley, Mr. Lindsay, and the rest of their suspects, Ashley admitted that they'd all been in and out of the dining room. Including the ritzy Kuneman and Baker, as it turned out. Everyone, it seemed, had time to dash downstairs and shut them in the hidden room.

"What about the two of you?" Amelia demanded suspiciously, not sure what to make of her sister's odd behavior.

"Oh, ha-ha. You're so fun!" Ashley forced out a laugh and then slammed the door shut.

They could hear her on the other side of the door, waiting for them to go.

In a loud voice, Sloane said, "I don't know why your family thinks *you're* the weird one, Amelia. They've easily got you all beat."

"Thanks," Amelia whispered as they walked along the long, upstairs hallway, "but the only part of that they probably heard was that they won."

They found the back servant stairs at the far end of the hallway. Unlike the wide, impressive main stairway that made a box around a huge crystal chandelier, this was a sensible set of stairs. Rather than being showy, they made it up and down as quickly as possible.

The lights at this end of the hallway weren't as bright, and outside, the sun had set with the approach of ten o'clock. A bit of inky-blue light spilled in through a tall window, the last of the daylight that had made it in through all the trees surrounding Tangle Glen.

Standing at the base of the attic stairs, Sloane and Amelia looked upward.

Shadows gathered thickly, like bats in a cave.

Waiting to swoop down on anyone brave enough or foolish enough to enter.

Sloane gulped, palms sweaty.

Amelia shook out her selfie stick and attached her phone to it. "In case anything horrible happens to us."

"How will filming us help with *that*?"

"It won't. But it will prove to the world the existence of haunted dolls."

Swallowing hard, Sloane wondered if maybe the life-changing event she should be worried about wasn't the Seife's stealing away her family. It was getting eaten by haunted dolls.

However, Sloane hadn't earned the nickname "Slayer" on the volleyball court for nothing. She balled up her fists and marched upward, into the darkness. Amelia followed just a few steps behind, determined to film whatever was about to happen, even if every hair on her body stood at attention, screaming at her to turn around or at the very least turn on some lights.

Actually, there was one light they didn't need to turn on. An eerie violet light.

Trickling out from underneath the attic door.

A ghost light.

9

THE HORROR IN THE ATTIC

"Ghost dolls!" Amelia shrieked. "Sloane, they're coming for us. Run!"

She tried to do exactly that herself, but Sloane grabbed her friend by the bootlegger's jacket and held on tight. "Hang on! I think I recognize that light!"

"Of course you recognize it! Everyone recognizes the light of ghost dolls getting ready for dinner!" Amelia waved her arms about, trying frantically to get away. She accidentally dropped her selfie stick, blinding them both with the camera's light as it bounced onto the floor.

"Ow!" Sloane threw an arm up to block her eyes from the dazzling flash. "Amelia, I think that's a grow lamp!"

"What's a grow lamp?" Amelia demanded, snatching up her phone and selfie stick and clutching them to her chest. "Is that how they grow ghost dolls? Do they start out as just little action figures and then get bigger?"

"Will you stop with the ghost dolls?" Sloane cried, rubbing her eyes to clear them of the spots the camera light had made dance in front of her pupils. "Gardeners use grow lamps to grow flowers and plants indoors in places where there isn't enough sunlight. You know, like attics?"

Amelia went still, considering this. Still wheezing a little from panic, she asked suspiciously, "Are you sure of this?"

"No, but I know a couple of experts we can call." Pulling out her phone, Sloane FaceTimed her grannies. "If we get attacked by ghost dolls, I think my grannies will find a way to save us. Even if they're forty-five minutes from here in Wauseon."

Amelia had a great deal of faith in Granny Kitty and Granny Pearl too. So, she stayed with Sloane on the landing. Though she positioned herself close to the stairs in case she needed to make a swift getaway.

"Sloane-y!" they cried in delight. "And Amelia, too! Look, Tia. Look, Timothy! See, the girls are having a marvelous time down at the peony festival not stealing anything. Er, investigating."

To both Sloane and Amelia's surprise, they appeared to have caught Granny Kitty and Granny Pearl in the middle of a card game with Nanna Tia (Sloane's great-grandmother) and Timothy Neikirk (Nanna Tia's ninety-year-old boyfriend). All four of them wore green visors on their heads for some reason, and they each had a pile of striped, round plastic chips in front of them. Nanna Tia's pile was the biggest, and it must be an intense card game because Nanna Tia was also burning chamomile incense, which she usually only did when she thought her bingo games were going to get rowdy.

"Bah!" Tiny Timothy Neikirk thrust out his chin above the green bow tie he was wearing. He always reminded both Sloane and Amelia of a leprechaun. "They'd better find that missing two million dollars of Jacqeline Yaklin's! Don't forget you promised me ten percent of whatever they get, Pearl, if I stepped down and let that blowhard Judge Alexander Poe take over for me!"

"What?" Sloane and Amelia gasped together.

"Oh, ha-ha-ha-ha!" Granny Pearl tittered. "You are a card, Timothy. And speaking of, that's gin rummy!"

Granny Pearl laid down her cards. Timothy Neikirk went red in the face, while Nanna Tia patted his shoulder soothingly. Before he could say anything, Granny Kitty chirped, "We'll just pop out into the kitchen to take this phone call!"

Once both Granny Kitty and Granny Pearl were in their peach-and-turquoise kitchen, Granny Pearl hissed, "Look, Sloane. We had to offer him something to give up his role as judge at the peony competition! He's been doing it for over fifty years."

"But we don't even know if we'll get to keep any of the money!" Sloane protested, while Amelia clutched her own phone and peered over her friend's shoulder.

"Don't worry, Sloane." Granny Kitty smiled slyly. "Pearl just promised him ten percent of whatever you get. If you get ten percent of nothing, then he gets ten percent of nothing."

Sometimes, Sloane wondered what would have happened if her grannies had become friends earlier in their lives. Before their children met and got married when the grannies were both in their fifties. Sloane's mom used to say that they probably would have taken over the world by now.

Either way, given how crafty they were, Sloane was glad that Granny Kitty and Granny Pearl were on her side.

And hoped they'd forgive her for not stealing those peonies for them.

"Grannies, we need your help," Sloane began before Amelia interrupted her.

She grabbed Sloane's phone and swiveled it toward the attic door. "There's a good chance there's an army of haunted dolls on the other side of that, and they're coming for our souls."

Sloane grabbed her phone back. "That's one possibility! Another possibility is that someone has a grow lamp on the other side of the door."

Haunted dolls didn't hold much interest for the grannies, but grow lamps did. Granny Kitty looked at Granny Pearl. Granny Pearl looked at Granny Kitty and said, "Ooo! Secret peonies!"

To Sloane and Amelia, Granny Pearl explained, "Technically, you can still enter peonies into the competition tomorrow, as long as they're there by the evening. I bet someone is keeping their peony hidden until then to avoid sabotage."

"People sabotage peonies?" Sloane asked in surprise.

"Oh, yes." Granny Kitty and Granny Pearl both nodded wisely. Granny Kitty added, "The competition is quite cutthroat. Now, let's bust open this attic and see what comes out."

"Sounds great." With Amelia peering around her back, Sloane turned the thick, old-fashioned iron doorknob. It went CA-CHUNK! and released the latch. Sloane leaned against the heavy wooden door, pushing it open with her shoulder.

More violet light greeted them, filling the attic.

Mustering up her courage, Amelia jumped from behind Sloane and went in first. As she did so, she called out, "Nothing to eat here. Just a couple of bootlegger ghosts, come to, ah, visit with the other ghosts."

To Sloane and the grannies, she whispered, "Just in case."

"I appreciate it, but I don't look much like a bootlegger." Sloane gestured from Amelia's suit, fedora, and spats to her own pajamas.

Revising her story a bit, Amelia ventured farther into the attic. "Yup, I'm just a bootleggin' ghost. With the human I've kidnapped to eat. She's all mine. So don't you ghost dolls get any ideas about attacking her. Or us."

If there were any ghost dolls in the attic, Amelia's ruse fooled them. She sagged in relief when nothing porcelain wobbled out across the floorboards with its arms stretched. (With old attics, you just never knew.)

Sloane followed Amelia into the attic and looked around. It was largely empty of anything other than dust and cobwebs. The only furnishings were right inside the door. The purple light they had seen did, in fact, come from several very ordinary grow lamps. They were all projected onto large tubs filled with dirt and big, lovely peonies. Potting soil, clippers, and garden gloves lay on a long wooden table nearby. Next to these sat a stack of very old, yellowing newspapers, along with the remains of compost and—ew, gross—*fish guts.*

"Ooh . . . now there's a thought, Kitty!" Granny Pearl peered through the phone, settling a pair of half-moon glasses on her nose so she could take a closer look. "Swing the phone over there, Sloane-y. I bet all those guts help add nitrogen to the soil!"

"Yuck." Grimacing, Sloane did as her granny asked.

Meanwhile, Granny Kitty had grabbed her own phone and FaceTimed Amelia. Who made the mistake of answering, cutting off the video she'd been recording for their next YouTube episode.

"Forget the fish guts, Pearl! Have you ever seen such a soft shade of pink? Amelia, see if you can turn off those grow lamps and turn on some regular lights."

Amelia ended the call but did as she was asked. There was a rather scary button light switch just inside the door. She grimaced and stood as far back as she could, stretching her arm out to poke gingerly at the switch, more than half convinced she was about to be electrocuted. Several hanging light bulbs hissed and crackled to life.

Sloane turned off the purple grow lights. In normal lighting, they could all see that Granny Kitty was right.

"Oh, it's lovely! Creamy white at the center and baby pink at the edges." Granny Kitty leaned in until her nose was practically pressed against the lens as she tried to get a better look at it. "Whoever is growing those knows what she's doing. I'd swear that's an heirloom breed."

"What's an 'earloom'?" Amelia asked, not liking the sound of it. She hoped it wasn't anything like "earwig," because just the thought of bugs made her feel scratchy.

"'Heirloom,' not 'earloom.' That means old, vintage-y breeds of plants that you can't find easily," Granny Pearl explained, pushing Granny Kitty slightly out of the way so she could get a better look at the table. "What about that stack of newspapers? Do you think whoever is growing them is using those as compost? I wonder if that's part of why those blooms are so gorgeous. Maybe it has something to do with the old ink."

"Forget compost." Sloane picked up the top newspaper. "It

looks like it's dated to May eleventh, 1932. Amelia, that's only a month before the feds arrested Ma Yaklin. And—oh! The headline is about Eli winning a sniffing competition Ma Yaklin arranged."

"I didn't know she arranged the competition Eli won." Amelia took the newspaper from her friend and propped it up against the bucket of fish guts so they both could look at it without getting their fingers all over the fragile, crumbly newspaper.

Leaning her elbows on the rough wooden table while her grannies continued discussing the peonies, Sloane looked at the old article. "That doesn't seem super fair, does it? I mean, that seems kind of rigged to me."

"Seems like the sort of thing my family would do," Amelia said darkly. "Set up a competition they know they could win."

"Well, I do think your family would make very successful bootleggers. If it was the 1920s and they wanted to be bootleggers."

Together, they turned their attention to reading. The headline screamed:

MA YAKLIN'S DOG WINS
SNIFFING COMPETITION!
RIGGED TEST?

Jacqueline "Ma" Yaklin's dog, Eli, is known to be the best sniffer around. The bloodhound makes sure that every batch of her illegal hooch can pass the sniff test. Neither the feds nor the Digits

Gang have been able to smell out her shipments. But is that reputation deserved? An inside source told us that Ma recently held a sniffing competition to show off Eli's skills. But doesn't it seem suspicious that she set up the competition, only for her dog to win? Do we catch a whiff of cheating?

Several surly, unhappy-looking men stood behind Ma Yaklin, their dogs all next to them. The caption beneath the photograph listed the names of each one.

"Sloane, look." Amelia pointed at the man standing behind Ma Yaklin. "His name was Anderson Lindsay, owner of a bloodhound named Elizabeth."

"Mr. Lindsay did say that his family had been raising bloodhounds for generations," Sloane said.

"Yeah, but he didn't say that his family worked for Ma Yaklin. And he *definitely* didn't say that his grandfather lost a competition to her because Eli was a better sniffer than Elizabeth."

There was no mistaking the sour look on Lindsay's face. Whether Ma had cheated or not, he clearly didn't appreciate his dog losing out to Eli.

"Nobody likes being made to feel inferior," Amelia observed unhappily, rubbing at her stomach as it twisted with the memory of feeling exactly that way.

Sloane gave her friend a sympathetic look and said gently, "I don't think that's what Ma was trying to do. Any more than that's what I think your family means to do to you. I think she was just supercompetitive."

"Yeah, well, just because you don't *mean* to do something doesn't change the fact that you *did* do it." Releasing her stomach, Amelia flipped through the stack. She found a newspaper from a week later, announcing that partiers had broken into Ma Yaklin's house using her secret tunnel. Someone had leaked that bit of information, and now Ma Yaklin had all sorts of unwanted guests creeping in and out.

Apparently, everybody assumed that Toledo's biggest bootlegger was always throwing a party in her mansion.

Sloane reached forward and flipped back to Anderson Lindsay's angry face. "Think he told people about the secret tunnel?"

Amelia shrugged. "I think it could've been any of those guys standing behind Ma Yaklin and—"

At Granny Kitty and Granny Pearl's request, Sloane swung her phone around the attic so the grannies could get a good look at it. Then, while they took notes, she and Amelia kept going through the stack of old newspapers. On June eighth, a new headline announced the results of the Tenth Annual Ohio Peony Enthusiasts Competition:

MA YAKLIN WINS AGAIN!
Gangster Wins Second Competition in a Month

It's well known that Jacqueline "Ma" Yaklin has to be the best at what she does. Everyone knows she's the most successful bootlegger in town. However, maybe it's not such a good idea to always be showing off. Not only has the Digits Gang taken notice— so have the feds.

An enormous picture showed Ma Yaklin holding her prize-winning bloom. The newspaper described the flower as having a "delicate oyster-shell white" at its heart, fading out to "antique pink" at the edges.

"That sounds exactly like the peonies in that attic!" Granny Kitty cried as Amelia read this bit aloud. "Pearl, we were right! Those *are* heirloom peonies!"

"Can't be," Sloane said absently. "All of Ma Yaklin's prizewinning bushes were destroyed by Two Thumbs Lundquist and the Digits Gang."

But that wasn't what interested Sloane and Amelia.

Because there, in the far background, was Anderson Lindsay again.

This time, he didn't have his bloodhound, Elizabeth, with him. He *was* clutching a vase with a peony in it.

He had that same bitter look on his face.

A newspaper from a week later announced that Eli had been kidnapped and Ma's prize-winning peony bushes had been destroyed. It was the same headline and picture Sloane and Amelia had seen downstairs. The one that made it clear that everyone assumed that Two Thumbs Lundquist and the Digits Gang were to blame.

This time, however, they spotted something they hadn't noticed before.

A distraught Ma Yaklin held her hand up to the photographer's lens, trying to block it. Several of her gang members stood behind her. Most of them looked very serious.

But one—all the way to the side and almost out of view—was caught looking very pleased.

Anderson Lindsay.

"Okay. You're right," Amelia squeaked. "He definitely did it."

"Amelia," Sloane said after a moment's stunned silence. "I think we may have solved a ninety-year-old dognapping."

"What's that?" The grannies looked up from the detailed notes they'd been taking.

Sloane explained about the destroyed peonies and Eli's disappearance. With Amelia finishing, "And no one at the time suspected Anderson Lindsay because Ma and everyone else assumed the rival gang members were to blame."

What had happened to Eli after that? Sloane wondered. Nothing horrible, she hoped. It wasn't Eli's fault that Ma Yaklin had to be the best at everything. Besides, Ma Yaklin loved her dog and seemed to take really good care of him. She hoped Lindsay took good care of Eli, too.

Hopefully, Eli and Elizabeth got along.

"Hey, why are you drawing a diagram of the attic?" Amelia asked Granny Kitty and Granny Pearl.

"No reason!" they cried together, and ended the call.

"Hey! There could still be ghost dolls in here, you know!" Amelia cried in alarm.

"Come on, Amelia." Sloane turned back on the purple grow lights. "I don't think there's anything more to find up here."

Sloane gestured at the empty attic. Amelia took a few more pictures of the newspapers and then nodded. "Hey, what do you think about making like bootleggers and breaking into the kitchen for some peanut butter and pickle sandwiches?"

"I'll agree to half of that." Sloane led the way out of the attic, unaware that just a day and a half later, she'd be in here again.

Only, next time there would be a kidnapper hot on her heels.

10

Fish Guts and Suspicions

By now, Tangle Glen had settled down for the night. It actually seemed to sigh and roll over contentedly, like all the guests in its many rooms. Overhead, the chandeliers slept like birds in their nests, swaying slightly in the breeze from the open window at the end of the hallway. Small lamps gave off dim circles of golden light on tables spaced evenly along the length of the hallway. Shadows stretched long and deep across the wooden floorboards and flowery carpets. Far outside, a symphony of frog croaks arose from the forest, rather like a lullaby, hopefully keeping everyone else asleep.

"Do you think my grannies were acting suspicious?" Sloane asked Amelia as they tiptoed down the servant stairs and into the kitchen.

"I dunno. We caught them in the middle of a card game after they got done running an illegal bingo ring. And they were doing it with Mr. Neikirk, who they're scamming." Amelia thought it over as she turned on her phone's flashlight and swung it around the kitchen. "So, they seemed pretty much like their normal selves to me."

"I guess," Sloane admitted.

The kitchen had a black-and-white tile floor, sort of like the dining room floor only not as expensive-looking. Unlike the dining room, there were lots of stainless steel appliances, and old-fashioned-looking cupboards. Sloane, knowing a thing or two about old houses, having grown up in one, pointed toward a butler's pantry. Going inside it, they saw lots of huge jars and cans, as well as boxes of onions and potatoes. Finally, at the very back, they spotted a tub of peanut butter large enough to feed an entire elementary school, and several bags of bread.

"No pickles, though." Amelia sighed regretfully. (Peanut-butter-and-pickle was Amelia's favorite sandwich. Little did she know it, but there *was* a jar of pickles in the pantry. Before she could spot it, Sloane tucked the glass jar behind the bin of onions out of fear that Amelia would become overly enthusiastic and insist that she have pickles on her sandwich too. It had happened before, and Sloane was determined that it would not happen again.)

"Here, try my favorite way to have peanut butter sandwiches," Sloane said. She grabbed a bag of potato chips and took it out into the main part of the kitchen along with some bread, with boot-legger Amelia lugging the giant tub of peanut butter after. Having scrounged up a knife, they spread everything out on one of the stainless-steel counters. Amelia smeared the bread with peanut butter and then Sloane crumbled up potato chips over the goo. Then she smushed the second slice of bread on top, cut each sandwich in half, and handed a slice to Amelia.

"Not bad." Amelia crunched her sandwich thoughtfully. "Hey, Sloane. Hot take here, but what if Anderson Lindsay, Sherwood Lindsay's grandfather, *already found Ma's missing two million dollars years ago?* What if that's the money he used to buy Tangle Glen?"

Sloane crunched her own sandwich unhappily. "Ugh. I don't like to admit it, but you may have a point. After all, he worked for Ma Yaklin. He knew about her hiding spots, if he was the one who revealed them to people. Maybe he knew where she kept her money, too. Only, if so, why wouldn't Ma admit that? Why just say, 'When I lost Eli, I lost everything,' and not 'Anderson Lindsay robbed me, the jerk'?"

Amelia opened her mouth to explain that people didn't really call other people "jerk" back in the 1920s and 1930s, they called them "gongoozlers." However, before she could, something caught her eye.

She and Sloane had sat down on one of the stainless-steel counters while they ate, their legs swinging clear of the floor. It gave them a view out the window.

Across the dark, open sea of the backyard, she could see into the trees at the back of it. That was where grass gave way to the surrounding forest.

Light flitted through the shadows between the trees.

A silver light.

A ghostly light.

"Sloane, there's something out there," Amelia squeaked, sliding off the counter and going over to the window.

Sloane joined her, a mouthful of sandwich sticking in her throat.

It wasn't a ghost. Obviously, it wasn't a ghost.

They'd already been through this with the attic.

Except . . . that time, Sloane had figured out pretty quickly what the light probably was.

This time, she had no idea.

"It's not a ghost," she declared strongly, to reassure both herself and Amelia.

It didn't reassure either one of them.

Probably because something grabbed them from behind.

"GAH!" Sloane shrieked, spinning around to kick at their attacker. While Amelia screamed, "Don't turn me into a ghost! I haven't even won an Oscar for best picture yet!"

"OW!" Their attacker released them so she could grab her knee while hopping around on one foot. "What are you two doing in my kitchen? Why do you have food out on the counter? *Are those crumbs on the floor?*"

It was Chef Zahra Abu-Absi, wearing a pair of pajamas that looked remarkably like her work clothes. Minus the floppy chef's hat and apron covered in terrifying stains. There was a bucket that hadn't been there a moment before on the counter behind her.

Oh, and also a meat cleaver.

A meat cleaver again! Who carried a meat cleaver around with them in the middle of the night like it was a teddy bear?

"We didn't leave those crumbs!" Amelia squeaked, words belied by the sandwich in her hand, still shedding potato chips onto the floor. "Somebody else must have broken into the kitchen and gotten out the peanut butter. But not us. And my parents will definitely want their money back if either Sloane or I end up in that bucket."

"What are you talking about?" Releasing her knee, Chef Zahra regarded them as though Sloane and Amelia were the most bizarre things she'd ever seen in her life. It wasn't particularly flattering coming from somebody who apparently wandered about in the middle of the night with a deadly weapon and a bucket for cleaning up the mess it left behind.

Sloane tried to decide if, when dealing with a homicidal maniac, it was better to apologize or run like heck. She'd just settled on "run like heck" when the back door burst open without warning.

Once again, everyone in the kitchen screamed. This time, that included Chef Zahra.

Who grabbed both Amelia and Sloane and pulled them backward. Apparently in case she needed to protect her ingredients from any forest ghosts who'd also decided to break in for a snack.

Instead of a forest ghost, however, Shakespeare Wikander burst through the door.

Not expecting to see anyone either, he shrieked as well.

"GAAAAHHH!!! Who are you? What do you want?" he gasped, falling back against the wall and clutching a hand to his heart. He still wore his tuxedo, and his top hat fell at a crooked angle. "Oh. Chef. It's *you*. What are you doing down here with two of the guests?"

He didn't sound particularly pleased to see Chef Zahra. Craning her neck backward to get a good look at the chef, Amelia noticed that she looked equally sour to be encountering the house manager.

"Helping them clean up from a midnight snack, apparently." She let go of both girls so she could turn and look pointedly at the mess they'd made on the counter.

Immediately, Sloane and Amelia rushed to put away everything they had gotten out. As they did so, Chef Zahra asked, "What were *you* doing out in the backyard so late at night?"

"Oh. Er. Um. Just . . . dusting the lawn." Shakespeare did one of his magic tricks and pulled an old-fashioned feather duster out of one sleeve. He swept it across the nearest counter as though to prove his point.

Chef Zahra crossed her arms and narrowed her eyes suspiciously. "You don't dust the lawn. No one dusts a lawn!"

Recovering from his shock, Shakespeare made the feather duster disappear with a clap of his hands. "And *you* don't fix late-night snacks for the guests. What's in the bucket, chef?"

Chef Zahra went all shifty as she positioned herself in front of the bucket like she thought Shakespeare Wikander might take it from her. "I was, er, cleaning my meat cleaver."

"Ha! You were heading up to the attic, weren't you?" Shakespeare accused. "I know fish guts when I smell them."

"And you were out in the forest! Don't think I don't know what you were doing out there with those rhubarb leaves and potato peelings I see poking out of your pockets!"

"They're part of my magic act! Since I'm entertaining gardeners, I plan on showering them with compost like, uh, confetti!"

As they argued, the two of them inched closer and closer together until their noses were practically pressed together. Sloane and Amelia both squeezed themselves out of the way and back against the kitchen cupboards. Neither one of them wanted to get caught in the crossfire if either fish guts or rotten potato peels started getting thrown.

Before it came to that, Chef Zahra let out a huff, grabbed her bucket, and stormed away. Over her shoulder, she called, "Don't think I don't know what you're up to! And it isn't going to work! That money is mine!"

"Over my dead body, Abu-Absi! We'll see who ends up with it when this is all over!" Shakespeare marched off as well, though he took a different door out of the kitchen.

Left behind and completely forgotten, Sloane and Amelia collapsed in relief.

"I guess they're looking for the missing money just like us," Amelia said. "If it was Chef Zahra who locked us in the hiding spot, maybe we should be glad she didn't turn us into guts too."

"Maybe. We know Chef Zahra is re-creating Ma Yaklin's award-winning peonies." Sloane went over to where Shakespeare Wikander had been standing and turned on her phone's flashlight. Sweeping it across the floor, she bent over and picked a petal off the tile. "This fell from Shakespeare's sleeve when he took out that feather duster. It's a peony petal, I think."

It was a large petal, a deep, inky purple in color.

"I haven't seen any peonies that color," Amelia said. "Not out in that big vase in the hallway, anyhow."

"I'm betting that makes it a rare color," Sloane observed. "So, maybe the two of them are competing against each other in the peony competition. You know, like maybe there's an award for 'Most Unique Flower' or something weird like that?"

"Maybe," Amelia agreed reluctantly as she and Sloane finished tidying up the kitchen and started back up the stairs to their room. "But I'm sure the peony competition isn't handing out two-million-dollar awards. I still think both Chef Zahra and Shakespeare could be using the peony competition to cover their search for the money. Maybe that's what Shakespeare wasn't doing out in the woods tonight."

"And we still can't rule out Mr. Lindsay, Mr. Boening-Bradley or Sergeant Pepper—GAH!" For the second time in the night, Sloane let out a strangled shriek and recoiled in horror.

Two figures formed out of the darkness on the stairs above them.

However, it was only Aiden and Ashley. Dressed all in black and scurrying down from the attic like they'd found that pack of creepy haunted dolls Amelia had been convinced was up there.

"What are *you* doing?" everyone said all at the same time.

"Just getting in some cardio!" Ashley claimed, running up and down a couple of steps to prove it.

"Then why are you carrying a bucket?" Amelia pointed at the one in Aiden's hands.

"To . . . practice for the . . . bucket-throwing team." Aiden started off lamely, then got into his story. Puffing out his chest, he bragged, "I *am* the best at it at the University of Toledo!"

"Only because I don't compete!" Ashley cut in quickly. "If I did, you'd be second best."

"Ha! Let's see you throw it half as far as me!"

"You're on!"

Still squabbling, they headed off to their room. Sloane and Amelia watched them go in astonishment. Amelia asked, "Sloane, does it seem like they're acting suspiciously to you?"

Sloane considered this and then ticked off some points on her fingers. "Let's see, someone in your family is engaging in a ridiculous competition and bragging about being good at something they've clearly never done before. No, that seems pretty normal for them to me."

"Normal," after all, is really just a matter of opinion.

Neither Sloane nor Amelia thought they'd be able to sleep. After all, they would be doing so under the same roof as the person who had shut them into Ma Yaklin's old bootlegging hiding spot. Who knew what else that person might try in the night? Plus, Sloane's anxieties were still wiggling about in her stomach like she'd eaten a whole mouthful of worms. She'd made the mistake of checking Instagram one more time, only to spot a picture of her dad and Cynthia snuggling together on the patio of the Red Rambler coffee shop, lattes in hand.

Big grins on their faces.

All while Skye and Brighton stole away her grannies' affections.

"What we do is, we turn the skunk loose in their house," Amelia explained as she wedged a chair under the doorknob of their room. That way, even if someone like Shakespeare Wikander had a key to their room and was unable to unlock it, that person still couldn't open the door. "But I'm thinking that we might want to get more than one skunk. Like, in case only Cynthia gets sprayed but Skye and Brighton still smell okay."

Sloane smiled weakly as she sank down onto her bed. "You want to get a backup skunk?"

"I was actually thinking about a surfeit of skunks. That's what you call a whole pack of skunks. A surfeit of skunks." Amelia went into the bathroom to change out of her bootlegger outfit and into pajamas. "Though, if we do happen to come across any creepy, haunted dolls, I think we might want to think about using one of those instead."

Sloane's limp smile grew into a full-on grin. "Yeah, but then we'd have to take it back to Wauseon with us in the car."

"I know. Just think how terrified my family would be." Sighing happily, Amelia returned to their room, turned off the lights, and went to sleep.

Miraculously, Sloane quickly fell asleep too.

There was something comforting about knowing that she had a friend to count on no matter what. Someone who would turn either a skunk or a haunted doll loose on people if that's what it took to keep you safe.

Knowing it reminded Sloane that she could count on her grannies to do the same thing. No matter how cute Skye and Brighton might be, her grannies would never choose them over Sloane.

Nor would her dad. Sloane knew that, too.

But all that sickly squirming in her stomach kept her from feeling it. Even if she could sleep.

Morning arrived bright and hot and early, the way it always did in June. Tangle Glen's enormous plate-glass windows seemed to let in even more dazzling golden light than normal windows did. For all the thick woods surrounding Tangle Glen, the mansion's wide lawn made the perfect runway for the flight of the rising sun.

"Wake up, sleepyheads!" Amanda Miller pounded cheerfully on their door. "I thought we could all go kayaking this morning before the Judge has to start—er—judging. Meet you in the entry hall after breakfast. And—er—Amelia? Try to wear something . . . appropriate? For kayaking?"

The normally hyperconfident Amanda Miller sounded more than a little hesitant. Sloane got the sense that Amelia's mom was trying not to hurt her daughter's feelings. Trying but not succeeding very well.

Amelia immediately went all hot and bristly, feeling very much as though someone had poked an especially tender bruise deep in her soul. She knew perfectly well that what her mom meant by "appropriate" was really "normal." The Miller-Poe definition of normal.

Which meant looking like you'd just stepped out of an Instagram ad for athletic wear. Everyone was supposed to look at you and wish they could be you.

Miller-Poes were supposed to be the people everyone else wanted to be.

But Amelia just wanted to be herself.

"I'll show them 'appropriate for kayaking'!" she snarled, and stormed into the bathroom.

She returned a few minutes later in overalls, a tan shirt, boots, and a tan cap.

There was a corncob bubble pipe clenched between her teeth.

Sloane blinked at her friend in surprise. Reaching up, she twisted her ponytail round and round her fingertip, trying to figure out who Amelia had dressed as now. Finally, she admitted, "I give up. How is this 'appropriate for kayaking'?"

"I'm a bootlegger again," Amelia explained with great dignity. "Last night, I was a boss bootlegger. You know, like Ma Yaklin? Now,

I'm just a worker bootlegger. Like Anderson Lindsay. Someone who got bossed around and did the actual work. I'm wearing overalls and boots because I'd be doing the hard work of moving barrels and crates around on boats."

"And a kayak is a type of boat," Sloane concluded. She didn't think that the rest of the Miller-Poes were going to love this reasoning, but she didn't say it.

All the other guests at Tangle Glen still thought Amelia was part of the entertainment arranged for the One Hundreth Annual Ohio Peony Enthusiasts Competition. Several of them handed her bottles of ginger ale or root beer, warning her to keep them out of sight. Then, they'd take swigs out of their own bottles before tucking them into their purses or under hats.

At first, Sloane and Amelia just blinked at each other in confusion. Breakfast time seemed awfully early to be drinking sugary, carbonated drinks. Then, Sloane got it.

"Oh—because it's 'beer' and 'ale,'" she explained to Amelia. "You know, the types of things Ma Yaklin would have bootlegged."

Amelia sighed. "If we can't figure out what happened to her money, maybe we can start renting ourselves out as party entertainment. We'd do better at it than poor Shakespeare."

Having just entered the dining room, they watched as the tuxedoed, top-hat-wearing house manager pulled a coin out from behind Mr. Boening-Bradley's ear. In return, the president of the Ohio Peony Enthusiasts Club glared at him. It occurred to both Sloane and Amelia that they had been wrong to compare Mr. Boening-Bradley to a grasshopper. Grasshoppers were essentially gentle creatures.

What the president of the Ohio Peony Enthusiasts Club looked like was a praying mantis.

An aggressive, swaggering, cranky praying mantis.

One who'd like to clip its claws around the tip of Shakespeare's nose.

Wilting like a peony, the house manager scurried off. Only to almost collide with Chef Zahra as she came into the dining room. Once again, Sloane and Amelia had to press themselves off to the side to keep from getting caught between the two of them.

"Eat fish guts," Shakespeare sneered.

"Go shove a feather duster someplace uncomfortable," Chef Zahra shot back.

Before either one of them could do something they regretted with guts or dusters, Mr. Boening-Bradley clinked his spoon against his orange juice glass and announced that it was last call to enter peonies into the competition.

Both the chef and the house manager shot out of the room.

Just as the rest of the Miller-Poes stormed into it.

Once again, Sloane and Amelia had to jump backward to keep from getting crushed.

"What do you mean you can't go kayaking?" Amanda Miller cried. As expected, she was wearing brand-new clothing and looked like she'd stepped out of an Instagram ad for kayaking.

"I need to be prepared!" the Judge replied, eyes just visible above the book he held in front of his face. His pupils scanned the words frantically, knuckles going white as he clenched the pages. "Have you seen the way that Hayden Boening-Bradley fellow looks at me? Like I'm some sort of worm?"

"He looks at everyone that way," his wife assured him.

She should have known better, being a Miller-Poe. Miller-Poes didn't do "like everyone else." They only did "better than everyone else."

The Judge let out a horrified sob and dashed from the room. "I'll eat and kayak after the competition is over!"

"Me too!" Aiden grabbed a muffin and a banana from a bowl near the door and sprinted after his dad. "I'd better study those peonies, too!"

"Not without me, you don't!" Ashley snatched up a cup of yogurt and a bagel and dashed after him.

"What?" Amanda gasped. "*Why?* You two aren't judging!"

However, the other Miller-Poes had already disappeared into the portrait gallery where individual peony stems were being set out on little pedestals.

"Hm. I guess people really don't like to be looked at like there's something wrong with them," Amelia observed pointedly to her mother.

Amanda Miller swiveled her attention to her daughter. She looked Amelia up and down, taking in the overalls, the cap, and the heavy boots. Amelia stared defiantly back at her and stuck the corncob pipe into her mouth.

She blew several large, shimmery bubbles out of the pipe.

Her mom watched them in a daze and then clapped a hand to her forehead. "I have a headache."

With that, she bolted back up to her room.

Amelia cracked her knuckles. Managing to sound both smug

and sad, she said, "All right. That's the Miller-Poe kayaking trip taken care of. Let's go find us some millions."

She grabbed a blueberry muffin from the bowl by the door and took a savage bite out of it. Then she stormed out of the dining room just like the rest of her family had.

For some reason, her eyes suddenly itched.

Her throat did too.

Because there was some tiny part of her that had wanted her mom to look at her and say, "Well, looks like it's just you and me, kiddo!"

And not care that Amelia didn't look like she'd stepped out of an Instagram ad for sports equipment.

Sure, her family had stopped bossing her around and trying to change her.

So why couldn't they actually enjoy being around her?

11

Into the Woods

Amelia marched all the way out of the mansion, mainly because she needed room to breathe. She was sick to death of the smell of peonies. Why was it totally normal for her family to get all competitive about some flower competition but totally weird for her to be into detective work and old movies? The rules felt completely random to Amelia, and the unfairness of it weighed as heavily on her as the mansion did on the grounds of Tangle Glen.

Sloane hurried after her friend with her arms full of muffins and fruit.

"So, I take it we've definitely decided to check the grounds for Ma's missing money?" Sloane asked, biting into an apple as they walked around the side of the house and toward the formal rose garden.

"It has to be out here somewhere. It just *has* to be." Amelia gestured toward the woods with her muffin.

"What's that, then?" a voice asked as Sloane and Amelia pushed open the white gate and went through the brick archway into the garden.

Looking down, they saw Mr. Lindsay on a wooden bench next to the long reflecting pool. As usual, he didn't seem to be sitting on it so much as growing out of it. His brown clothes matched the wood and his floppy hat looked more than ever like a mushroom cap. He was leaning on his walking stick and watching the Koi fish flit about beneath the lily pads. Chiave lay at his feet, sopping wet and panting, a lily pad sliding from her ear. Mr. Lindsay's socks, shoes, and shorts were wet too, and he looked completely exhausted from fishing his bloodhound out of the reflecting pool.

Peering up from beneath his grubby hat, he asked, "Did the two of you lose something?"

Sloane and Amelia exchanged a look, not sure how much to tell him. Mr. Lindsay did not seem the most likely person to have shut them in the old bootlegger hiding spot simply because he couldn't move very quickly. However, *someone* had done it, so maybe Mr. Lindsay was looking for Ma Yaklin's missing money too.

Maybe that was why he'd posted information about it on Tangle Glen's website.

Maybe he wanted his guests to look for that money.

Maybe he was using them the same way Sloane and Amelia had been used when the whole seventh grade was looking for the long-lost Hoäl jewels.

Maybe he was just faking his injured back. Pretending to be helpless so no one would suspect his nefarious plan.

Then Chiave sneezed, leaped to her feet, and took off running. Her leash slipped easily from Mr. Lindsay's damp fingers, and before anyone could stop her, the dog shot out of the garden gate and back toward the front of the house.

"Chiave, no!" Mr. Lindsay cried, struggling—and failing—to get to his feet in time. He fell heavily back onto the bench with a whimper of pain.

"Don't worry! I'll get her!" Sloane sprinted after Chiave, determined that some bloodhound was not going to get the better of Slayer Sloane the Volleyball Queen. She tackled Chiave as the dog stopped to snorf one of the many peony bushes lining the front of Tangle Glen.

The dog didn't seem to mind that Sloane had pinned her to the ground. Chiave kept her nose buried in the bright pink blossoms, tail thumping happily.

It took all of Sloane's strength to drag the bloodhound back to Mr. Lindsay.

"See? Got her," she panted, wiping mud and grass stains from her legs.

Chiave grinned up at her person, doggy lips curling back so her tongue could dangle out and give him a slurp. Mr. Lindsay massaged her ears. Without any resentment, he admonished, "What a bad dog you are, Chiave. Who's the bad dog? You are! Yes, you are!"

"What kind of name is 'Chiave,' anyhow?" Amelia asked, blowing a few more bubbles from her pipe. Chiave snapped at them, trying to catch them in her mouth. It confused her when it seemed she couldn't.

"Don't know," said Mr. Lindsay. "But we've always had a Chiave in the family. Even when my daddy was a little boy, they always had a Chiave about. I think it might be Italian for 'cheese.' The family name was originally 'Linzi,' you know. Granddaddy changed it to 'Lindsay' to make it sound more English, but he spoke fluent Italian."

"Yeah, I had a great-great-grandpa who did something like that too," Sloane said. After a moment's pause, she asked, "Mr. Lindsay, what would you do if someone found that missing two million dollars of Ma Yaklin's?"

"I don't know." Mr. Lindsay swiped the hat from his head and scratched at his wild tangle of hair. It looked like roots growing upside down. "Honestly, I probably wouldn't tell anyone. It's been too good for business."

Amelia wasn't at all certain that she liked the sound of that. "Would you lock us in a basement hiding spot to keep us from finding it?"

"Good heavens, no!" Mr. Lindsay looked aghast at the thought. "No, I'd just offer you some of the money to keep quiet about it."

Both Sloane and Amelia sagged with relief after hearing that. If Mr. Lindsay was looking for the money too, at least they probably didn't have to worry about him doing something terrible to them over it.

You know. Probably.

Chiave the cheese-named dog slipped from Mr. Lindsay's grasp again. She dove back into the reflecting pool, emerging with another lily pad clamped happily in her jaws. Mr. Lindsay groaned, wincing in pain as he leaned on his cane and tried to get up.

Sloane and Amelia exchanged a look as Sloane fished the dog out of the water.

This time, their looks actually meant the same thing.

Heaving a martyred sigh, Amelia said, "Hey, why don't we take Chiave for a walk for you again?"

"Oh, would you?" Mr. Lindsay asked, pathetically relieved. "I was going to ask Sergeant Pepper. I thought I'd find her out here trimming the rosebushes since she's the only one around who hasn't gone peony-mad and she loves to play fetch with Chiave. But I think I she's off trimming some of the honey locust trees. Terrible creatures."

Neither Amelia nor Sloane knew what a honey locust tree was or why it was terrible, and were afraid to ask. It made Amelia imagine a tree covered with gross insects that had been glued to it with honey.

Sloane took Chiave by the leash. As she did so, she had one more question for Mr. Lindsay. "Where do *you* think the money is hidden in Tangle Glen?"

Mr. Lindsay shrugged his squat shoulders. "Wherever Jacqueline Yaklin hid it, I think it was long gone by the time Granddaddy bought the house. Over the years, we've put in all-new plumbing and electricity. Every wall and floor in this house has been torn up, and no one ever found a thing."

"What about the woods?" Amelia asked, earning her a nudge in the ribs from Sloane. No sense in giving Mr. Lindsay ideas of where to look before them. Just in case he was faking that back injury of his.

However, Mr. Lindsay just shook his head and waved a dismissive hand at the idea. "Nah. Too easy to lose. Even back then, the woods around here were a tangled mess. Why do you think it was called 'Tangle Glen'? I've grown up here, and I still get lost out there sometimes. We have to tie bits of cloth to the trees to mark the path from one place to the next. Why would a smart, successful bootlegger hide her money someplace she couldn't easily find even with a map?"

That was an excellent question. One to which neither Sloane nor Amelia had an answer.

Still, they were determined to at least take a look at the woods themselves. They headed toward the nearest path, with Mr. Lindsay calling after them, "Mind you, follow those ribbons and stick to the path! If you're not back by sundown, I'll send out a search party for you!"

That wasn't exactly super reassuring.

Overhead, clouds began to gather, blocking out the sun. However, Sloane and Amelia hadn't gone more than a few steps into the woods when the thick green canopy of leaves blocked out even that bit of grayish light. They were plunged into a humid twilight with ferns licking at their ankles, brambles at their clothing, and branches at their hair.

As Mr. Lindsay had promised, strips of colored cloth had been tied to the trees, helping Sloane and Amelia spot the narrow trickle of dirt that formed the path.

"He's got a point about this being a terrible hiding spot," Sloane admitted, wiping sweat from her face. "Even with a map, you'd have to look around for landmarks, and they just wouldn't be easy to see in the daytime. Let alone at night."

Amelia nodded unhappily.

"And it wouldn't even have been any good to have, like, a mathematical map in your head. You know, like, 'Walk fifty paces forward and then twenty paces to your left.' Even using the path, you have to zig and zag all over the place."

Sloane opened her mouth, but before she could say anything, Chiave spotted a chipmunk. She tore off after it, yanking the leash free from Sloane's fingers

"Chiave, no!" Amelia cried, clamping her hand onto her hat to keep it from flying off her red curls as she and Sloane raced after the bloodhound.

"Bad dog!" Sloane yelled desperately. "Bad! Dog!"

The chipmunk must have thought Sloane was talking to it. Because the chubby little rodent shot into a hole.

Rather than stopping to snorf it, Chiave kept right on romping through the undergrowth, sending last autumn's leaves flying through the air and squirrels racing up the tree trunks.

On and on, Chiave ran, letting out happy woofs and occasionally turning around to make sure that Sloane and Amelia were following her.

"*Very* bad dog!" Sloane pushed back at all the whippy little branches smacking at her face as she tried to catch up with the bloodhound. She'd been in track, but hurdles were not exactly her thing.

At least she was doing better than poor Amelia, who tripped over a mossy log with a "WHOA!" She threw her arms up into the air, both her bubble pipe and her cap disappearing into the thornbushes as she crashed into the mud.

Sloane ran back to help her now-very-dirty friend up. They both thought they'd lost Chiave, but the dog must have realized she'd taken things too far. She sat down under an oak tree by some wild blackberry bushes and whined apologetically.

"Oh, it's okay," Amelia assured the dog, going over to her as Sloane searched about for the lost cap and pipe. "I know you didn't mean it. You just get a little too enthusiastic sometimes. I do that too."

Apparently deciding that she was forgiven, Chiave tried to dig after another chipmunk that must have been hiding in the rotting leaves and old acorn caps beneath the tree.

Amelia took Chiave's leash firmly in hand and pulled her away. "Nope. No more chipmunks for you. If they organize with the squirrels, we'll never make it out of these woods alive."

Chiave whined guiltily, muzzle and paws both covered with mud.

"Good news: I found your hat and pipe." Sloane held them up with a wince. The pipe was broken in two and the hat now had a long rip in the top. "Bad news: I think they're ruined. Worse news: I don't know where the path is."

Both Sloane and Amelia looked around helplessly.

This deep in the woods, they couldn't see a single bit of the mansion or the lawn or the river. Heck, five feet into the woods, you couldn't see those things. The bits of torn cloth they'd been following were bright yellow, easily seen against the brown of the tree branches and the green of the leaves. However, in chasing after Chiave, they'd lost sight of the scraps.

And neither one of them could remember what direction they'd come from.

Or how far they'd run.

"Sloane, do coyotes come out in the daytime?" Amelia asked in a small voice.

"No, I don't think so," Sloane assured her, managing to sound far more confident than she felt.

"We really have to stop getting into situations in which we have to worry about getting eaten by coyotes." Amelia handed the quivering, straining Chiave over to her friend.

"On the bright side, there aren't any bears in our part of Ohio." Sloane exchanged the ruined hat and bubble pipe for the leash.

"Getting eaten by coyotes isn't any better than getting eaten by bears," Amelia countered. "I don't want to be on the menu for *anything.*"

Hot and sticky, Sloane turned round and round, trying to decide which direction they should go. Maybe if they could see the sun, they could tell what direction it was moving? And that would somehow tell them where north was?

Except that Sloane didn't know how it would tell them that.

Or how knowing where north was would get them back to the mansion.

Plus, between the clouds and the leaves, the sun was impossible to spot.

"Look, over there!" Amelia gripped her friend's arm and pointed toward a bit of red tied to a tree branch. Walking over to it, they were able to see another red cloth tied up ahead.

"Yeah, but the markers for our path were yellow." Sloane made a face.

"Does it matter? A path is a path. It'll take us *somewhere.*"

Deciding Amelia was right, they followed the trail from one red flag to the next. Chiave kept trying to break away to chase after more chipmunks, squirrels, and a very alarmed snake, but this time, both Sloane and Amelia held on to her leash.

Finally, up ahead, they spotted a gap in the trees and grassy lawn beyond.

"It's Tangle Glen!" Amelia sagged in relief.

Only to discover that they hadn't left the woods at all.

They were just in a clearing.

"At least there aren't any chipmunks out here." Sloane tried to find something positive as Amelia flopped down onto the grass in despair.

"Nope. There's no good to any of this." Her hair streaming about her, Amelia lay on her back and folded her hands on her chest. Closing her eyes to complete the corpse look, she declared, "We shall die out here, Sloane! All that is left is to do it with dignity. Join me, Sloane! We shall face the grave together."

"There's a garter snake by your elbow," Sloane pointed out dryly.

Amelia shot straight up into the air with a shriek. She landed on Sloane's back, clinging to it like a monkey. Fortunately, the snake didn't turn to Sloane for protection too, sliding off into a patch of violets instead.

Less fortunately, the impact of Amelia against her shoulders caused Sloane to let go of Chiave's leash as she staggered about.

Amelia slipped off Sloane's back, and the race was back on once again. However, Chiave didn't go far, having encountered a patch of nearby peonies.

Inky purple peonies.

Joining the bloodhound, Sloane and Amelia looked them over. They hadn't seen anything quite like them at the competition so far. All the other peonies had mostly been different shades of pink, red, orange, or white. Some of them had been magenta, but nothing as deep and dark and dramatic as these.

"What are these doing, growing all the way out here?" Sloane wondered. "I'm pretty sure I heard someone say that peonies don't grow in the wild, when they were all showing off how much they know."

"How much do you want to bet these are Shakespeare Wikander's?" Amelia guessed. "He was out in the woods last night, right? And it seems pretty clear that he and Chef Zahra are both entering the peony competition."

"I'm betting you're right. The peony petal that fell from his sleeve matches these," Sloane agreed, pulling with all her might to get Chiave away from her favorite plant. The dog only agreed to leave after she had peed on one of the bushes, marking it as her territory. "But, just like Chef Zahra and the peonies she's growing up in the attic, it's a pretty good cover for looking for Ma Yaklin's missing money. Maybe last night he was out here digging for it. When Chef Zahra saw him, she assumed he was taking care of his secret peonies just like her. Maybe she assumed it because that's what he wanted her to think."

"We still have too many suspects and not enough clues," Amelia said unhappily as they walked back across the meadow and toward the red marker tied to the tree. Since they'd followed the cloths in one direction and it had led them here, it seemed likely that following them in the opposite direction would take them back to the mansion.

"What I've been thinking is that maybe we're going about this all wrong," Sloane said, keeping a firm grip on the leash as Chiave tried to make friends with more forest critters. "Maybe we don't need to figure out what Ma Yaklin was thinking or how she planned on finding the money. If she buried it in the forest, I bet she would have put it into a metal box first. You know, to keep it from getting damp and falling apart? I read about that in a book once. Maybe we just need to get a metal detector and walk all over the woods with it."

It was a lot of woods, but Sloane was running out of ideas.

Amelia, however, hadn't.

"And what *I've* been thinking is that we need to interrogate our suspects!" She rubbed her hands gleefully. "Really rake them over the coals! Make them sing like canaries until they squeal and tell us all that they know!"

"Canaries squeal?" Sloane asked doubtfully.

"Not the point!" Amelia waved a hand dismissively, her eyes going glassy. A dreamy smile slid onto her face. "We'll question them all like we're 1920s detectives and they're bootleggers! You know, shine lights into their faces and call them 'Mac' a lot! Then, we'll upload the interviews to YouTube and let our subscribers decide who shut us in that room!"

Amelia didn't mention that at least it might get them a few more clicks.

And hopefully prevent anyone from noticing that they hadn't really found out anything about where Ma Yaklin's missing millions could have gone to.

So far, all Osburn and Miller-Poe Detective Agency had found were some empty crates, old newspapers, and a pack of obsessive peony enthusiasts.

Little did they know that they'd already seen all the clues they needed to solve the mystery.

Then again, those clues had been right there in front of lots of people for the last ninety years.

And no one had ever noticed.

12

WILD ACCUSATIONS

Dirty, stinky, and tired, Sloane and Amelia returned Chiave to Mr. Lindsay once they found their way back to the mansion. Aiden and Ashley were slinking about the entry hall, whispering to each other and eyeing up the enormous museum vase full of peonies.

When Amelia passed by them, covered in mud and grass and looking like she'd just crawled out of a movie about the Great Depression, both of her half-siblings barely gave her a glance.

"Don't you have anything to say?" she demanded.

Aiden and Ashley jumped guiltily. Then they immediately started acting extremely, aggressively casual.

"Hey, sis!" Aiden stretched and then did some lunges. "Nothing to see here! Just doing my stretches before a run!"

He wore a pair of dress pants, a collared shirt, and a tie. Definitely not running clothing.

"Yup! Me too!" Ashley stretched her arms high above her head in spite of the fact that she wore a dress and heels. "Think I'll get in a five-kilometer run."

"I was going to do a ten-kilometer run!"

"Yes, but I was going to do my run *after* I'd kayaked ten miles," Ashley countered smugly.

"In your dress and heels?" Amelia asked, confused. "And you in your tie and dress shoes?"

Both Aiden and Ashley started, then went bug-eyed at being caught out in lies.

"Yup!" they both agreed.

And took off running to prove it.

Amelia stared after them, dazed.

"I could be wrong," Sloane said, "but I think my grannies have somehow manipulated them into collecting peony-growing information from the competition."

Returning to their room, they took turns in the bathroom to scrub the mud, heat, and humidity of the woods off their skin. Sloane also strongly recommended that they check themselves over for ticks, but fortunately, neither one of them found anything.

Clean and smelling much fresher, they got around to lunch. As they did so, Amelia checked their YouTube channel. What she saw pleased her immensely. "We're back up over a thousand now, Sloane. Though one of them is QueenMac329, and I'm pretty sure that's Mackenzie Snyder because that user posted that we're super lame and should just give up."

Pulling her long dark hair back up into a ponytail, Sloane peered over her friend's shoulder. "And I think that one there is her grandma. You know, 'QueenMacGramma'? The one who says we have stinky butts and are dumber than her granddaughter?"

Both Sloane and Amelia stared at the screen, considering this.

"Sloane?" Amelia said. "Are we being bullied *by a grandma*?"

"I actually think it's more that Mac's grandma is trying to

bully my grandmas, and we're sort of in the way." Sloane twisted the tip of her ponytail around her finger, thinking. "Hm, or maybe Mackenzie and her grandma *are* trying to bully us, and my grannies are in the way."

"Either way, I'm blocking them." Amelia blew a dismissive sound, tapping at her tablet with her finger.

As soon as she'd done it, Amelia tossed her tablet easily aside and began rooting around in her suitcases for the perfect outfit to wear. Sloane watched her friend, confused.

"Doesn't it bother you that Mac and her grandma posted that?" she asked.

"Not really." Amelia shrugged. "I mean, don't get me wrong. It was awful when we were in school, and she was always making fun of me. But now... well, I guess I feel like snobby Mackenzie Snyder isn't the person I want to like me."

Amelia started out sounding casual and indifferent, but by the time she'd finished, hurt bled into her words. She tried to toss them off like they didn't matter, but her voice got thick and soggy, betraying just how much she ached inside.

"Amelia," Sloane said hesitantly, trying to be as careful as a doctor examining a wound. "I don't think it's that your family doesn't like you."

"Oh yeah? Then what is it?" Amelia demanded, scrunching up the dress she'd picked into a tight ball. "Because they sure act like it!"

"Honestly? I think they know that you're super creative and smart in ways that they aren't." Sloane felt so awkward saying it that she kept twisting and twisting her hair. "And it's surprised them and made them feel unsure about themselves. And I don't think that's something your family is used to feeling."

Amelia released the dress she'd squeezed in her fists. She thought about what Sloane said. "I like your version better than my version. But I don't know that I believe it."

That wasn't exactly true.

Amelia desperately wanted to believe that Sloane's version was the correct version.

That she was wrong when she was convinced that her family was laughing at her behind her back. Or rolling their eyes at her.

The trouble of it was, she wanted it to be true so badly that Amelia didn't think she could bear it if she believed it only to find out that Sloane was wrong.

It was easier not to feel loved and cared for than to think that you were and have it taken away from you.

Some of this showed in Amelia's face, but before Sloane could figure out what to say to it, her phone rang. Relieved that she wouldn't have to figure out how to deal with something that felt too big, Sloane pulled out her phone and opened a FaceTime call from her dad.

"Hi, Sloane!" he cried happily. "Are you having fun with Amelia and her family? Are you discovering lots of clues about what happened to that yak-leaning lady's money?"

"'Yaklin'," Sloane corrected, grinning. She was sure that her dad knew that and was just making a dad joke.

"Hey, do you know where the pizza cutter is?" her dad asked, the camera swaying back and forth as he looked through the kitchen drawers. "Weren't you using it for something the other day?"

"I couldn't find the scissors, so I was using it to cut apart some paper." Sloane made a face. "It didn't end well. I think it's still up in my room. Why?"

Before he could answer, a woman's voice called out, "Pizza is here!"

Cynthia.

Seife.

"Yay!" children's voices cried. David Osburn turned around, giving Sloane a clear view of Skye and Brighton as they crowded eagerly around the table. Smiling at them, Cynthia set down two steaming cardboard boxes. Brighton immediately lifted the lid to peer inside.

"Bacon and banana peppers? Ew—*gross!* Who eats bacon and banana peppers?" He wrinkled his nose in disgust.

Sloane and her dad ate pizza with bacon and banana peppers, that was who.

Sloane and her dad.

And now her dad and Cynthia ate it too, apparently.

"That's not for you, silly. But it is Sloane's favorite, so David wanted me to give it a try." Cynthia ruffled her son's hair affectionately. Then she opened the lid on the other box. "Here's a cheese pizza for you and Skye."

Brighton and Skye both sagged in visible relief. Picking up a piece of the cheese pizza and biting into it, Brighton leaned into the phone's camera. From around a mouthful of mozzarella, he mumbled at Sloane, "You eat gross stuff? I didn't know that you eat gross stuff."

Actually, Sloane had once bitten into a ghost pepper on a dare. (And then immediately regretted it.) However, that had nothing to do with this. "Bacon and banana pepper pizza isn't gross! It's delicious! Look, Dad, I've gotta go."

Before he could answer, she ended the call.

Clutching her phone in both hands, Sloane stared at the room in front of her.

Her dad was eating bacon and banana pepper pizza without her.

Was he about to watch old episodes of *Doctor Who* with Cynthia and her kids too? That was their thing—her and her dad's and her mom's, back when Maisy Osburn was alive. They'd eat pizza and watch the cheesy old episodes from the 1970s. The Osburns were the only ones in the whole world who did that, and even after her mom died, Sloane and her dad had kept right on doing it.

Her dad was replacing her and the memory of her mom with Cynthia Seife and her kids.

It wasn't that Sloane didn't want her dad to move on. She did.

But she wanted him to take her along.

Instead, she'd only been gone two days, and he'd already moved an entirely new family into the house.

"Breathe," Amelia encouraged her once again, finding Sloane curled up on the tombstone bed. She tugged the phone out of Sloane's clenched fingers as her friend hyperventilated. "Breathe. They're just eating pizza, okay? It's just pizza."

"Our pizza!" Sloane cried between gasps. "Our special *Doctor Who* pizza! They're eating it without me!"

"Maybe that's because your dad likes bacon and banana pepper pizza too," Amelia pointed out. "Maybe he just ordered what he likes on a pizza. And you don't know that they're watching *Doctor Who* together. Did you even see the TV turned on?"

"Well . . . no," Sloane admitted, breath calming. She realized that she'd wrapped a strand of hair so tightly around one finger that it had cut off her circulation. Sitting upright, she released it. "Do you really think that's it? That it's just pizza?"

"I'm positive," Amelia assured her. "My family would mail me back to the stork if it accepted returns, but your family would turn the stork into a Thanksgiving turkey if it ever tried to take you back."

In spite of herself, Sloane grinned. "Thanks. That's really horrifying. But thank you. And you're wrong about your family, you know. They just don't know what to do now that they aren't bossing you around all the time. And from what I've seen, Miller-Poes do *not* like it when they don't know something."

"That's an understatement." Amelia scowled.

Still, they both felt a bit better.

Not completely better. But better enough. For now.

Amelia had changed out of her hobo overalls and into a tie, button-down shirt, jacket, and fedora. Instead of a corncob bubble pipe, she'd stuck a toothpick in her mouth, explaining, "This is how all gumshoes dressed in the twenties and thirties."

"What's a gumshoe?" Sloane felt she should know but couldn't remember.

"A detective. The detective is for chomping on while I squint at the suspect like I don't believe a word he's saying."

"I thought we were already detectives."

"We were girl detectives before. Smart and stylish. Now we're bitter and hard-boiled," Amelia explained, cheering up. "When we question people, I scare them by pounding on the table. Or maybe flipping it over. I haven't quite decided which just yet."

Quickly Sloane assured her, "I think pounding will be scary enough. No need to flip anything."

For her own part, Sloane pulled on a jersey dress, feeling she needed to be fancier than shorts and a shirt. But not feeling like she could pull off the 1920s detective look herself.

Starting downstairs, they jerked to a halt at the balcony over-looking the entry hall. Below, the mansion was filled with people, all elegantly dressed. Not tuxedos-and-gowns elegant, but summery, *Who, me? I just threw on this fabulous outfit* casual. Flowy dresses for the women and pressed pants and pastel shirts for the men.

All of them were milling about the marble-topped table with its enormous vase of peonies. Smiling at each other in the way adults sometimes did when they secretly wanted to smash pies into each other's faces.

But—being adults—they didn't.

Even if privately they desperately wanted to start a food fight.

If they did, there would be plenty of food to pick from. Waiters in 1920s–style tuxedos circled among the guests, carrying silver trays heavy with snacks. Kuneman—the woman in the pink dress from dinner the night before—"accidentally" almost sloshed a glass of punch onto Baker's shoes. That was the woman in the blue silk dress who seemed to be Kuneman's sworn enemy. Once again, they wore pink and blue, with Kuneman preferring diamond jewelry and Baker, pearl jewelry.

In exchange for Kuneman's attempted assault, Baker also "accidentally" sloshed her glass of punch onto one of Kuneman's peonies in the museum vase on the hall table, staining it from orange to red.

Both Shakespeare and Mr. Boening-Bradley had to intervene to tear the two of them apart before anyone's silk gown could get torn to tatters by garden shears. Not needing any shears of his own, the president of the Ohio Peony Enthusiasts Club clicked his fingers menacingly together the same way a praying mantis clapped its claws. That seemed to unnerve even the two warring competitors.

"Maybe now isn't the best time to grill our suspects about what they know," the normally drama-loving Amelia admitted. She liked her skin in one piece.

"No, no, no—now is good." Sloane started down the steps, taking her friend by the elbow and dragging her along. "They'll all be busy and distracted, so maybe they'll let something slip. Besides, even if we get—I don't know—shanked with a garden hoe by some ritzy peony-obsessed weirdo, it still beats sitting upstairs in our room feeling sorry for ourselves."

"I wasn't feeling sorry for myself!" Amelia protested hotly as they reached the bottom of the stairs and were swallowed up by the crowd.

The portrait gallery was closed off for the moment. Based on what they could hear from people talking, the Judge and the rest of the peony judging committee were inside, inspecting the peonies. That was why everyone outside was so tense. Both Amelia and Sloane got the sense that, if one of the gardeners was murdered, their peony might be disqualified.

Or at least the other gardeners seemed to think that.

"Let's split up," Sloane whispered to Amelia. "You go question Chef Zahra and Shakespeare. I'll take Mr. Boening-Bradley and Sergeant Pepper."

"Why do I have to take the person armed with a meat cleaver?"

"Fine. I'll trade you Chef Zahra for Mr. Boening-Bradley."

Amelia thought that over for a moment, then shook her head. "No, I'll take my chances with the chef. At least she needs a meat cleaver to murder me. Mr. Boening-Bradley seems like he could do it with his bare claws. Er, hands."

They went their separate ways. Amelia found Chef Zahra in the kitchen but was too intimidated by the way she was confidentially banging pans and flipping things in skillets to try to flip over anything herself.

"Yes, that's my office down the hall, and yes, those newspaper clippings are mine," the chef said absently when Amelia questioned her.

"I looked you up online," Amelia said, feeling this was a thing a 1920s detective normally wouldn't say. "You were working at a pretty big hotel in Chicago before you took this job here at Tangle Glen about a year ago."

"So?"

"So, isn't this kind of a step down?" Amelia swallowed nervously, keeping an eye on a nearby set of knives. "Why would you leave there to come here?"

Several of the junior chefs were leaning toward the two of them, clearly trying to listen to what Chef Zahra would say. Noticing it, she let out a hiss, grabbed Amelia, and hustled her into the pantry.

"Please don't fillet me!" Amelia squeaked, snatching up a baguette loaf with which to defend herself in case Chef Zahra tried.

"What are you talking about? Get your hands off my food!" The chef yanked the bread loaf out of Amelia's hands. Then, lowering her voice, she said, "Look, kid. If I tell you, will you get out of my kitchen?"

Amelia nodded.

Chef Zahra sighed, rolled her eyes, and straightened her apron. "You're right. Technically, coming here is a step backward. But my mom is a professor of horticulture over at the University of Toledo." When Amelia frowned in confusion, Chef Zahra explained, "That means she teaches the science of growing plants. She's the one who first told me about this peony competition. They give out some pretty big awards, with the top one being for fifty thousand dollars. I want to open my own restaurant, and winning that money would help me do it. Mom knew that Jacqueline Yaklin had an award-winning breed of peonies, and I thought I'd re-create it. Even if it doesn't win, I can sell it to a gardening company and make decent money. So, yeah, I never planned on sticking around here very long, but I'd rather not tell all of my chefs that, okay? What's it to you, anyhow?"

Scrounging up her courage, Amelia said, "Fifty thousand is a lot of money. But if you were researching Ma Yaklin's peonies, then you have to know that there's also two million dollars hidden somewhere around Tangle Glen. Tell me you don't want that money for your restaurant!"

Just in case she'd made the chef mad, Amelia snatched up a jar of pickles and held it threateningly.

However, Chef Zahra just laughed. "Are you kidding me? Kid, that money is long gone! Unless it's locked up tight in a metal box, mice ate it a long time ago if it's anywhere in the house. And if Jacqueline Yaklin buried it anywhere outside, it's rotted away. No thanks! I'll stick with the money I can actually get. Not some ghost money."

Still chuckling, Chef Zahra went back to her pots and pans in the kitchen. Amelia slunk out of the kitchen, feeling a bit embarrassed and confused.

Could the chef be right?

Were they chasing ghost money?

Amelia imagined posting a video to YouTube of her and Sloane finding tattered scraps that had once been Ma Yaklin's money. She could only imagine the comments they'd get about that. And not just from Mackenzie Snyder and her mean grandma.

Then Amelia remembered Sloane saying something about Ma Yaklin hiding her money in a metal box too. Bootleggin' Ma Yaklin had been a smart woman. If both Chef Zahra and Sloane could think of storing the money safely in a metal box, then Ma Yaklin would have known to do it too.

Shakespeare Wikander likewise admitted to growing the

purple peonies out in the clearing in the woods. However, when Amelia pressed him on whether he was digging for something else out there, he denied it.

"Look, I don't really like nature," he said as he practiced turning his feather duster into a bouquet of Sergeant Pepper's roses and then back again. "Gardens are fine, but the only reason I grew my peonies in the clearing was so Chef Zahra wouldn't see them. Aside from taking care of my soon-to-be-award-winning plants, I'd rather stay out of the woods. Too many bugs and snakes."

Shuddering, he hurried off to break up Baker and Kuneman again as they swiped silver trays from the waiters and got ready to whack each other with them, tottering on their high heels, the chandelier light glinting off their jewels. The sight of the roses he was holding at least united the two of them in ganging up on the house manager and sneering at him for carrying around "such a common flower!"

Sloane similarly struck out with Mr. Boening-Bradley, who waved her away with his handkerchief held at the tips of his spindly, insect-like fingertips. "Shoo! Leave, you unpleasant child! Don't you know it's gauche to talk about money?"

"Go?" Sloane repeated in confusion, looking behind herself. He already had waved her all the way to the wall. "Go where?"

"Not 'go'! Gauche! It's French for—oh, never mind." Rolling his eyes, Mr. Boening-Bradley tucked his handkerchief back into his pocket. "The point is, one doesn't talk about money. One just has it. And one certainly doesn't go tromping about someone else's house, trying to find it!"

Sloane didn't know who this "one" person was, but she had one more question for him. Crossing her arms, she scowled and demanded, "Oh yeah? Well, tell me that you wouldn't lock me and Amelia in the basement!"

Looking about, Mr. Boening-Bradley lowered his face to Sloane's. She squeezed herself against the wall to keep away from it. His eyes looked more bug-eyed than ever. His jaw even more like a praying mantis's. "I would happily shut the two of you in the basement and throw away the key! Alas, I can't take credit for that absolutely brilliant idea. If you find out who did it, let me know so I can shake that person's hand!"

With that, he hopped away. Well, he walked. But somehow he managed to give the impression of a whole plague of locusts.

Glaring after him, Sloane resolved to get her hands on some bug spray and zap Mr. Boening-Bradley with it the next time he got close.

She had better success with Sergeant Pepper, whom she found out in the garden, trimming the rosebushes as rain began to fall from the heavy clouds that had gathered around Tangle Glen. The gardener wore a grubby pair of overalls and thick gloves. She grimaced up at the drizzle and started collecting her tools, placing them into a nearby wheelbarrow.

"Hey, Sloane!" Sergeant Pepper grinned at her, then winced as a raindrop smacked her in the eye. She'd snipped off one of the deep red roses and tucked it into her ponytail. Wiping the rain from her face, she offered one to Sloane, too. "Want a rose? I'm so sick of smelling peonies that I'm wearing one until the competition is over. All those peony competitors are driving me wild! I've never had so many people sneer and make snide comments about my gardens."

Sloane accepted the rose and tucked it into her ponytail too. For no other reason than because she was sure that it would annoy Mr. Boening-Bradley if he saw it. However, before she could question Sergeant Pepper on where she was when Sloane and Amelia had been locked in the basement or what she knew about where Ma Yaklin's money might be, Chiave came romping up, tail wagging.

With Sergeant Pepper's wallet in her mouth once again.

"Oh, you bad dog," Sergeant Pepper sighed, taking it back and wiping the slime off in the grass. To Sloane, she said, "She's just a great big puppy, always wanting to play."

"At least when she's stealing wallets, she isn't crawling all over the peonies or peeing on them," Sloane pointed out as she followed Sergeant Pepper and Chiave back to a large gardening shed.

"True," the gardener admitted as they went inside. Once there, she tucked her wallet into a backpack while Chiave sniffed everything in sight. (But, fortunately, did not pee on any of it.)

Sloane looked around. The room was pretty grungy and full of junk, with old, smeared windows and lots of rough wooden tables and benches. Dirt and dead garden clippings covered the floor, and rusty equipment sat everywhere. Clay pots and metal pails jostled for space on warped wooden shelves with old books, a typewriter, lots of paintbrushes, a broken lamp, and about three dozen other things that no one seemed to want anymore but couldn't bear to throw out. Off to one side, a rickety set of stairs led upward, probably to more storage on the second floor.

A large, tattered photo album lay open on one of the tables, next to a seed catalog.

"Hey, that's Tangle Glen back a long time ago, isn't it?" Going over to the album, Sloane pointed at a water-stained black-and-white picture.

"From the early 1930s." Sergeant Pepper nodded, joining her as she took off her muddy gloves. "Mr. Lindsay gave it to me. He'd like me to try to re-create what the gardens looked like back when his grandfather first bought the place." She flipped the page. "See, there he is."

Anderson Lindsay stood in front of the mansion, smiling smugly and pointing at the holes were Ma Yaklin's peonies used to be. There was just no denying that he was pleased by the destruction—if you knew what had happened.

Sergeant Pepper clearly didn't, because she said, "I think he must have been getting ready to plant some peonies in there. Mr. Lindsay said his grandfather was runner-up at the Annual Ohio Peony Enthusiasts Competition back in 1932. Those are the same bushes that are out front now. Did you know that they can live to be a hundred years old? I had a great-aunt who was a pretty good gardener, too."

Sloane did not, and wasn't sure when that information would come in handy. Still, she made a polite noise and flipped a page. There was another picture of Anderson Lindsay, this time with a little boy who Sloane assumed was probably Mr. Lindsay's father, and a bloodhound who must have been the first Chiave. Or, at the very least, another Chiave.

Only—hang on a second.

Under the picture, someone had handwritten names. They were:

Anderson, Clyde, and Elizabeth

Elizabeth? Who was Elizabeth?

"Isn't that dog's name Chiave?" Sloane asked, poking at the picture.

"Oh—no, he shows up later. See, here he is." Sergeant Pepper flipped through the pages until she found a spread of dog pictures. In one, two bloodhounds licked a laughing toddler Clyde. In another, one dog dug at some freshly planted peony bushes while the other one watched. In yet a third, a dog sniffed sadly at a fence that had been staked around the bushes.

In the fourth photograph, both dogs panted happily at the camera, surrounded by a pack of puppies.

"Mr. Lindsay said that Elizabeth was runner-up in a money-sniffing competition," Sergeant Pepper explained, as Elizabeth's great-great-great-great-great-great-great-granddog tried to paw her way into the gardener's backpack again to steal her wallet. "Back then, both the police and bootleggers would train their dogs to sniff out things like that. Actually, the police still do that today, sometimes. Anyhow, Mr. Lindsay's grandfather must have decided that Elizabeth's super-sniffer was worth hanging on to. So, he got another bloodhound and the two had puppies."

"Uh-huh," Sloane agreed distractedly. "Hey, mind if I borrow this picture? Thanks, I'll bring it right back!"

Before Sergeant Pepper could actually reply, Sloane plucked the stiff old photograph out of the triangles sticking it to the page.

"What? Hey, wait! That's Mr. Lindsay's photo!" Sergeant Pepper cried.

However, it was too late.

Sloane was already sprinting out of the gardening shed and back toward the mansion.

Because she was pretty sure of two things.

One, that Elizabeth was the dog Anderson Lindsay had been holding in the old newspaper clipping when he'd been in the background after the sniffing competition in 1932. The one where he'd been glaring jealously at Ma Yaklin.

The second thing Sloane was sure of was that the first Chiave looked exactly like Eli.

Anderson Lindsay had dognapped him.

13

PIECES FALL INTO PLACE, BUT THE PICTURE STILL ISN'T CLEAR

Half an hour later, a stunned Sloane and Amelia were back in the attic as rain drummed steadily on the roof outside. Amelia had taken the fedora off her head and flipped her tie over her shoulder. She scratched at her hair as Sloane held the picture of Chiave and Elizabeth next to the newspaper photograph of the bootleggers and dogs from the 1932 sniffing competition that Ma had won right before Eli disappeared.

"It wasn't Two Thumbs Lundquist and the Digits Gang who dognapped Eli after all!" Sloane declared excitedly. "If you read the article, you'll see the reporter talks about Elizabeth being the second-best sniffer in the Toledo area. And you can tell from the photograph that he is *not* happy about that."

"Just like he was clearly mad about having the second-best peonies at the 1932 Annual Ohio Peony Enthusiasts Competition." Digging through the stack of newspapers, Amelia pulled out that newspaper, too. They laid both papers down on Chef Zahra's potting table, along with the photograph of Chiave, Elizabeth, and their puppies.

There was no denying that Eli and "Chiave" looked identical.

They both had the exact same dark markings above their eyes and at the tips of their long, droopy ears.

"Anderson Lindsay worked for Ma Yaklin, but really, he wanted to *be* her, not just work for her," Amelia summarized as lightning sizzled across the sky outside. Thunder rumbled immediately after, as the attic lights flickered but stayed on. "He hated that she was better than him at everything. She won the peony competition, so he dug up her prize-winning peonies and let Two Thumbs take the blame."

"And I bet that Two Thumbs was more than happy to take credit for anything that upset Ma," Sloane continued, picking up the thread of the story as the wind shook the attic windows. "So, Ma doesn't realize that she has an enemy right in the heart of her operation. She sets up the money-sniffing competition—"

"Which still seems super unfair to me, since she planned on entering Eli into it," Amelia cut in.

"True, but anyhow, Eli wins that. So, to get revenge, Mr. Lindsay kidnaps Eli. Maybe Ma would have finally figured out that it was someone close to her who was doing things like letting people into the mansion through her tunnel and telling them where her bootlegging spot was hidden—but she never got the chance. The feds arrested her."

Both Sloane and Amelia fell silent, considering this.

All of Ma's misfortune could be blamed on someone close to her. Someone she thought she could trust.

Someone who had been silently working against her.

To destroy her prizewinning flowers. To steal away her beloved dog. To ruin her fortune and send her off to prison.

Could Anderson Lindsay have been angling to find her money as well?

If so, had he succeeded?

In the hush that had fallen in the attic, the door slammed open.

Both Sloane and Amelia shrieked and clung to each other. They'd been so deep into the thoughts of the past, they half expected to see the angry ghost of Anderson Lindsay charge into the attic.

Instead, it was Aiden and Ashley.

They both wore gardening gloves and held trowels as they shoved at each other.

"I was here first!" Aiden cried, pushing Ashley backward. "I win!"

"Was not and did not!" Ashley hooked him by the shirt collar and whipped him behind her.

Then they spotted Sloane and Amelia.

Once again, everyone exclaimed, "What are you doing here?"

"This isn't the bathroom?" Ashley asked innocently, yanking the gloves off her hands and stuffing them into her pockets to hide them. "Our bad! We both really, uh, have to go."

Automatically Aiden boasted, "I have to go more than you do!"

Sloane and Amelia looked at each other. Amelia asked, "How badly do you have to go that you need gloves and a trowel?"

Aiden opened and shut his mouth several times, eyes going big. He looked like a gasping fish. One that wasn't able to come up with a decent answer.

Instead, he turned around and fled downstairs.

After a second's thought, Ashley joined him.

Sloane watched them go, one hand on her hip. "Yup, my grannies are definitely using your brother and sister to collect peony-growing information from the competition."

Amelia shook her head. "It sort of feels like they're both competing to see who is easier to manipulate, and they don't even know it. I'm betting they were coming up here to get soil samples or something."

Collecting a copy of each newspaper plus the photograph Sloane had snatched from Mr. Lindsay's album, Amelia headed toward the door after her siblings. Even with the lights on, the rain made it gloomy and spooky up here, and she was pretty sure they'd gotten everything they needed.

As Sloane followed her, Amelia said, "As long as Aiden and Ashley aren't trying to find Ma Yaklin's missing millions or looking at me like they can't believe they're related to such a weirdo, I don't care what they do. Meanwhile, do you think Anderson Lindsay found Ma Yaklin's missing money and used it to buy Tangle Glen? If so, then we're looking for money that doesn't exist anymore."

"Yes, *but*—if we can prove that, then we'll still solve the mystery of what happened to it," Sloane pointed out as they walked down the servant stairs to the bedrooms on the more brightly lit second floor. "And also, I'm not sure he did find her money. At least, not before he bought the house. I'm going to see if I can get ahold of

Belinda Gomez at the Wauseon Public Library and have her check how much Anderson Lindsay paid for Tangle Glen. If it really wasn't very much, like Mr. Lindsay said, then there's no reason to believe he found it. I bet he bought the mansion thinking that two million dollars was still here, and that he'd have plenty of time to find it if he lived here."

The rest of the day passed by more or less uneventfully. Amelia put together another video for their YouTube channel, detailing everything their investigation had found since the last video. They were now up to almost two thousand subscribers and Amelia excitedly announced that she'd gotten a message that it was the number-one watched video in Nauru.

"Where's that?" Sloane asked.

When they looked it up, they discovered that it was a small island in Oceania with a population of about twelve thousand people.

"Well, so what?" Amelia asked defiantly. "How many people do you know who have a number-one most-watched YouTube video anywhere?"

Sloane felt she had a point, and was absurdly proud. She reached for her phone to brag to her dad.

Then stopped.

She didn't think she could stand it if Cynthia Seife was with him.

When Sloane thought about FaceTiming her grannies instead, her insides only got more anxious.

What if Brighton and Skye were there? She didn't want to see that, either.

Sloane didn't want to be number one in Nauru.

She only wanted to be number one in the Osburn family.

At supper in the fancy dining room downstairs, Amelia told her family the good news. They all froze with their soup spoons halfway to their mouths and stared at her like they thought she might be choking.

"Nauru?" Ashley repeated uncertainly. "Never heard of it."

"Are you sure that's a real place?" Aiden asked.

"Do you feel well?" Her mom laid a hand against her daughter's forehead. "Maybe you have a temperature."

"Maybe it's a cold," the Judge suggested. "Isn't 'nauru' German for 'bless you' after you sneeze?"

"Oh, forget it!" Amelia cried, and that was pretty much the end of it. Partly because Baker flipped her bowl of tomato bisque onto Kuneman's tiara and then Kuneman dumped a bread basket down Baker's silk dress, setting off a riot among warring factions of well-dressed peony enthusiasts.

Two of whom tried to take the Judge and the rest of the Miller-Poe family hostage to demand an early release of the competition's winners. Fortunately, the athletic Miller-Poes were able to fight off their fur-and-diamond-wearing attackers with nothing more than their soup spoons and a lot of scary determination that involved curling back their lips to show their teeth and growling.

Eventually, everyone made it out of the dining room in one piece.

Back upstairs in their room, Sloane saw that she'd gotten a text message from Belinda Gomez, who was the children's and young adult librarian at the Wauseon Public Library. Sloane and Amelia had gotten to know her pretty well while they worked on the case of the Lost Hoäl Jewels. She was more than happy to help them and had been able to use the library's subscription databases to find out that Anderson Lindsay had paid just five thousand dollars for Tangle Glen back in 1932.

"So, *maybe* he *did* find Ma Yaklin's missing two million dollars, *but* he wouldn't have needed them to buy Tangle Glen," Sloane summarized.

She and Amelia looked back unhappily at the text message.

They'd figured out what had happened to Eli, but once again, it didn't feel like they were any closer to finding Ma's money.

On the bright side, whoever had shut them into the old boot-legger hiding spot must have felt the same way. Since they hadn't been attacked again.

Bedtime finally arrived, and with it, one more night away from home for Sloane. She wondered despairingly if she lost more parts of her life with each night she stayed away or if two nights would be the same as one. All around Tangle Glen, the tree branches thrashed about, wild and angry in the summer storm. Lightning lit up the sky as the thunder broke it apart. Yet Amelia fell easily asleep, feeling very safe in such a large house that had stood firmly against both the wind and the rain for so many years.

Even Sloane had to admit that the rhythm of the rain against the plate-glass windows was soothing and cozy. So soothing and cozy that she found her eyelids drooping in spite of the too-hard mattress, the too-soft pillows, and the too hot/too cold blankets. . . .

Then, through the blankets wrapped around Sloane, the sound of scratching reached her ears.

Something is trying to get in, she thought blearily, and rolled over.

Then her brain fully realized what it had just thought.

Something is trying to get in!

Sloane shot upright in bed. Through the shadows, she watched the door quiver.

"Amelia!" she squeaked, but it was too late.

The door creaked open, and the something scuttled inside.

Sloane opened her mouth to shriek into the darkness.

Before she could, it pounced on her.

14

A Nighttime Disappearance

Slayer Sloane screamed.

Screamed as a demon dog with razor-sharp teeth and drool like acid tried to devour her.

This—this is why she should have stayed in her own bed, in her own house, in her own room. She knew every creak and groan of every settling wall and floorboard in her home. There weren't any horrors in her house.

Here, there were nightmares.

Across the room, Amelia shot up out of bed too. In fact, she moved so quickly that she practically floated in the air over her bed, clutching her blankets to her chest and matching Sloane's scream of terror with one of her own.

However, rather than treating Sloane like an oversized Snausage, the demon dog pawed past her face to wriggle down beneath the blankets. Once there, it pressed itself against Sloane's leg, shivering and whining.

"What is it? What is it?" Amelia screamed. "Is it a doll? *It's a doll, isn't it?*"

"It's not a doll!" Sloane peered under the covers. "I think it's Chiave."

Two droopy eyes stared back pleadingly at Sloane, begging

Sloane not to make her come out as the rain picked up, rattling furiously at the windows.

"Oh." Amelia dropped her phone and rubbed at her eyes, still only half awake. "That's too bad. I bet we could have made a lot of money off a video of that."

Before Sloane could figure out why there was a bloodhound in her bed and what she should do about it, Amelia's parents stumbled into their room, switching on the lights and causing Amelia to shriek all over again. The Judge wore a long black nightshirt that looked very much like his court robes. He brandished a particularly large book about peonies, as though trying to intimidate their attacker with his knowledge. Amanda Miller wore black pajamas that looked like a suit. She clacked a flat iron menacingly, similar to a crab snapping its claws.

Hair awry, eyes bleary, they swung their heads about, looking for someone to attack.

"What is it? Who is it? What's going on?" Amanda Miller demanded, while the Judge threatened the lumpy pile of Amelia's clothes with "I'm a judge, I'll have you know! How dare you attack my Amelia!"

Before he could have Amelia's costumes arrested, Sloane said, "I think it's Chiave."

She tried to roll back the blankets to show them, but the dog whimpered and scooted farther down the mattress.

The Judge looked around in confusion. "Chiave? There's cheese in your room? Why is there cheese in your room? We didn't get any cheese in our room!"

"No, Dad. That's the name of Mr. Lindsay's dog." Amelia slid down off her bed and came over to join Sloane in comforting Chiave.

Outside, lightning flicked through the night sky, turning the trees of the woods into long, pale ghosts. Thunder snapped immediately afterward, harsh and too-close. Like it wanted to crack those trees apart. Everyone in the room jumped, Chiave included. The dog howled, scurried out from under the blankets, and buried her face in Amelia's mass of hair.

"I think Chiave got out of Mr. Lindsay's room somehow," Sloane observed. "I guess she was frightened and sniffed her way over to me and Amelia."

Lightening flared again, thunder snapping across the roof. Once more, everyone flinched. If it had sounded before like it wanted to break the trees, it sounded now like it wanted to tear right into the roof. Amelia's hair was no longer enough for Chiave. The bloodhound frantically dug her way back under Sloane's covers until only her tail could be seen. The mass of blankets quivered and whined.

"We'd better call Mr. Lindsay," Amanda Miller said briskly. "We don't want him out in the storm, looking for his dog. Listen to that wind! There will be tree limbs down tomorrow."

As if hearing her words and wanting to show off, the wind blew harder than ever. It wailed and wrapped itself around the house, shaking at the windows as though begging to be let in. When no one let it, the wind rattled the siding and swept upward to tug at the roof like a spoiled child determined to break a toy.

Each burst of lightning showed branches waving wildly back and forth as though the trees were shaking their fists at the wind.

Shaking...

And shaking...

And...

Falling.

The trees around Tangle Glen had stood for over a hundred years. That made them very big. And very tired.

In the angry, flickering light of the storm, Sloane, Amelia, and her parents watched in horror as an enormous old oak tree collapsed toward the mansion.

"Everyone away from the window!" Amanda Miller cried, grabbing both Sloane and Chiave and yanking them backward to the far side of the room. The Judge likewise pulled Amelia along and away from the room's enormous plate-glass windows.

The oak tree fell against the mansion with enough force to make the sturdy brick structure shake, knocking Sloane and Amelia's phones to the floor. A branch broke through one of the window panes, sending glass tinkling onto the floorboards below. Having expected much worse than that, everyone in the room cringed and half covered their faces.

Fortunately, however, the tree mostly didn't land against their room.

The attic broke its fall.

Plus, a big chunk of its massive trunk hit the room next door.

"Aiden and Ashley's room!" the Judge gasped, and took off to check on his son and stepdaughter.

Amanda, Amelia, Sloane, and Chiave all followed, hot on his heels.

(Well, Sloane had to drag along a very reluctant Chiave. The rest of them were hot on his heels.)

"Aiden! Ashley!" the Judge and Amanda cried together. He pounded on the door with his fists while she tugged at the doorknob, desperate to get inside. Sloane and Amelia joined them in crying out Aiden and Ashley's names...

... only to step back when the Judge snatched a lamp off a nearby hallway table and brandished it about. "Stand back, Amanda! I'm battering this door down!"

Expecting her mom to be the voice of reason, Amelia was shocked to hear her instead let go of the doorknob and cry, "That lamp won't do it! Grab a chair!"

However, before the Miller-Poe family could run up an enormous bill at the inn by smashing its furniture, Aiden and Ashley came scuttling up the servant stairs.

They each held a vase of peonies in their hands.

Realizing everyone was standing outside their room, they both jerked to a guilty, horrified halt.

Exchanging a panicked look with Aiden, Ashley said, "We were—"

"We can explain—" Aiden said at the same moment.

Rather than letting them explain anything, the other Miller-Poes rushed forward to hug them.

Sloane hung back with Chiave, relieved that Amelia's half-siblings were all right but not really eager to get in on the hugging. She narrowed her eyes at those two vases of flowers. Which Aiden and Ashley both slid onto the hallway table without explanation. Neither their parents nor Amelia thought to ask them why they were lugging around peonies in the middle of the night. They were just happy to discover that their children/siblings were in one piece.

Again, Sloane was happy about that too.

But she also really wanted to know why Aiden and Ashley had those vases full of peonies.

Not just any peonies, either.

Competition peonies.

Now wasn't the time to ask, however. When Aiden and Ashley opened up their door, everyone let out a cry of horror. A large branch lay across one bed, glass shards sprinkling the pillows and covers. More branches had torn through the ceiling, snapping the chandelier off and dropping it onto the other bed. Chef Zahra Abu-Absi's work bench had half slid through from the attic above, spilling dirt, leaves, and blossoms onto the floor.

Rain poured in through the shattered window, pooling against the dust and broken bricks. More joined it from the attic, leaking in from the hole where the roof had once been.

The wind swirled into the opening, sending the tattered remains of the curtains flying.

Sloane and the Miller-Poes took in the damage.

"If—we'd been here—we would have been crushed," Aiden said in a much smaller, more hesitant voice than he normally spoke. Amelia reached out and took his hand reassuringly. He squeezed it tight, pulling her close.

By now, the other guests staying at Tangle Glen had begun to come out of their rooms. They all rubbed at their eyes and looked around blearily, trying to figure out what was going on. Shakespeare Wikander, Chef Zahra, Sergeant Pepper, and Mr. Boening-Bradley were all last to arrive.

With earthy, mushroomy Mr. Lindsay nowhere in sight.

It made sense that it would take the house manager, the chef, and the gardener a minute to get there. Their rooms were on the other side of the mansion, one floor up and next to the attic in the old servant quarters. Fortunately, that was at the opposite end of where the oak tree had bashed into the house, but it would still take them a bit to get to Aiden and Ashley's room.

Mr. Boening-Bradley made less sense. As head of the judging committee, his room was just down the hallway from the Miller-Poes' rooms.

Yet instead of coming out of his room, he came up the stairs from the entry hall below.

Sloane pointed this out to Amelia when she finally managed to pull her friend off to the side. Everyone was on their phones and talking excitedly, trying to decide if the mansion was safe to stay in for the rest of the night, if they could still have the awards ceremony the next day, or if the whole building was about to come tumbling down.

"Where is Lindsay?" Mr. Boening-Bradley kept crying, hopping around in agitation, his hands clamped nervously behind his back. He wore green silk pajamas and looked more than ever like an enormous praying mantis. "Blast that man! His house is falling down, my peony competition is falling apart, and he's nowhere to be seen!"

Shakespeare tried to soothe him by saying that Mr. Lindsay

actually lived in the old carriage house closer to the road, but that only upset Mr. Boening-Bradley more.

"Then what's his *dog* doing here?" He waved a hand at Chiave in disgust. Probably because dogs also tended to eat bugs and were therefore Mr. Boening-Bradley's natural enemies.

All the same, the president of the Ohio Peony Enthusiasts Club had a good question that no one had an answer to.

Sergeant Pepper assured the nervous guests and judges that she'd already contacted a building inspector and repair crew and that the mansion was well built and not likely to tumble down from one itty-bitty wallop from a tree. Chef Zahra encouraged everyone to come downstairs for a comforting cup of hot chocolate. Shakespeare promised that he and Sergeant Pepper would move some mattresses downstairs. Between those and the many couches on the main floor, there would be plenty of places for people to sleep for the rest of the night until the inspector and repair crews could make sure everything was safe.

Everyone thought this a terrific idea, especially after Chef Zahra promised to whip up some gourmet s'mores to go along with the hot cocoa. As they followed her downstairs, Amelia noticed that the hems of the chef's pants were wet, and her shoes were squishing damp imprints down into the rug.

Like she'd been outside.

But why would she be outside in the middle of the night? Let alone during a storm?

She thought back to the others upstairs. It was hard to remember through her sudden panic that her annoying, exasperating, beloved siblings might be hurt, but Amelia was pretty sure that Sergeant Pepper's hair had been wet, the rose she always seemed to have stuck in her ponytail sodden and wilted.

And... she'd been wearing heavy work boots with her pajamas.

Why would the gardener be wearing boots if she'd just gotten out of bed?

Having collected China cups filled with hot cocoa and delicate plates heaped with s'mores, Amelia grabbed Sloane by the elbow and led her out of the kitchen. Everyone else seemed to be relieved to be nestled in the kitchen's cozy, golden light while the storm raged on outside. The rest of the mansion hulked large and cavernous like a bear curled up in its cave as they tiptoed through it to the portrait gallery.

"In here." Amelia jerked her head toward the double glass doors, confident that no one would be sleeping in there tonight. They flipped on the lights, finding the long room now jam-packed with tables covered in white cloths. Pedestals sat on top of the cloths, a vase with a single peony bloom on each.

It smelled heavenly as the many portraits of Chiave's great-great-great-great-great-great-great-grandpa, Eli, looked down at all the floral competitors.

Sloane and Amelia wedged their way past one of the narrow tables to sit down on a velvet couch in front of the enormous portrait of Jacqueline Yaklin, the peony-sniffing Eli, and her roadster. As they drank their cocoa and ate their s'mores, Amelia told Sloane what she'd observed about Sergeant Pepper and Chef Zahra.

"And where is Mr. Lindsay?" Amelia concluded. "Why hasn't

anyone been able to get in touch with him? Everyone has been calling and texting him, but he's not answering."

"Maybe he's a heavy sleeper," Sloane suggested, crunching a bit of graham cracker thoughtfully. "But that doesn't explain how Chiave got out. *Or* how she ended up at the house. Unless someone let her out. Maybe because they were looking for the money at the carriage house where Mr. Lindsay lives? It would make sense for Ma to hide her money there. Her roadster would have been there too, so she could have just grabbed her money and driven off."

"And yet she didn't. Which makes it seem to me that the money isn't there." Amelia frowned at the gooey marshmallow sticking to her fingers. "But whoever let Chiave out wouldn't necessarily have known that. My bet is Sergeant Pepper or Chef Zahra, since they both were definitely out in the storm."

"Y-e-e-e-s-s-s," Sloane agreed hesitantly. Now it was her turn to frown up at Ma Yaklin and Eli, before finally saying, "But, Amelia, Chiave was dry when she hopped up in bed with me. If she was out in the storm, *why was she dry?*"

That surprised Amelia and caused her to choke on the sip of hot chocolate she'd just taken. Sputtering into the back of her hand, it took her a minute to speak. Hoarsely, she said, "That means Chiave was in the house for a while! Why wouldn't Mr. Lindsay have her with him? Sloane, do you think someone dognapped Chiave?"

"You can't kidnap someone if they're still in their own home," Sloane said.

"Which Chiave is," Amelia agreed, as more thunder rolled across Tangle Glen and lightning lit up its grassy lawn.

"Yeah, but as far as we can tell, Mr. Lindsay *isn't*. Amelia, I think someone might have kidnapped him."

They both turned and looked out through the windows at the thrashing trees and threatening, storm-streaked sky.

If someone had kidnapped him, where could Mr. Lindsay be? Both Sloane and Amelia worried about the answer to that question.

Little did they know that it was themselves they should be worried about.

Because the person who had taken care of Mr. Lindsay now worried that Sloane and Amelia had gotten a little too close to solving the riddle of what happened to Ma Yaklin's missing money.

In fact, that person was peering in at them right now, hidden in the darkness behind the vase of peonies in the entry hall.

Watching them—and plotting.

Planning how to take care of Sloane and Amelia for good.

15

Language Lessons

The Miller-Poes burst in on Sloane and Amelia as the two of them discussed who could have taken Mr. Lindsay and where they might have put him. If the Miller-Poes had been less focused on themselves, they might have spotted the person lurking in the shadows of the entry hall. However, being Miller-Poes, they announced themselves very noisily and didn't notice anyone or anything that didn't give them a chance to brag or show off. The other person searching for Ma Yaklin's missing millions shrank back into the darkness by the zigzagging stairs, unseen.

"Amelia! Sloane! Here you are!" Amanda Miller bellowed. She carried an entire tray of s'mores plus a pot of hot chocolate. "We were worried about you!"

"This whole house could cave in at any moment!" the Judge declared, making a gavel-banging motion with his hand—only to realize there wasn't a gavel in it. "We need to find someplace safe to sleep tonight. I'm thinking the basement, in case there are tornadoes."

Amelia's mom agreed. Fortunately for Sloane and Amelia (neither of whom were super excited about sleeping someplace damp and spider-infested), Aiden and Ashley jumped in.

"Or we could stay here!" Ashley suggested, jamming an elbow into Aiden's ribs.

Getting the hint that he should say something, he nodded his head vigorously. "Yes! To prove that we're the best at protecting the peonies!"

"Or saving them, if the house collapses!" Ashley suggested. "I bet we'd be the best at that, too."

All of which was like catnip to their parents. The two elder Miller-Poes agreed that this was an excellent idea. Dropping the tray of hot chocolate and s'mores, they hurried off to find Shakespeare, to bully him into carrying mattresses into the portrait gallery.

"Excellent!" Ashley cackled as Aiden rubbed his hands together gleefully.

"Why are you two so happy?" Amelia scrunched up her face at them.

"No reason!" they cried together, and darted from the room.

Amelia turned to Sloane. "Again, how am *I* the weird Miller-Poe?"

Instead of answering, Sloane said, *"Et clavem intus est occultatum."*

Amelia blinked in confusion. "Uh, what, now?"

"Et clavem intus est occultatum," Sloane repeated. She'd grabbed another s'more off the tray Amanda Miller had left for them because she found that the warm, melted chocolate helped her think as she stared at the portrait of Ma Yaklin and Eli. With smeared fingers, she pointed at the brass plate fixed to the bottom

of the heavy gold frame. "We never did figure out what that means. It could be important."

"'Et' is probably Latin for 'eat,' and 'clavem' probably means 'clams.' I bet the whole thing says something like, 'Eat clam intestines and taters,'" Amelia said gloomily. But she took out her phone to find out for sure. She googled "Latin translator" and then ran the phrase through it as Sloane poured them both more hot chocolate and the rain kept rattling the windows.

As soon as she tapped the translate button, Amelia squeaked and dropped her phone.

"What? What is it?" Sloane asked, sloshing cocoa onto the tray. "Is it really something about clams?"

"No! *Look.*" Amelia held up her phone so her friend could see the English translation.

The key is hidden within.

"'The key his hidden within,'" Sloane repeated. Setting down the hot chocolate pot, she got up so she could inspect the painting of Ma and Eli more closely. "The key to what? Her money?"

"It has to be!" Amelia said confidently, scooping up her phone and joining Sloane to press her nose close to the canvas. "Somewhere in here, there has to be a key to where Ma hid her money!"

"But if so, then she'd have been able to find it the night the feds came for her," Sloane objected. "Unless . . . she knew where it was but couldn't get to it?"

"Probably because the feds were after her!" Amelia danced with enthusiasm. "But there aren't any feds after us, Sloane. If we can just figure out how the key is hidden in there, then we can find the money!"

Unbeknownst to them, the other person after Ma Yaklin's missing two million dollars had already figured this out. That person also had a pretty good idea as to where to find the key. What that person hadn't had was a good opportunity to grab it and use it.

At least, not until now.

Sloane and Amelia were still a few steps behind but determined to get to the money before anyone else. While the rest of the Miller-Poes bossily coerced Shakespeare, Sergeant Pepper, and Chef Zahra into carrying blankets and pillows into the portrait gallery (and to convince an outraged Mr. Boening-Bradley that this was for the good of the peony competition), Sloane and Amelia tried to figure out how to "read" the painting of Ma and Eli.

There was Ma Yaklin in her big, velvet-collared coat and bell-shaped hat, leaning against her roadster. And there was Eli at her feet, snorfing a prizewinning peony. Behind the roadster, Tangle Glen's grassy lawn stretched out toward the mansion's white columns and brick walls, tiny in the background. Swallowed up by the forest.

Given how huge the forest looked and how small the house was, Sloane and Amelia agreed that this was a clue that the money was definitely out in the woods. But they'd already suspected that, and what they couldn't figure out was, what key were they supposed to see?

Amelia tried to spot actual key shapes hidden within the swirls and globs of the oil painting. Sloane tried to make words out of the first letters of everything shown: "dog," "car," "flower," "house," "woods."

D, C, F, H, W.

"No vowels," she groaned. "Maybe it's a code?"

"Or maybe the key is hidden in the frame?" Amelia kept squinting and flexing her eye muscles, making her vision go blurry and then sharp. Finally, she gave herself such a terrible headache that she had to give up.

It was time to lie down and try to sleep, anyhow. The Miller-Poes had arranged beds made out of pillows and blankets on the floor, while the rest of the peony committee and the other guests stretched out in the dining room. The storm was finally settling down, and the house seemed as sturdy as ever in spite of the damage to the attic. Sergeant Pepper tried to get Chiave to go back to the old servant quarters with her, Shakespeare, and Chef Zahra, but the dog insisted on curling up with Sloane and Amelia instead.

"We don't mind," Sloane assured her, ignoring Amelia as her friend mouthed, *Yes, we do.*

Amelia might not be a huge fan of getting dog fur all over her satin 1920s-style pajamas, but Sloane felt like she could understand the dog.

Chiave had lost her family in the night, exactly like Sloane worried she might.

Someone had taken Chiave's person away.

Sloane didn't want anyone taking her people away.

As they all made nests out of the blankets and pillows and turned off the lights, Amelia thought about losing her people, too. There had been about one truly horrible minute there when she'd thought that Ashley and Aiden had been crushed by the tree inside their room. Having been both blessed and cursed with a very vivid imagination, Amelia had been able to picture it all too clearly. Her brain had fast-forwarded through finding them in there, squashed between the branches and their mattresses to rushing them off to the hospital to the doctors not being able to save them to standing over two sad graves as the wind blew through the cornfield at the edge of the Wauseon Cemetery.

Amelia's entire body had gone cold and stiff with terror at the thought. What if she never saw her brother and sister again? What if she never set things right with them? Never got them to stop giving her the side-eye or swallowing up the things they wanted to say?

What if she never got them to understand her?

Accept her?

Living or dead, maybe she could never get them to do any of that. But in the moment Aiden and Ashley appeared in the hallway, Amelia had almost buckled to the floor in relief.

In that moment, she knew that if it didn't happen, it wasn't going to be for lack of trying on her part.

No more disasters disturbed anyone for the rest of the night. Still, the wooden floor of a picture gallery wasn't a particularly comfortable place to sleep no matter how many blankets or pillows you heaped on top of it. Everyone woke up with cricks in their necks or pains in their backs or tasseled pillow marks on their faces at about six in the morning. They might have slept a bit longer, but both a building inspector and construction crew had already arrived and were pounding on Tangle Glen's thick, heavy front doors.

As the Miller-Poes shook themselves grumpily up from the floor, Sergeant Pepper dashed down the stairs and across the entry hall to let in the inspector. She was already dressed for the day in overalls and work boots, another rose in her ponytail to fend off the bad omens of the peony festival.

"Come on in!" she cried, throwing open the door. "Close to a hundred people are supposed to be coming back this afternoon, and we want to make sure it's safe to have them in the house."

Both the inspector and the construction crew seemed taken aback by the enormous museum vase filled with peonies. Towering, as it did, so high above the entry hall that it practically met the chandelier swooping down to greet it.

"Are you sure *that* thing is safe?" a woman in a hard hat asked uncertainly, nodding at the vase.

Sergeant Pepper made a face. "Nothing has felt safe in this house since this peony competition started!"

Looking around as the gardener led the crews upstairs, Amelia realized that Aiden and Ashley were missing.

"Probably off for an early-morning run." Amelia's mom shrugged, not particularly worried about it. Like Sergeant Pepper, she and the Judge disappeared upstairs, though they went in search of showers and clean clothing.

Still sitting in the nest of blankets she'd wrapped herself up in for the night, Sloane blinked blearily at the room. The storm seemed to have passed in the night, with bright, golden sunshine flooding the room as though pretending the storm had never happened and there wasn't now a giant, elderly oak tree collapsed against the house.

Sloane rubbed at her already-wild hair. "Where's Chiave?"

"I don't know. She probably wandered off to go sniff some peonies. Or pee on them." Amelia wasn't very interested in what dogs did first thing in the morning. She checked the s'mores tray for leftovers and came up empty. The pot of hot chocolate was likewise empty. Amelia grimaced, feeling a strong need for breakfast before she could deal with either missing money or her family.

"I'd think she'd be more likely to wake me up so I could take her outside." Sloane lifted up a blanket, thinking that maybe Chiave had wiggled down beneath it again to feel safe after the night's storm.

Instead, she found a pillow.

With a note attached to it . . .

. . . by the spike of a meat thermometer.

"Amelia!" Sloane cried, jumping backward as though it were a bomb that might go off and cover her in feathers.

Amelia hopped over the various pillows, sprinting across the floor to join her friend and stare down at the note. She clutched Sloane's arm for reassurance.

Someone had tapped it out on an old-fashioned typewriter, it would seem. The letters were slightly crooked upon their lines, the paper itself thin and yellow with age.

Forget about the dog. This is none of your business. That money isn't yours.

It might have been a note from the past. Left by an angry ghost.

An angry ghost with a meat thermometer.

Finding her courage, Sloane reached forward and yanked the

long metal spike out of the pillow. As expected, it caused a few wispy feathers to drift up into the air.

Holding the thermometer up to her face so she and Amelia could inspect it more closely, Sloane asked, "Do we think this makes it more likely to be Chef Zahra who's also looking for the money? Or less likely because it seems way too obvious, which means that it's someone else trying to frame her?"

"I don't see her using a typewriter," Amelia said. "Was there one in the attic?"

Neither Sloane nor Amelia could remember if there had been. Given the wreck that it was right now, there didn't seem to be any chance they could go back and find out.

"Mr. Boening-Bradley seems like the sort of person who would use a typewriter," Sloane said. Picking up the note, she folded it and tucked it into the pocket of the hoodie she was wearing. "I bet he learned to type on one."

"No way." Amelia shook her head. "Insects don't type."

The note left them both with a creepy-crawly sort of feeling. Someone had been in the portrait gallery with them while they slept. That person had pulled Chiave away into the night and left behind that threatening note for Sloane and Amelia to find. With all the many Elis staring down at them from the wall, both Sloane and Amelia found the hairs standing up on the backs of their necks.

This mansion was exactly the sort of place that would have more hidden passageways. And secret viewing spots behind the portraits. The sort where a person slid aside a bit of the wall so they could peer out through the portrait's eyes without being noticed.

"Let's get out of here," Amelia suggested. Sloane was in complete agreement with this idea, and they both scurried from the room and into the entry hall.

Which they looked over for foot- or paw prints, hoping to get some clue as to where Chiave could have gone or who could have taken her.

It would seem that the dognapper would have to be Shakespeare Wikander, Sergeant Pepper Arroyo, or Chef Zahra Abu-Absi. After all, the dog had gone quietly, so that would seem to imply that she knew her kidnapper.

Then Sloane pointed out that the Mr. Boening-Bradley could have lured Chiave away with a wave of a peony or two. The bloodhound would have gone willingly with anyone carrying her favorite snorfing object.

"It could even be Mr. Lindsay," Amelia suggested unhappily as their search of the entry hall turned up nothing. "Maybe he faked his own disappearance so he could search for the money without anyone realizing. Uh, Sloane? Didn't there used to be more peonies in that vase?"

She nodded toward the enormous museum vase.

Sloane considered this, before shrugging and giving up. "Maybe? I mean, it's sort of hard to tell the difference between two hundred and one hundred and ninety."

Amelia supposed her friend had a point.

But she still felt certain there was something off about the peonies in the vase.

Before either getting dressed or eating breakfast, Sloane

managed to talk Amelia into walking over to the carriage house where Mr. Lindsay lived on the chance that he'd returned, collected Chiave, and left the note as a joke.

(Sloane admitted there wasn't a very good chance that this was the case.)

They trooped out onto the lawn in their bare feet. The grass felt refreshingly cool and damp against their skin as they walked. Sticks, leaves, and entire branches littered the normally perfect lawn. Most of the peonies along the front of the house had been squashed pretty flat by the pounding they'd taken, their pink blossoms torn free and sprinkled around the garden.

When the oak tree fell, it had brought most of its root system out of the ground, too. A crater now carved out a chunk of the yard, gnarled roots grasping at the air. Workers were already desperately trying to remove it, attacking the trunk with chain saws as cranes and pulleys were used to right it.

Watching it all, Sloane shook her head. "There's no way they're going to get the mansion looking good again before the awards ceremony this afternoon. Safe, maybe. But not good."

"Yeah, yeah, yeah." Amelia had very little interest in either peonies or the awards they might receive. She pulled at Sloane's arm. "That's great. Let's go talk to Mr. Lindsay. I want to change out of my pajamas and into something more normal. Like a silk flapper dress. Plus, I want to check our YouTube channel. Maybe we're number one in Nauru again!"

However, when they reached the carriage house, no one was home. Neither Mr. Lindsay nor Chiave. The large two-story building (larger than many houses) sat empty and silent, its windows blank and its door like a closed mouth guarding a secret.

Trying to pry loose some of those secrets, Sloane and Amelia pressed their faces against the glass pane of the closest window, hoping to catch a glimpse of someone inside.

If there was anyone in there, they remained well hidden.

The only interesting thing either Sloane or Amelia could see was a bunch of photographs of bloodhounds on the wall. In them, they could see both Mr. Lindsay and his father grow from babies to adults, and then from young adults to old adults. Funnily enough, they both kind of looked like mushrooms right from the start, growing from itty-bitty button mushrooms into solid portabellas. Along the way, they always had at least one bloodhound with them.

In the oldest of them, they could clearly see the distinctive markings of Eli-Chiave, Ma Yaklin's dog, and Elizabeth, Anderson Lindsay's dog.

Many of the photos showed that Eli's love of peonies had lasted down through the generations. Half the photos showed bloodhounds sniffing peony bushes, peeing on peony bushes, holding peony bushes in their mouths, or throwing up on peony bushes.

"I guess it's good to have a hobby," Amelia said as they returned to the house.

"Hm. One of Chiave's seems to be stealing people's wallets."

"I guess that's what happens when you're the something-great-grand-dog of a bootlegger." Amelia winced, thinking of something. "Though we're both descended from thieves, and *we* don't steal anything."

"It's probably a dog thing."

They both hoped to see Chiave back at the mansion, but the dog was still nowhere to be seen. More chunks of the tree had been removed, but about a quarter of it still stuck out of the attic in the place where a chunk of the roof had once been. Workers scuttled about, frantically trying to heave parts of the tree into a truck to be carried off. It all still looked like a huge mess.

Everyone must be using the back entrance to stay out of the workers' way because when Sloane and Amelia stepped into Tangle Glen's entry hall, it was unusually quiet.

Quiet, but not empty.

Aiden and Ashley each had a hand in the museum vase.

They both froze when Sloane and Amelia spotted the door.

"What the—" Amelia began.

"Nothing to see here!" Ashley cried, yanking a fragrant yellow blossom out of the vase. Clutching it, she whipped around and sprinted back up the stairs.

"Oh, no, you don't!" Aiden snatched a peony of his own from the vase and pounded up the stairs after her.

"Are my brother and sister . . . stealing peonies?" Amelia asked in bewilderment, laying a hand against her own forehead to check for a fever. "Or am I hallucinating? I thought they were just spying for your grannies, not committing felonies for them!"

"Oh, Granny Kitty and Granny Pearl are very good at sweet-talking people into all sorts of crimes," Sloane gritted through clenched teeth. "Come on, Amelia. I think we need to have a little chat with Aiden and Ashley—and my grannies!"

Amelia hurried after Sloane. They both went up the wide, zig-zagging steps to the second floor. Yellow caution tape roped off the hallway by Aiden and Ashley's room, but their voices came through the other side of the door. Along with the slightly warbly sounds of someone else talking to them through FaceTime.

Ducking under the tape, Sloane threw open the door.

To reveal a room full of peonies.

Specifically, competitors' peonies.

The cleanup crew called in by Sergeant Pepper and Shake-speare had removed the chandelier from Aiden's bed and the tree branch from Ashley's. The debris had been swept up, and Chef Zahra's worktable no longer threatened to slide down into the room. But the enormous chunk of tree that had landed in the attic still hung there threateningly.

"What are you doing in here?" Amelia clapped a hand to either side of her face and dug her fingers into her hair. She looked around the room at the hundred or so blooms filling it.

Aiden and Ashley looked about as guilty as a Miller-Poe was capable of looking. Which was to say, not very. Deciding the best way out of this mess was to act like Amelia was the one doing something wrong, Ashley put her hands on her hips, stuck her nose up in the air, and said, "Uh, excuse me, but this is *our* room. What are *you* doing in it?"

Sloane stepped in furiously. "Stopping my grannies from manipulating the two of you into committing a crime! Or at least, any more crimes! Granny Kitty! Granny Pearl! Turn your camera back on! I heard the two of you talking!"

Aiden's tablet was propped up against a heavy marble-and-silver lamp, its screen blank but the FaceTime app clearly up and running. At Sloane's demand, her grannies switched it on.

Like Aiden and Ashley, they tried to pretend nothing was wrong.

"Oh, hello there, Sloane-y!" Granny Kitty cried casually. "How're you doing? Quite a storm last night, wasn't it?"

"Don't try to change the subject!" Sloane walked farther into the room, testing the floor with her toes as she went. It all seemed solid. "You manipulated Aiden and Ashley into stealing peonies for your garden, didn't you?"

"They did no such thing!" Aiden cried indignantly. "Ashley and I are just having a friendly competition to see who can collect the most peonies for them."

"And I'm winning!" Ashley cut in.

From the tablet, Granny Pearl warned, "Just remember, they have to have a root still attached to them to count. Seems to me, Aiden, that several of yours don't."

Ashley crossed her arms smugly and threw her stepbrother a triumphant look. Aiden appeared almost humble for a second.

Then he shot out of the room, clearly determined to fix this problem.

"No, you don't!" Ashley ran after him.

Dazed, Amelia watched them go, while Sloane shook her

finger at the camera. "Bad grannies! Very bad grannies! It's one thing to commit your own crimes! It's quite another to get someone else to do them for you! Just wait until I tell Dad!"

However, she should have known better than to try to shame her grannies. They both put on sweetly innocent faces. The type they used when they were up to no good and knew they could rely on people thinking that they were just a couple of harmless, kindly old ladies to get away with whatever they were doing.

"Sorry, Sloane-y! Can't hear a word you're saying!" Granny Kitty said in a voice thick with honey.

"Must be because us old folks get confused so easily!" Granny Pearl agreed in a quavery little voice very unlike her normal speaking tone. She hunched her shoulders pathetically. "Half the time, we just don't understand what anyone's saying or doing!"

With that, she very obviously reached forward and ended the call.

"Grrrr." Sloane grabbed her ponytail, twisting its tip tightly around her finger. "My grannies are the best when they're on my side, but when they're plotting, they can be very frustrating!"

Amelia took her friend by the shoulders. "Sloane, we don't have time to deal with your grandmas' crimes. We still don't know where Ma Yaklin's money could be hidden, someone is threatening us, and now Chiave has been kidnapped too. We have to solve all of those riddles before it's time to leave tonight."

"You're right! You're right!" Sloane tugged on her ponytail in distress. "Let's get dressed, and then I want to ask your thieving brother and sister some questions since they got up before anyone else this morning. Maybe they caught a glimpse of whoever left that note."

Since their room was on the other side of the yellow caution tape, Sloane and Amelia figured it was safe to go inside. Sloane changed into a shirt and a comfortable pair of shorts. Amelia, being Amelia, pulled on a filmy pale green dress, pearls, white gloves, and another bell-shaped cloche hat.

"It's a morning dress," she explained airily, twirling the pearls around a fingertip. "Perfect for breakfast."

They went back downstairs to find that breakfast. As they went, Amelia checked how their last video was doing on YouTube. "Hey, we've gotten three hundred more likes! *And* in Liechtenstein, we're the number-two most-watched true crime historical mystery series done by kids!"

Yesterday, they had missed an elaborate meal of omelets and Belgian waffles because of their investigations. Today, both Sloane's and Amelia's stomachs growled eagerly as they approached the dining room. They couldn't wait to see what fabulous dishes Chef Zahra had to offer. However, when they reached the room itself, they found it mostly empty. The serving staff were setting up fancy tables all around the black-and-white checkerboard floor, but those seemed to be for later in the day.

Breakfast itself appeared to be on a long, narrow table by the windows, overlooking the cliff down to the Maumee River. Sunlight sparkled on silver coffee- and teapots, as well as crystal glasses and China plates. Fancy—but not for eating.

The food itself was just cold cuts of meat, cheese, fruit, and pastries.

No omelets. No Belgian waffles.

Sloane checked hopefully for some bacon and came up empty.

"They're too busy setting up for the awards ceremony this afternoon," Aiden explained. He and Ashley appeared to be taking a break from stealing peonies to stuff pastrami, grapes, and cheese wedges into their mouths.

"Yeah, that's great." Amelia helped herself to a pear and a chocolate croissant. "Hey, when the two of you got up early to go rifle through the competitors' prizewinning flowers, was Chiave still in the portrait gallery with us?"

Both of her siblings opened their mouths in outrage. Before either one of them could deny what they'd been doing, Amelia added, "Tell us, or *I'm* going to tell Mom and Dad what you've been up to."

Aiden choked on the grape he'd just swallowed. Ashley pounded him on the back until he horked it out onto the floor.

"Fine," he gasped. "I don't remember if Chiave was still there or not. Do you, Ash?"

"She was definitely still there." Ashley used her toe to slide the spattered grape under the table's skirt so they could pretend it wasn't there. "She was drooling on my wrist when I woke up."

"What time was that?" Sloane asked.

"About five thirty."

Sloane and Amelia had gotten up around six. That left half an hour for someone to sneak in, lure Chiave away, and leave behind the threatening note staked to the pillow. Amelia asked, "Did you see anyone else awake?"

Aiden shrugged. "There were people in the kitchen, getting all of this around."

He waved at the food. That meant Chef Zahra was a suspect.

"Oh, and that Boening-Bradley guy was yelling at that Wikander guy about something."

Which meant it could be either one of them, as well.

Or even the two of them working together, just like Sloane and Amelia were. Not that they had any reason to think that Shakespeare and Mr. Boening-Bradley had ever met before the peony competition, but that could all be a ruse.

Neither Aiden nor Ashley had seen Sergeant Pepper, which seemed to at least clear her from the list of suspects. Besides, as Amelia pointed out, the gardener would have been more likely to stab the note to the pillow with a pair of gardening shears or some-thing else outdoorsy-but-terrifying.

No, the person who would have had the easiest time grabbing that meat thermometer was Chef Zahra.

Who came into the room to see how everyone was enjoying the breakfast spread.

For once, her apron wasn't covered with horrifying stains. She did, however, look distinctly nervous. Twitchy and glancing around and having a hard time concentrating, exactly the way Sloane did right before a big volleyball game.

In Chef Zahra's case, was this because she was anxious about how her peony was going to do in the competition?

Or because she'd kidnapped Chiave and was hot on the trail of Ma Yaklin's missing two million dollars?

Sloane and Amelia didn't know which.

As the chef came over to the table, Amelia froze with a

chocolate croissant halfway to her mouth. Sloane picked up a fork, just in case she needed a weapon.

"How's the croissant?" Chef Zahra asked Amelia distractedly.

"Not poisoned, right?" Amelia squeaked, a bit of chocolate stuck in her throat. Her body was trying to push it back out again, just in case.

That got the chef to focus. She gave Amelia the exact same what-is-wrong-with-you look that her family frequently gave her. "Of course not!" Lowering her voice, she added, "And would you please not say things like that? It makes the other guests nervous."

She glanced around to see if anyone else had heard. Baker and Kuneman had. They immediately tried to get each other to eat, hoping a poisoned muffin might take out the competition.

Not wanting to get on the bad side of someone who may have kidnapped a dog and stabbed a pillow while they slept, Amelia tried to fix things. In a loud voice, she declared, "Everything is super great! Cheese for breakfast! What an idea, huh? Cheddar and, uh, especially the *chiave*."

Chef Zahra blinked at Amelia in confusion. "What are you talking about? Wait—what are you implying? Do you think I would put *dog drool* on my food?"

"No—no!" Amelia went beet red. "You know, *chiave* cheese! I was wondering if any of these are *chiave* cheese."

The chef continued to stare at Amelia as if she was talking in a different language and Chef Zahra was trying to figure out which one. "Do you mean *chevre* cheese?"

"Maybe?" Amelia glanced uncertainly at Sloane. But Sloane

just held her hands up in a shrug. She didn't know anything about cheese. "Isn't Chiave named after a kind of cheese?"

"Chiave?" Chef Zahra repeated. "No, *'chiave'* is Italian for 'key.' It's a variation of the old Latin word *'clavem.'* My mom is a botanist, you know, so she made me learn Latin."

As a stunned Sloane and Amelia took this in, Shakespeare Wikander rushed in, the black tails of his tuxedo flying and one hand pressing his top hat to his head. "Zahra, do you have a spare key to the basement? Some dunderhead has gone and locked it! We're going to need some extra chairs from down there for the awards ceremony, and no one can get in!"

Exasperated, the chef said, "Shakespeare, I don't have the house keys! You're in charge of that sort of thing, not me!" However, she went with him all the same.

Left alone, Amelia and Sloane looked at each other.

Amelia dropped the croissant she'd been holding.

Sloane dropped her fork.

"*'Chiave'* means 'key'!" Amelia gasped.

"The painting of Ma and Eli says, 'The key is hidden within.' Amelia, what if *a bloodhound* is the key to finding Ma Yaklin's money? What if you don't need a map to find the money, you just need a super-sniffer?"

A super-sniffer that someone had just kidnapped.

16

KIDNAPPED DOGS AND CONCRETE GEESE

Sloane and Amelia ran back to the portrait gallery. In the back hallway, they had to shove their way past Shakespeare, Chef Zahra, and a whole crew of people trying out various keys in an effort to open the basement door. Through the entry hall they went, screeching to a halt in the portrait gallery.

Amelia jabbed a gloved finger toward the portrait of Ma Yaklin. "Just look at it, Sloane! Aside from Ma and her roadster, the only things you really notice are Eli and the woods around Tangle Glen."

Sloane picked up the thread of the idea. "Sergeant Pepper said that both the police and bootleggers used bloodhounds to sniff out money and booze during Prohibition. Eli was supposed to have the best sniffer around, so maybe *he* was the only dog who could smell where she hid her money out in the woods!"

"As one of the bootleggers working for Ma—and also having gone up against her in the sniffing competition—Anderson Lindsay probably knew that Eli was the 'key' to finding Ma's money. After he kidnapped Eli and bought Tangle Glen, he had to rename Eli something different. Calling him 'Chiave' in Italian must have been his idea of a joke," Amelia said as Mr.

Boening-Bradly hopped into the portrait gallery in his green suit with his hands clasped behind his back. He looked over the peonies with a great deal of pleasure, jaw moving as though he was imagining nibbling on their leaves like a good insect.

"But the problem was, he only picked up on half of the clues," Sloane finished. "He knew that Eli was the key to sniffing out the money, but he thought it was hidden somewhere inside the mansion. Just like everyone else did."

"Now someone has figured out that Chiave is descended from Eli—and wants to use her super-sniffer to sniff out the money. If the money is still somewhere close by, then she must be, too. But where?"

Before Sloane could answer Amelia, Mr. Boening-Bradley scurried over to them. "Out! Out, both of you! This peony competition is going to be a disaster! There's still a branch sticking out of the attic! Children in the judging chamber! Now no one can get into the basement to get enough chairs! Worst of all, I have you two smarming up the tablecloths with kid goo! I'll be laughed out of the Ohio Peony Enthusiasts Club! I'll have to join the Petunia Enthusiasts Club! *Can you imagine the shame?*"

He put a hand to each of their backs, and with each word, nudged Sloane and Amelia closer to the doorway. Reaching it, he gave them one final shove out of the room, slammed the glass doors shut after them, and turned the locks. His big, round eyes blinked slowly at them, daring them to try to get back inside.

Or call an exterminator for that bug spray Sloane kept wanting to get her hands on.

"Well!" Amelia puffed up with outrage, but Sloane had more important things to think about.

"Amelia! The basement! Why can't anyone get in the basement?" She dragged her friend across the entry hall, past the enormous vase (with noticeably fewer flowers in it).

"Because someone lost the key?" Amelia suggested sullenly, arms crossed and still offended.

"Or because no one wants anyone else to go down there. Possibly because there's a kidnapped dog hidden down there!"

That finally got Amelia to forget about Mr. Boening-Bradley's unkind words. She joined Sloane in running to the back hallway. "We get this solved, we won't just be number two in Liechtenstein, we'll be number one!"

The crowd of workers was giving up on opening the basement door. Shakespeare pushed past the two of them with a phone clipped to his ear as he spoke with some sort of rental company about getting a hundred chairs delivered right away.

"No luck?" Sloane asked Sergeant Pepper as the gardener hefted a garden hoe up onto her shoulder. From the dirt stains on the paint around the frame, it looked like she'd tried to use the hoe to pry the door open for Shakespeare.

Sergeant Pepper shook her head, then tucked the rose back into her ponytail as it started to slide out. "No luck. We'll have to get a locksmith here later, after the ceremony. Hey, shouldn't you two be getting ready for it?"

"We will," Amelia assured her, face going flinty with determination. "Just as soon as we get that door open!"

"All right." Sergeant Pepper looked taken aback by Amelia's ferocity. "Uh, good luck? Just don't take any of my axes to it, okay? All of that woodwork is expensive to repair."

Amelia swore that they wouldn't be hacking their way into anything. Relieved, Sergeant Pepper went to take care of her rosebushes. Leaving Sloane and Amelia to commit a little breaking and entering in peace and quiet.

"I know where her garden shed is. Do you want me to go get one of those axes?" Sloane turned to do just that, but her friend stopped her.

Amelia had pulled up a YouTube video on how to pick a lock using a bobby pin.

(Fortunately, Amelia also knew that a bobby pin was something people used to hold their hair in place. Sloane did not know this, having never used a bobby pin in her life.)

"I've got one." Amelia slid it out from under her cloche hat and held it up smugly for Sloane to see. She bragged, "It's the sort of thing women always had in their hair back in the 1920s."

Snapping the hairpin in two, Amelia had Sloane hold up her phone so she could watch the video's instructions on how to insert the two pieces into the lock. Holding one still, she wiggled the other one around until . . .

Click-click-click.

The lock slid open.

"Woof?" Deep in the basement, a dog barked excitedly.

"You were right! She's in there!" Flicking on the lights, Amelia took off down the basement steps. In her excitement, she managed to be faster than Sloane for a change, hitting the bottom of the steps and running through the basement's many rooms. Sloane lagged behind, picking up the broken bobby pin pieces Amelia had tossed to the floor.

As Sloane reached the bottom step of the basement, her phone buzzed in her pocket. Taking it out, she saw that it was from her dad. Worried that something was wrong, she swiped open FaceTime. However, rather than her dad, she saw her concrete goose staring at her from her room back home.

Startled, Sloane jerked to a halt.

Why was her concrete goose calling her? And also, *how?*

Finally—and this wasn't the most important thing, but it was still weird—why was her goose wearing a pink princess dress and crown?

Then Skye's face dropped into view.

She wore a princess crown, too, and was holding a china teacup in her hand. Specifically, one of the china teacups Sloane and her mom had used for tea parties when Sloane was about Skye's age.

"Oh, hiya, Sloane." Skye took a sip of water from her cup. She'd also laid out some very smeary jam sandwiches on a "picnic blanket" made out of Sloane's favorite fuzzy blanket. "Bertram and I were trying to call Santa Claus, but I guess we got you instead."

There were many confusing things about what Skye had just said. Still reeling from the fact that Cynthia's youngest child had invaded her room, Sloane was only able to gasp, "Bertram?"

"Yeah, that's what I named the goose."

Sloane went rigid with outrage. "Her name isn't Bertram! It's Cordelia!"

"Oh." Skye looked surprised. "Why?"

"Why? *Why?* It just is!" Sloane sputtered, going rigid with outrage.

"Sloane!" Amelia cried from farther in the basement. "Sloane, hurry up!"

Skye perked up. "Is that Santa Claus? Can I talk to her? I've got a long list of what I want, so I thought I'd better talk to her while it was still summer so the elves would have enough time to get started."

"No, that's not Santa Claus! And why are you in my room, anyhow? And where's my dad? Why do you have his phone?"

"Sloane!" Amelia shrieked.

"Oh, never mind! You'd better not get any jam on Cordelia!"

With that, Sloane ended the call. Though not before she heard Skye protest, "Bertram says he likes the name 'Bertram' better!"

Sloane squeezed her phone in despair.

Her concrete goose probably really did like the name Bertram better than Cordelia.

Just like how her dad seemed to like hanging out with his new Cynthia family better than he did with his Maisy and Sloane family. He was letting Skye the super-annoying gremlin hang out in Sloane's room. Play with her things.

How could he do that?

How could he replace his daughter so easily?

"Sloane! The kidnapper is escaping out the bootlegger's tunnel!" Amelia shrieked in despair. "Help!"

Shaking furiously away the tears forming in her eyes, Sloane forced herself to concentrate on what was happening right now. She couldn't do anything about her dad or Skye or Cordelia the concrete goose.

But she could help her friend.

And rescue a dog in need.

Sloane rushed through the basement, finding her way into the room that led to the old tunnel. Amelia was already there, trying with all her might to squeeze open the dusty shelf hiding the entryway. Leaping over the old wooden crates still scattered about, Sloane joined her. She yanked the door the rest of the way open, allowing herself and Amelia through. The old antique light bulbs showed them the way down through the dank, narrow tunnel. Slime oozed from between the bricks, a sludge made of mildew and rainwater that had seeped down through the ground from the yard and woods above. The tunnel angled downward. The other day when Mr. Lindsay had come through here, the tunnel had seemed cool and dry. Now, after last night's storm, it seemed positively freezing and very, very wet.

"Woof!" Far away, Chiave barked.

Through the murky gloom, they ran. Overhead, the ancient lights buzzed. The damp chill seemed to wriggle all around them like worms. At first, the air tasted musty, but the closer they got to the Maumee River, it turned fresher.

Like a door had been opened ahead of them.

Sloane saw it first, that rectangle of watery blue light. Putting on an extra burst of speed, she left Amelia behind as she sprinted faster and faster.

Because that rectangle of light was getting skinnier and skinnier.

Someone was closing the door.

"Stop!" Sloane yelled, but of course, the kidnapper didn't listen to her. Chiave's tail disappeared through that crack of light.

And then it vanished entirely.

The door slammed shut.

Sloane reached it a second later. She yanked at the handle, but it wouldn't give. Bracing her feet against the door, she tugged harder but still had no luck. No matter how much she pulled or pushed, it wouldn't open. Finally, Sloane slammed her fist against the metal door in frustration.

"It's a twist handle!" Amelia panted, finally reaching the end of the tunnel. She wobbled down the last step to fall against the door. "Look!"

Amelia was right. Sloane had just tried to pull the handle, but she actually had to twist it to the side. She did so, and the seal gave, allowing her to shove it open. Together, Sloane and Amelia stumbled out into the bright sunlight. They both threw up their hands to shield their eyes. Reflecting off the water, the light glittered and danced, dazzling them. It took a moment for their eyes to adjust to the sunlight, but by the time they did, there was no one to be seen.

Sloane looked around frantically, trying to guess where Chiave and her dognapper could have gone. There were a few boats out on the water, but they were all far away. If the kidnapper was already on one of them, he or she had done a great job of blending in.

Several paths zigzagged their way along the waterfront or else back up the hill toward the woods and the mansion. The grass and tree branches stirred along all of them—but from someone running past or the breeze off the river, it was impossible to tell. Old, wet leaves made a matting over the paths, preventing Chiave's paws from leaving marks in the mud underneath.

"Gah!" In frustration, Sloane kicked at a rock, but that did nothing more than knock it free from where it had been lodged in the hill. It tumbled down the slope to splash into the river below while pain flared through Sloane's toes. She slumped down onto the stone door ledge, overwhelmed by a wave of frustration.

To her horror, tears began to leak out of her eyes.

Sloane tried to snuffle them back in before Amelia saw, but they wouldn't stop.

As Amelia sat down next to her with her face crinkled in concern, Sloane scrubbed at her face with the back of her hand.

"Sloane, what's wrong?" Amelia asked.

"N-N-N-*othing!*" Sloane tried to say, but it came out as a sob. Then her nose was leaking too, and her face had gone all puffy, and more words kept boiling up into her throat only to get caught there. "I'm f-f-fine! Really!"

But her shoulders shook, and she buried her face in her hands.

Then it all came pouring out of her. She told Amelia about Skye in her room, and her continuing fear that she was losing her family.

Having heard it before, Amelia listened thoughtfully. She sat down next to her friend, resting her chin on her fist. When Sloane finished, they sat together in silence for a while, Amelia letting her friend wipe the tears from her eyes.

Finally, she said, "Do you want to take my family? You can

totally have them. You're super good at sports, so they'll love you."

Sloane snort-laughed. She picked up a stick and used it to poke around in the underbrush, lifting up old leaves. "Thanks, but I saw your face last night when you thought Aiden and Ashley were hurt. Don't try to tell me that you wouldn't care if you lost them."

"True," Amelia sighed, looking out over the glittering ribbon of the Maumee. "They can be annoying, competitive jerks. But they're *my* annoying competitive jerks."

"And they don't mean to be jerks," Sloane pointed out. "They're kind of like Chiave, honestly. Just so super excited about whatever it is they like that they don't really notice when other people aren't excited about it too."

In her mind, Amelia pictured her parents and siblings with tennis balls stuffed in their mouths. Drool dangling from their lips and surprised, doggy expressions on their faces. She cracked up.

"I still don't know how to talk to them," she confessed. "I mean, yeah, I know that I did that one time with my mom. But just because you do something once doesn't mean you suddenly become good at it."

"Yeah, I know." Sloane sighed, stirring the old, dead leaves with her stick. Something bright and red swirled with them. At first, Sloane thought it was blood, but when she poked at it with the stick, it turned out to be a red flower petal. "I guess we're just going to have to keep practicing it until we become good at it."

"Experts in talking to our families." Now Amelia sighed too.

"I think we're even less likely to do that than find Bootleggin' Ma Yaklin's missing two million dollars by the time we go home tonight."

"At least we're number two in Liechtenstein."

"And number one in Nauru."

Absently, Sloane picked up the red flower petal and rubbed it between her fingers. How did a peony blossom get all the way out here? Something clicked in Sloane's head. "This must have been dropped by whoever dognapped Chiave!"

Amelia leaned forward and sniffed it. "No, that's not a peony petal. The smell is wrong. And the size and shape of it too, and OMG . . . I sound just like my family."

As her friend made a face at this realization, Sloane sniffed the petal too. Amelia was right. The smell was all wrong. Too strong, too perfumy, too . . .

Too much like a rose.

This was a rose petal, not a peony petal.

And there was only one person in the house who had any interest in roses.

"Sergeant Pepper Arroyo!" Sloane gasped, leaping to her feet. "Amelia, she's always wearing a rose in her hair. And she was fully dressed this morning when those workers arrived, meaning she could have sneaked into the portrait gallery after Ashley and Aiden left but before we got up. Because Mr. Lindsay stuffed a bunch of his old family albums and newspaper clippings in the shed, she could have put together the same clues as us!"

"Oh-oh-OH!" Amelia accidentally dropped her shoe.

"Sloane, Chiave kept going after Sergeant Pepper's wallet! I bet she trained Chiave to use her bloodhound skills to scent out money—*just like Eli could!* She would have had lots of opportunities to train the dog because poor Mr. Lindsay needed so much help with her. Only, rather than training Chiave to sniff money, Sergeant Pepper accidentally just trained her to sniff out *her* money!"

Sloane nodded grimly. Picking up Amelia's shoes, she handed them to her friend.

"Come on. Let's go check out her apartment in the carriage house. If she just lost her hiding place in the tunnel, she can't have many other places to keep Chiave."

"Let's just hope Mr. Lindsay is there too." Amelia shuddered. "Let's hope that she hasn't done anything terrible to him."

Little did they know they didn't need to worry about Mr. Lindsay.

They needed to worry about someone doing something terrible to them.

Because in less than an hour, Sloane would be slipping toward her death on the mansion's roof.

With Sergeant Pepper close behind her.

17

Not Surprisingly, a Plan Goes Awry

Sergeant Pepper wouldn't have many places where she could easily hide Chiave, what with the peony awards ceremony happening at the house. That pretty much left Mr. Lindsay's house and the gardening shed.

Sloane and Amelia were betting on the gardening shed.

"Do you think she has Mr. Lindsay tied up in there too?" Amelia asked as they ran back through the tunnel.

"I wouldn't be surprised." Sloane gritted her teeth.

They tore through the basement, up the stairs, and out into the back hallway, almost knocking over Shakespeare Wikander.

"Hey, how'd you get the door open?" he asked in surprise, grabbing his top hat as it tumbled off his head. Two canaries burst from it and took flight down the hallway.

"We're girl detectives," Amelia bragged. "We've got skills."

"Come on, Amelia! We'll tell people all about it later!" Sloane dragged her friend through the mansion. They had to dodge the rest of the Miller-Poe family, who were all dressed in extremely fancy clothing.

"Amelia! Why are you wearing that?" Amanda Miller clasped her hands to her head in despair.

"Oh, look!" Baker cried. "It's the entertainment! Isn't she cute!"

"I'm not cute! I'm the bee's knees!" Amelia cried as Sloane propelled her out of the house.

They made their way through the rose garden to the large shed at the edge of the woods. With its sloping, mossy roof, cheerful red bricks, and beveled glass windows, it looked way too charming to just be used for storage and messy gardening supplies.

And way, *way* too charming to be used as a prison for a defenseless dog and an injured old man.

"Can you see anything?" Amelia asked as they both pressed their faces against a smudged glass pane in one of the windows. No one had bothered to clean them in years, so everything inside seemed to be covered in a milky brown film.

"Not really," Sloane confessed. "I don't see either Chiave or Mr. Lindsay. But I'm betting she'd have them upstairs anyhow."

She pointed at the rickety wooden stairs leading upward to the shed's second floor. It didn't have much in the way of windows, and they were obviously far too short to see into the ones it did have. Anything could be up there.

Anyone could be up there.

They tried the door, but it was locked up tight.

"Drat." Amelia felt in her hair for another bobby pin while Sloane jiggled the handle in the hopes that it was just stuck. "I'm all out of bobby pins."

They walked around the back of the building, hoping to find another way in. This time, they were in luck. A window had been cracked open, and together, they were able to lift the old, swollen pane up a little bit more.

"I'm not sure I can make it through that." Sloane scrunched up her face uncertainly.

"I can. I'm smaller than you." Amelia swept the hat off her head and handed it to Sloane for safekeeping. Her gloves and pearls quickly followed. "Besides, if I get caught, you can run faster than I can."

"Okay, but be careful in there. I want to live to see us hit number one in Liechtenstein." Sloane gave her friend a boost up and through the open window.

Amelia's flailing legs disappeared through the crack. Sloane tugged anxiously on her ponytail, worried that Amelia might have fallen on a rack. Or stand up with a trowel sticking out of her skull.

But after a moment, Amelia got woozily to her feet, no trowel sticking anyplace uncomfortable. She gave Sloane the thumbs-up and headed toward the door to open it so Sloane could come inside too. Sloane scurried through the weeds growing along the side of the shed, planning on doing just that.

Only to screech to a halt and flatten herself against the brick wall.

Sergeant Pepper was walking across the yard, toward the shed.

Before Sloane could run back to the window and warn Amelia, the gardener reached the front door. She took out an old-fashioned iron key and used it to undo the lock.

"Hey, what are *you* doing in here?" she demanded, stepping inside and shutting the door behind her.

Oh no. Oh no, oh no, oh no.

Not only was Sloane losing her dad to a new family, her best friend was about to be murdered.

In a panic, Sloane cast about for something to do. She had to save Amelia—she had to get her friend out of there—she had to get help—she had to—she had to—to—

Without any coherent thought, Sloane picked up a large rock near the shed's door.

And hefted it right through a window.

Glass shattered with a force that was both satisfying and caused Sloane to recoil. She covered her ears and turned her face away to avoid any shards. The stone crashed onto the floorboards beyond, smashing a small crater into them and sending splinters flying. Glass tinkled after it like confetti tossed at a party.

As the sound died away, Sloane uncovered her ears and looked in through the window.

Sergeant Pepper gaped at Sloane in astonishment.

And rage.

At least she forgot about Amelia. She yanked open the door as Amelia darted up the stairs to the shed's second floor.

Sergeant Pepper stormed toward Sloane, shrieking, "What do you think you're doing?"

From inside the building, Amelia shouted, "Sloane! I can hear barking upstairs!"

At that, Sergeant Pepper whipped back around. Then she turned to face Sloane again, clearly unsure which girl was the bigger threat.

Sloane scooped up another rock out of the garden and pulled her arm backward.

"I'm the pitcher for my softball team," she warned the gardener. "Undefeated in our league."

(Granted, that was partly because they'd only played two games this season. But Sloane didn't see any reason to get into the specific details right now.)

That seemed to decide Sergeant Pepper.

She shot back into the shed and up the stairs, after Amelia.

"No! Stop!" Sloane cried after the gardener.

Going even deeper into the evil gardener's lair hadn't been quite what Sloane had in mind. She'd been hoping Sergeant Pepper would just freeze in place until Amelia could free Chiave. Then the three of them could run back to the mansion together.

Sloane was super fast. She launched herself after the gardener, determined to tackle her before she could harm Sloane's friend. Amelia, however, had a talent of her own.

She was super clumsy.

(This might not seem like a talent to the average person, but it could sometimes come in handy all the same.)

In this case, Amelia tripped right as she reached the top step.

Having tripped, she skidded downward, selfie stick flying, arms up in the air and crying "WHOA!" as she went.

In the process, she ran into Sergeant Pepper. Who was not expecting a budding YouTube star to suddenly be bodysurfing toward her.

Amelia slammed into the gardener, knocking her off her feet as well. Sergeant Pepper cried out as the two of them slid their way down the stairs with the *thump-thump-thump* of two people who were about to be bruised and achy in places they'd rather not be bruised and achy.

Having been friends with Amelia long enough not to be entirely shocked by this turn of events, Sloane jumped to the side in time and managed not to be wiped out as well.

"Don't try to save me!" Amelia shrieked as she bounced past. "Let my sacrifice mean something, Sloane! Upload my video to YouTube! Our subscribers will exact vengeance for me! Save Chiave!"

By now, Sloane could hear the barking that had sent Amelia up the stairs in the first place. She sprinted upward as Sergeant Pepper struggled to untangle herself from Amelia's arms and legs.

Reaching the top of the stairs, Sloane discovered a short hallway cutting the second floor in half. There was a door on either side. Both of them were shut, but a desperate clawing and woofing came from behind one of them.

Down below, Sergeant Pepper cried, "Stop!"

Sloane ignored her and threw open the quivering door.

Chiave bounded out of it and thumped her happily in the chest. She slurped and snorfed Sloane's face as Sloane tried to look past her into the room. It was dingy and gray, stacked full of more unwanted junk from Tangle Glen. There was a water dish and a bowl with dog food on the floor, but no Mr. Lindsay.

"Erf—Chiave! Get off!" Sloane pushed the dog's face away from her own and sat upright.

Just as Sergeant Pepper staggered up the stairs.

Panting, she stood at the end of the hallway with her back and arms bent. As Sloane hugged Chiave, she thought that the gardener looked very much like the villain in a Wild West show.

She had the posture of someone about to draw from a holster and the facial expression of someone who had just been knocked down the stairs.

Given that she was capable of kidnapping a dog and had no doubt done something terrible to Mr. Lindsay, Sloane's stomach twisted with fear. She squeezed Chiave tighter, determined to find a way to protect them both as that fear spread out across her entire body. Every muscle in Sloane's body tensed, hardening with determination.

If this was the end for Sloane, then she was at least going to make her dad, her grannies, and her mom proud.

Slayer Sloane never turned her back on a teammate. Not even a furry one.

So, she got up slowly, threateningly, to her feet herself.

Everything about Sloane's own posture said, *Go ahead. Make my day.*

Only, Sergeant Pepper didn't.

Because a selfie stick shot into view from around the corner, whacking one of Sergeant Pepper's legs out from under her.

"Run, Sloane! Run!" Amelia wheezed, having crawled her way back to the top of the stairs. "Tell the poets to sing the praises of my exploits!"

Grabbing Chiave by the harness, Sloane did just that.

Sergeant Pepper tried to grab Sloane's ankle as Sloane vaulted over the collapsed gardener. But Sloane easily cleared her. Shoving the bloodhound down the stairs first, Sloane hooked Amelia by the neck of her green dress and dragged her along too.

"Come on, Amelia!" she cried. "Our subscribers will have to get vengeance for you another day!"

"*STOP!*" Sergeant Pepper screamed behind them. Horrible thuds hinted that she was getting to her feet and was still after them.

By the time they reached the bottom of the stairs, Amelia had managed to fully right herself. Together, they burst out of the shed and toward the mansion with Chiave in the lead. The dog romped over the grass and through the garden with her tongue hanging out and her ears flapping in the breeze. As she reached the first brick pathway leading around the mansion, Chef Zahra came out the kitchen door with a basket slung over her arm.

Chiave changed courses and bounded over the chef to give her a lick and a snorf.

"Chiave? What are you doing out here?" Chef Zahra asked. "Is Mr. Lindsay back?"

"Help!" Amelia shrieked, still waving her selfie stick and camera about, filming it all. "Murder! Kidnapping!"

Chef Zahra startled at that, but before either Sloane or Amelia could explain, Chiave shot into the house.

Looking back over their shoulders, they watched as Sergeant Pepper altered her path.

Now she was running toward the front of the mansion, face grim.

She had to be planning to get to Chiave before Sloane and Amelia could.

"*What* is going on?" Chef Zahra demanded.

"I told you!" Amelia waved her arms about frantically. "Murder! Kidnapping!"

Sloane pushed Amelia's arms down so she wouldn't accidentally whap either the chef or herself. "Not murder! No one has been murdered!"

"We don't know that!" Amelia argued. "We don't know *what* she's done to Mr. Lindsay! But we know that she kidnapped Chiave!"

They couldn't afford to offer more of an explanation than that. Sergeant Pepper had already disappeared toward the front of the mansion, and Chiave could be anywhere inside. (Normally, one might assume that a dog would get distracted and remain in the kitchen near all the food in the hopes of a snack. But given that they were dealing with a peony-obsessed pooch and a house full of peonies, there was just no way of saying where Chiave might end up.)

Chef Zahra cried, "Wait!" after them as Sloane and Amelia took off again. They dodged their way around various waitstaff, dipping and twirling when necessary. Shooting out into the back servant hallway, they looked about in a panic.

"Do you see her? Do you see her?" Sloane cried, ponytail whapping her across the face as she jerked her head this way and that.

"No!" Amelia clutched her white hat against her head in despair. "And I'm not dressed properly for a rescue! And there's no time to change! And Sloane, what are we going to do?"

A shriek from the portrait gallery gave them their answer.

They ran to the portrait gallery where Kuneman clutched her silken bottom and gasped at Chiave, "I *beg* your pardon!"

Baker snickered into a crystal glass of punch. A very rumpled Sergeant Pepper pushed her way through the crowd and said smoothly, "Oh, that's just how she says hello."

As ever, Kuneman was elegantly dressed in a sparkly gown, her hair swept up on top of her head and a choker of diamonds at her throat. She did not seem at all reassured by either Sergeant Pepper's words or her appearance. In fact, she put her hand to her throat in horror as the pearl-wearing Baker said, "Go on, Mrs. Kuneman. Say hello back. It's only polite!"

As Baker and Kuneman prepared to resume their usual death match, Sergeant Pepper took Chiave by the harness and started to lead her away.

Amelia fell to her knees and pointed dramatically at them. She let loose with a bloodcurdling scream. *"MUR*-DERRRRRRR!!!"

That got the attention of everyone in the room.

Several peopled dropped the stemmed glasses they had been holding. Gasps filled the air as everyone swung around to see what was going on.

Even the Judge looked up. Startled, for once, into noticing what was going on around him. He was holding Shakespeare Wikander's purple peony in his hands.

"Who's been murdered?" he asked. "This is supposed to be my weekend off. No one's supposed to get murdered. I didn't even bring my official robe. This is my casual-wear robe!"

Mr. Boening-Bradley pushed his way to the center of the

crowd, clicking his hands in a praying mantis–like fashion. He gave a hysterical laugh, his mustache-antennae twitching and his eyes huge and unblinking. "Nothing to worry about, ladies and gentlemen! No peonies have been murdered! It's just a dog!"

The crowd let out a sigh of relief, but that relief was short-lived. Chiave wriggled free of Sergeant Pepper's grasp and barreled happily forward.

Toward the enormous vase of peonies in the middle of the entry hall. The one that had all the peonies combined together into one arrangement.

Apparently, the dog had decided there was no sense in snorfing the flowers one by one when she could just roll about in all of them at once.

Realizing what Chiave was about to do, Sloane put on a burst of speed. She shoved past Amelia and Sergeant Pepper alike, diving through the double doors and toward the foyer.

As she did so, Sloane shouted, "NO! Chiave—stop!"

But the dog ignored her.

And leaped into the air.

Toward the vase loaned to the peony competition by the Toledo Museum of Art . . .

. . . and then into it.

The bloodhound swept the vase right off the marble table on which it had been set. It was big and heavy, but Chiave was bigger and heavier.

It tipped over the edge and smashed onto the floor.

Shards of china went everywhere.

Prizewinning (or at least potentially prizewinning peonies) were flung all across the foyer floor.

Behind Sloane, shrieks filled the air as competitors realized what was happening to their precious flowers.

Mr. Boening-Bradley fell to the floor with a thud, having fainted dead away.

Amelia switched off her camera for the moment, not at all sure she wanted proof that they had accidentally helped to break the art museum's loaned-out vase.

Chiave landed on the floor too. By then, she'd already figured out that she'd done something very bad. Shoulders hunched, tail between her legs, the bloodhound didn't even bother to sniff any of the flowers she'd worked so hard to reach. Instead, she took off up the curved stairway to the second floor.

Sergeant Pepper had recovered from the shock of being accused of murder. Sprinting out into the foyer, she pushed past Sloane and continued up the stairs after Chiave.

"Oh no you don't!" Amelia shouted, turning her camera back on as she dashed after the gardener. She accidentally knocked Sloane over as she passed by.

In the portrait gallery, someone screamed, "My Buckeye Belle!"

Someone else cried, "She's ruined my Chocolate Soldier!"

"Oh, just look at the state of my Julia Rose!"

As Sloane got to her feet, she could only assume these were the names of the various peonies scattered about on the floor in front of her. She checked her hands and knees for shards of china and was grateful to find none. A leaf was sticking to her leg. Baker dashed forward and snatched it from her.

"My Pink Derby!" she gasped. "You've destroyed my Pink Derby!"

Sloane opened her mouth to point out that she'd done no such thing. It was hardly *her* fault that Mr. Lindsay's dog was snorfing-obsessed. Then she caught a glimpse at the look on Baker's face and took a step backward as the woman pointed her finger at Sloane so dramatically that you would have thought she'd been taking lessons from Amelia.

"SABOTAGE!" Baker's finger shook as she accused Sloane. "This girl is sabotaging us all! And her father is the judge!"

"He's not *my* dad!" Sloane exclaimed automatically. Then, she took in the crowd of angry gardeners funneling into the foyer from the portrait gallery.

Not a single one of them looked happy.

It suddenly occurred to Sloane that, as gardeners, they might very well have pruning sheers and trowels hidden on them.

Spinning around, she took off up the stairs after Amelia, Sergeant Pepper, and Chiave. They were at the end of the hallway, grappling over the leash that Sergeant Pepper had managed to attach to the dog when Amanda Miller threw open her door.

"What on earth is going on out here?" she demanded, accidentally whapping her daughter to the side with the door.

Sergeant Pepper let out a triumphant yell.

Then she looked toward Sloane and froze in horror.

Glancing over her shoulder, Sloane realized that she had a mob of angry gardeners hot on her heels. Kuneman actually had a pair of garden clippers in one bejeweled hand, and Baker was waving about a golden trowel.

(Sloane had known it. She had *known* it. Never mess with a gardener. You just didn't know what they might be carrying.)

Putting on a burst of speed, Sloane made it down the hallway in seconds. She ripped the leash out of Sergeant Pepper's grip as Ashley and Aiden looked out from their room. Both of their jaws dropped open in horror.

Quick as lightning, Aiden ducked back into their room and returned to the doorway with an armful of vases. He began flinging peonies over the yellow caution tape and at the furious horde. "Here! Take them back! We never wanted them anyway!"

That caused most of the gardeners to draw to a halt in confusion. No one seemed to be able to figure out why flowers were raining down on their heads. (Especially since Ashley had started to chuck the flowers out of their room too. Meanwhile, Amanda Miller had the weary look of someone thinking long and hard about just closing her door, putting her earbuds in, and taking a nice long, hot bath while events sorted themselves out.)

Chiave seemed to think the crowd was coming for her (which it sort of was). She took off running even faster than Sloane, ripping her leash free from Sloane's grasp.

"Wait! No! Chiave, come back!" Rather than heading downward, toward the kitchen and people who might be able to help, the bloodhound headed up the kitchen stairs.

Toward the smaller rooms on the former servants' floor.

And past that to the attic beyond.

Or, at the very least, whatever remained of the attic beyond.

The attic door still hung open from when Sloane had helped Chef Zahra rescue her peonies. Beyond it, Sloane could see the shattered remains of the chef's potting table and grow lamps beneath the fallen branch. Chiave scampered right over all the little twigs and leaves littering the floor to scoot underneath the branch itself.

Disappearing into the attic on the other side.

A bit of a ruckus reached Sloane's ears, and then a very bedraggled Amelia appeared at her side.

"Managed to shove Sergeant Pepper into Aidan's room!" she panted. "But that will only give us a few seconds. She was already fighting her way out again, throwing vases like grenades at all of those gardeners."

Turning her attention back to the attic, Sloane walked carefully inside. She felt the floorboards with her sneakers, but they seemed firm. She was fairly confident she wouldn't fall through the ceiling into Aiden and Ashley's room below.

Fairly confident.

Bending over, she tried to peer through the green mesh of leaves arching over the floor. "Chiave? Come back here, girl!"

A whimper on the other side of the branch said that Chiave was still feeling like a bad dog for knocking over the vase in the foyer.

"I'm going in," Sloane said grimly, dropping onto her stomach so she could wiggle through the forest now sprouting in the attic.

"Not without me, you aren't." Amelia got down on her hands and knees as well. With a grimace, she added, "Oh, I'm definitely not dressed right for this, Sloane!"

"What would even *be* the right outfit for this?" Sloane grimaced herself as a branch whapped her in the face. Pokey little twigs tore at their hair and clothing as they wormed their way over the floorboards. Fallen slate shingles bruised their hands and knees, tearing a hole in the skirt of Amelia's green dress.

Finally, they reached the other side of the mess. Standing up, Sloane spat out a mouthful of leaves and tossed her ponytail back over her shoulder. Amelia emerged looking like some sort of nature spirit with entire branches caught in her hair.

Chiave huddled against the wall over on the far side of the attic, clearly convinced that she was in trouble. The girls ran over to the bloodhound and scooped her up into an embrace.

"Aw, Chiave. It's no big deal," Amelia assured her. "I break things all the time."

Whether the dog understood them or not, they petted her until she calmed down.

Which was right before Sergeant Pepper's voice rang out, "I know you're in there! You'd better come out before something terrible happens to you!"

Sloane and Amelia stiffened in fear. They looked at each other in desperation.

Now what should they do?

Leaping to her feet, Sloane searched about for an exit. Where was a good hidden passageway when you needed one? If there were any in the attic, she hadn't found any yesterday and couldn't spot any now, either.

"Fine! I'm coming in after you!" As soon as Sergeant Pepper said it, they could hear the sounds of the branches and leaves swishing and scraping at the gardener as she made her way toward them.

"The window!" Sloane whispered, pointing to an oval-shaped

opening. "We can crawl out onto the roof and then either get someone's attention or else climb down the side of the house."

They could see the tree branch shaking now, meaning that Sergeant Pepper must almost be through it. Together, they ran over to the window. It opened more easily than Sloane had expected, swinging to the side with one push.

"You first," Amelia said. "That way I can hand you Chiave."

Sloane slung her leg over the wooden ledge and eased her way out onto the damaged roof. The wood still felt soft from last night's downpour. Which didn't seem to be entirely over just yet. Rain spattered her face as she finished climbing through the window.

Of course it *would* start to rain again right when she needed a clear, calm day to keep from plummeting to her death. Sloane slid carefully on her bottom down the wet, sloping roof of the three-story mansion and toward a probably spattery death below. Definitely toward a bone-cracking, skull-splitting drop to the ground.

"Careful! Careful!" Amelia called from the oval-shaped attic window out of which Sloane had just escaped.

"That's not helping, Amelia!" Sloane clenched her teeth as the wind smacked her long black ponytail into her eyes, blinding her. Then it playfully changed directions and pushed at her back as though this was all a fun game.

At least the roof's broken, mossy shingles snagged her shorts, slowing her downward slide.

A bit.

A very little bit.

Hopefully enough of a bit.

"Sloane!" Amelia squeaked in terror from the attic window. "Sloane, don't die!"

Before Sloane could answer, her shorts tore free from the old, crumbling slate tiles. Instantly, she picked up speed on the slick rooftop, speeding faster and faster toward the abyss beyond the rain gutter. Just as she thought she was going to have to send Amelia a note from the afterlife, saying, *Whoops! Sorry!* her right foot hit the metal trough and sunk down into the soggy mess of old leaves still stuck there from last autumn.

Whew! Sloane's left foot joined her right foot to land softly in the gutter. Her knees bent, allowing her bottom to come to a gentle stop. Before Sloane could sigh in relief, she made the mistake of looking over the edge.

It was a long way to the ground.

Three stories, to be exact.

Long enough to make her very, *very* grateful for the rain gutter. Even if it was now filling her shoes up with water.

Soggy socks and ruined shoes were still better than ending up as a soggy, ruined mess yourself.

Sloane turned back around to find Amelia still peering anxiously out the window. Calling up to her friend, Sloane said, "I survived!"

"Oh, good!" Amelia's very freckled face relaxed.

Then, that face disappeared with a shriek as Amelia was yanked backward, deeper inside the attic.

"Amelia!" Sloane cried, twisting around to try to crawl back up the slick shingles to help her friend. "Amelia, don't you dare die, either!"

Barking covered whatever else Amelia might have yelled back.

Inside the murky gloom of the attic, Amelia and her attacker merged together into a misshapen beast with too many elbows and twirling backs—as well as the teeth and tail of a very angry bloodhound.

"OW!" Someone screamed as the dog sank teeth into an arm. Whether it was Amelia or their pursuer, Sloane didn't know.

"AMELIA!" she shrieked again.

But her friend didn't answer her.

Instead, the dog jumped out of the window.

Hurtling straight toward Sloane.

With enough speed to knock them both over the side of the building onto the patio stones three stories below.

When they did, Sloane's shoes wouldn't be the only soggy mess.

Thinking quickly, Sloane rolled to the side. She looped one arm around a vent pipe poking up out of the roof. With her free hand, she caught Chiave by the leash attached to the dog's harness. The bloodhound's paws scrabbled at the slick tiles, trying to get a foothold. Instead, her paws eventually sank into the leaf-logged gutter just like Sloane's feet.

It was too much weight for the gutter.

The ancient, rusty bolts holding it in place screeched in protest.

And then, one by one, they started popping out of their sockets.

"Amelia!" Sloane screamed. She clung more tightly to the vent pipe as the gutter pushed away from the house. The metal squealed as it twisted away, leaving her feet and Chiave's paws dangling in the air. The bloodhound threw back her head and howled.

As if that wasn't bad enough, Sloane realized that they were both still slooooooowly slipping downward.

The vent pipe was buckling under the weight of Sloane's grasp.

"Oh no. Oh no—oh no—oh no!" Sloane hugged Chiave more tightly as the dog howled again. "Amelia! Help!"

Down below, a crowd was gathering. Amanda Miller was on her phone, hopefully calling for a rescue squad. Aiden and Ashley were both attempting to climb the columns lifting up the porch roof in an attempt to get to Sloane.

There was no way anyone was going to get to Sloane in time.

The vent pipe twisted, dipping Sloane and Chiave farther over the side. By now, Sloane's legs were entirely over the edge of the roof. Feet swinging about, trying to get a foothold on *something* that might keep her from falling.

"Hold on, Sloane!" the Judge called up to her. Unhelpfully, he didn't tell her how or what to hold on to.

The vent pipe snapped.

Sloane felt the ancient, brittle metal give. Fear shot through her as she slid downward. Her heart fluttered upward as though trying to escape, while her brain tried to figure out some way in which this would all be fine. She wasn't really falling.

Except that she was—

—and yet her brain was right. It was fine.

Because someone caught her.

18

A Surprising Turn of Events

"I've got you, Sloane," Sergeant Pepper gasped. "I've got you!" The gardener had managed to snag Sloane by the shirt. Sloane, in turn, still had Chiave by the doggy harness as the bloodhound dangled over the edge of the roof, unhappy and howling louder than ever.

Behind Sergeant Pepper, Amelia gripped the gardener by the ankles. Straining with all her might, teeth clenched with effort, Amelia slowly tugged Sergeant Pepper backward. Inch by painful inch, they climbed back up the roof's slope. Once Sergeant Pepper was able to wiggle her way into the attic, both she and Amelia hauled Sloane inward too. Chiave came in last of all, whimpering and terrified.

"You!" Sloane staggered backward, away from the gardener. "You kidnapped Chiave! And Mr. Lindsay! *And* shut me and Amelia into that old bootleggers' room! *And* threatened us! Why did you save me now?"

"I did no such thing!" Sergeant Pepper exclaimed. Before guiltily adding, "I mean, not *exactly*, anyway. Not all of it."

Before she could explain any further, Amelia's family arrived to the rescue. Aiden and Ashley burst in through the window, having successfully scaled the outside of the house. A terrifying chopping sound ripped through the attic, causing leaves and sawdust to fly everywhere. A moment later, Amanda Miller appeared through the remains of the fallen tree. She was wielding a chain saw with the Judge, Shakespeare Wikander, and Chef Zahra following at a safe distance.

After that, there was a lot of exclaiming, even more barking, and lots of sawdust drifting through the air, causing everyone to cough and sputter. Eventually, they all agreed that there were much better places to be than this attic, and they all trooped quickly downstairs to the portrait gallery. The Judge ushered all the remaining gardeners out of the room, while Shakespeare Wikander hurried into the entry hall to oversee the cleanup of the broken vase and the reviving of Mr. Boening-Bradley after he fainted in the middle of the riot upstairs.

Having cleared out the room, the Judge returned to question Sergeant Pepper.

"Give me one good reason why I shouldn't have you arrested right now," he boomed in his courtroom voice. It echoed through the portrait gallery, causing everyone else to wince.

"Because I haven't done anything illegal!" Sergeant Pepper cried, gripping the armrests of her chair indignantly. "Mr. Lindsay is fine! I sent him out to a lovely spa in Wauseon for a countryside retreat. He's getting hot stone massages for his injured back and a chance to rest without all the worry of the peony competition."

Amelia spoke up. "Is this spa in an old mansion where they use fish to remove the dead skin from your feet?"

Startled, Sergeant Pepper said, "Why, yes. Have you heard of it?"

Both Sloane and Amelia had. In fact, they had recently broken into the manager's office and discovered a secret compartment hidden inside.

(Which had actually resulted in them both recently receiving restraining orders. That meant neither one of them were allowed inside the Hoäl house again.)

"And Chiave?" Sloane demanded suspiciously. "Why did you have her?"

"I actually promised Mr. Lindsay that I'd take good care of her while he was away." Sergeant Pepper scrunched up her shoulders sheepishly. "Then, Chiave went and got away from me last night because of the storm."

"Why not just tell us?" Chef Zahra asked. "If you were helping Mr. Lindsay out, why not just say so?"

Sergeant Pepper didn't answer right away, giving Amelia a chance to take charge of the interrogation.

"Because you weren't *really* helping Mr. Lindsay, were you?" she guessed. "You were getting him out of the way so you could look for Ma Yaklin's money!"

The expression on Sergeant Pepper's face confirmed Amelia's accusation. Realizing she'd already given herself away, Sergeant Pepper shrugged and gave away even more. "Only it isn't Ma Yaklin's money anymore. It's *my* money. Jacqueline Yaklin was my great-aunt. My mom was her sister."

Everyone gasped in shock at that. Amelia mentally cursed herself for not turning on her camera. What a great moment that would have been in their next YouTube video.

"And technically, Chiave is mine, too. Or, at least, half mine.

Since Eli was her something-great-grandparent, along with Anderson Lindsay's dog, Elizabeth."

"But why now?" Amanda Miller asked, turning from the dramatic to the practical. "Why not before the competition? Or after?"

Sloane cut in, pretty sure she had the answer. "Because she only recently figured out how to find the money! Using Chiave's super-sniffer!"

Everyone swung their attention from Sloane to Sergeant Pepper to confirm if this was true. Ma Yaklin and Eli watched it all, silent as ever.

Sighing, Sergeant Pepper admitted, "She's right. I realized that Great-Aunt Jacqueline must have buried her money out in the woods. That was why she was running through them the night she was arrested. The trouble was, without Eli's ability to sniff out money, my great-aunt had no idea where she'd buried the box holding all that cash."

"Sergeant Pepper was training Chiave to sniff out money too," Sloane explained. Turning to the gardener, she continued, "But it wasn't working, was it?"

"No. She just kept bringing back *my* wallet." Sergeant Pepper scratched the scruff of Chiave's neck. "But I thought that if I got her out in the woods without my wallet around, she'd finally sniff out Great-Aunt Jacqueline's money instead. It might have worked, too . . . except the storm did more damage last night than I thought it would. Suddenly, instead of having an entire day to go through the woods on my own, Tangle Glen was overrun with even more people! I needed Sloane and Amelia to stay out of my way until the competition was over.

"Great-Aunt Jaqueline had that painting of herself and Eli put together for my grandma, just in case anything happened to her. See, my grandma was a lot younger than Jacqeline and just a kid when Jacqueline was arrested. With the painting, at least some-one in the family would get the money she'd worked so hard for. However, by the time my grandma could talk to her sister, Great-Aunt Jaqueline was already sick. She kept saying the painting was the key, but not how to use that key. Then Anderson Lindsay bought Tangle Glen, and it didn't matter if the painting *was* the key. My family didn't have it anyhow. And since my grandma thought the painting was useless without Eli, she never bothered trying to get it from Anderson Lindsay."

"Only, Eli wasn't really lost," Amelia said. "Mr. Lindsay's grand-father had kidnapped him and then renamed him Chiave so no one would realize who his new bloodhound really was."

Chef Zahra spoke up. "Then Mr. Lindsay's family must have at least suspected that Eli was the key to finding Ma Yaklin's money, since '*chiave*' is Italian for 'key.'"

It was Sloane's turn to take over. "But at that time, everyone thought the money must be hidden somewhere in the mansion. Mr. Lindsay himself said it was, when we first met him. The Lindsay family had the right 'key' but the wrong 'lock.'"

"It took me forever to realize that the money couldn't be in the house," Sergeant Pepper said miserably. "And once I realized it had to be in the woods, I didn't know how I would ever find it. For the longest time, I tried taking a metal detector over the entire woods, but I never found anything more interesting than old pop cans and coins. I thought if Eli was the key to finding the money, then that

key was long lost. Until it finally clicked with me how Ma is showing off Eli's sniffing abilities in the painting. Sniffing for money is
something bloodhounds can be trained to do."

She'd already decided to take advantage of Mr. Lindsay's
injured back and send him off to the spa for the weekend so she
could "borrow" Chiave without anyone realizing what she was up
to. Then the storm hit, the tree fell onto the house, and suddenly
there were even more people wandering around Tangle Glen, and
Sergeant Pepper couldn't easily take Chiave out into the woods to
sniff for the money. So, she kidnapped Chiave to keep Sloane and
Amelia from using her sniffer and tried to scare them off. Her plan
had been to take Chiave out into the woods while the awards ceremony was going on. Then, she'd return the bloodhound to Tangle
Glen and run off with the money.

"What I don't understand," Amelia said, "is why you were wet
last night and Chiave was dry. Sloane and I thought it couldn't have
been you for that reason. We thought that whoever had dognapped
her wouldn't be out in the storm without her."

"She got away from me," Sergeant Pepper explained, taking
the rose out of her hair and plucking at the petals one by one. "I
thought she must have run back to Mr. Lindsay's home at the carriage house. I never dreamed that she'd run to the two of you."

"And the meat thermometer you used to pin the note to the
cushion?" Sloane asked. "Were you trying to frame Chef Zahra?"

"No!" Sergeant Pepper looked shocked as Chef Zahra crossed
her arms and said, "So *that's* what happened to it! I wondered."

"I'm telling you, that tree falling on the house ruined everything. Well, that and Sloane and Amelia poking their noses around.

I needed to get Chiave out of the portrait gallery and try to scare off the two girl detectives here. I didn't have much time, since I knew the tree removers and the building inspectors would be here early. I grabbed the meat thermometer on my way through the kitchen because it happened to be lying on the counter, that's all." Sergeant Pepper sighed, shoulders slumping. "I didn't even want it for myself. I wanted to open up the Jacqueline Yaklin Animal Shelter in my great-aunt's honor. My dad said it always really bugged his mom that her sister was only remembered for the bad things she did and how she died. It was always his dream to set up an animal shelter so people would remember how good she was to Eli. He died last year, and I thought making his dream happen would be one way I could still feel like he was around."

Sergeant Pepper looked so miserable that both Sloane and Amelia felt sorry for her. This was easier for Sloane to feel because she was very grateful to the gardener for saving her life. Amelia, on the other hand, was quite miffed that Sergeant Pepper hadn't been trying to kidnap or murder them and has simply wanted to get to the missing money first. Having a competitor was a lot less dramatic than having a kidnapper or murderer after you. (Obviously, Amelia didn't want to be either kidnapped or murdered. That would be terrible, and also terribly boring, as she'd never get to do anything ever again. However, she'd recently found out that being *almost* kidnapped or murdered was actually quite lovely, in her opinion. It made you the center of attention, and there was nothing Amelia enjoyed more than that.)

"Money back in the 1920s and 1930s must smell different than it does today," Sergeant Pepper sighed regretfully as Chiave slurped her face. "Because I'm sure that Chiave really is the key to finding it. Or at least Eli was. Maybe he didn't pass his super-sniffer on to Chiave after all."

As Sergeant Pepper rubbed Chiave's neck and back, Sloane gazed up at the painting of Ma Yaklin and Eli. A slight smile played about the gangster's face. An I-have-a-secret smile. One eye almost seemed ready to wink as she held that pink peony for Eli to sniff.

"Oh!" Sloane gasped. "Oh—oh—*oh!* I think I just figured it out!"

Throwing open the gallery doors, she dashed out into the foyer. Shakespeare Wikander had swept up most of the damaged peonies and tossed them into a large metal garbage can. All around him, gardeners were weeping. Mr. Boening-Bradley lay on a velvet couch with one hand pressed against his forehead. Baker held his other hand and was patting it soothingly, while Kuneman offered him a glass of punch in a crystal cup.

"The horror . . . the horror . . ." Mr. Boening-Bradley whispered, unblinking eyes staring straight up at the chandelier. His long, bent legs looked more than ever like a praying mantis's.

A shocked, sad, despairing praying mantis.

Ignoring them all, Sloane grabbed the garbage can from Shakespeare Wikander and dumped it out all over the floor.

"What are you *doing*?" he wailed, clutching his broom and dustpan to his chest. "Now that has to be cleaned up all over again! And this time, you're doing it! Not me! I've just about had enough of Tangle Glen and peonies and competitions and everything!"

"Sure—sure," Sloane agreed, not really paying attention. She rifled through the damaged flowers, finally finding Chef Zahra's recreation of Ma Yaklin's prizewinning peony and snatching it up.

"My poor peony!" Chef Zahra wailed as she returned. At the sight of so much hard work gone to ruin, the chef squeezed her hands together in despair.

Forgetting his competitiveness, Shakespeare Wikander patted her on the shoulder and reminded her, "That was just for display. You still have a stem in the competition."

Ignoring them both, Sloane shoved the blossom under Chiave's nose. The dog snorted it enthusiastically, tail thumping so hard that Amelia had to jump out of the way. "Now, come on! Let's take her out into the woods!"

Forgetting all about the peony competition, everyone did as Sloane said. They all trooped out the gallery's back exit so none of the gardeners would see them leave. Then, out through the kitchen they went and to the edge of the woods. Sloane let Chiave get another good snorf of the peony, and then she unsnapped her leash.

"Go, girl! Go find it!"

Chiave bounded off through the woods, quickly followed by Sloane, Amelia, Sergeant Pepper, Shakespeare Wikander, Chef Zahra, and various Miller-Poes. (Though, admittedly, Sloane and Sergeant Pepper had to keep grabbing Amelia to keep her upright and moving forward every time she tripped over a vine or fallen log or lost her balance when ducking under tree branches. Or somehow ended up with a chipmunk in her hair.)

The bloodhound ran with the certainty of a creature born to do this. Deep, deep into the woods she went, the humans crashing after her. Finally, she stopped by an oak tree that looked very much like any other oak tree—except that something had recently been digging there.

"Oh!" Amelia jerked to a stop and clapped a hand against her forehead. "Chiave brought us here yesterday when we got lost!"

As Amelia spoke, Chiave woofed and dug with enthusiasm. Mud spattered behind her, causing the rest of the group to jump off to the side as they joined Sloane, Amelia, and Sergeant Pepper.

"We thought she'd just spotted another chipmunk." Amelia bent down to look into the muddy hole.

"Here, we brought shovels." Aiden and Ashley pushed their way to the front. Sloane pulled Chiave out of the hole, allowing Amelia's half-siblings to take over. Chiave went reluctantly, lured out only by the promise of more snorfs of Chef Zahra's now-very-wilted peony.

Aiden and Ashley dug quickly, because of course they turned it into a competition to see who could get there first. Amanda Miller and the Judge cheered them on approvingly, while Chef Zahra gave everyone the side-eye, clearly wondering what on earth she'd gotten herself involved in.

After several minutes, their shovels went *ker-CHUNK* at the exact same moment.

"I found it!" Ashley cried.

"No, I found it!" Aiden countered.

Amanda Miller shook her head in disappointment. "It's a tie, I'm afraid."

"Ah, yes." The Judge nodded gravely. "A tie. Also known as a 'losers' draw.'"

Aiden and Ashley regarded each other in horror.

Then Aiden said, "My dirt pile is bigger than your dirt pile."

"No it isn't!"

They both leaped out of the hole, and then the entire Miller-Poe family (except Amelia) forgot all about any missing money as they focused on measuring the two piles.

Sloane peered down at what they'd struck. "I think it's a granite slab."

She and Sergeant Pepper picked up Aiden and Ashley's shovels and used them to remove a bit more dirt from around the top. (Amelia offered to help, but everyone was too afraid of what might happen to take her up on it.) Eventually, they uncovered enough to find a thin line going all the way around the top.

"It's a lid, I think," Amelia said, leaning in to get a better look. "WHOA!"

Losing her footing, she slid down the side of the hole. Sloane and Sergeant Pepper tried to grab her while Chiave barked encouragement, but Amelia still smacked into the granite slab with a loud "OW!" *That* caused the Miller-Poes to stop bickering long enough to make sure that she was fine. Then they went right back to arguing again.

The impact of Amelia against the slab caused it to scoot just the slightest bit. Proving that Amelia was right: it was a lid.

With the tip of her shovel, Sloane hefted the granite slab up enough that Sergeant Pepper was able to wiggle her fingers underneath. Together, they lifted it up and to the side.

Revealing a box.

A box filled with stacks and stacks of old-fashioned-looking cash.

Amelia scooped one up and climbed to the top of Aiden's dirt pile (squashing it down and cutting off any more conflict over whose dirt pile was larger). "Sloane! Turn your camera on!"

Sloane did as her friend asked. With everyone's attention on Amelia, she made a dramatic declaration.

"It's Bootleggin' Ma Yaklin's lost millions! Returned to their rightful owner by Eli's descendant!"

Epilogue

Whether or not Sergeant Pepper was the rightful owner of the money was up for some debate. After all, the money had been found on Mr. Lindsay's property. However, when he returned from his spa day at the Hoäl house out in Wauseon with his skin gleaming, his muscles relaxed, and his back no longer aching, he was inclined to be generous.

"Eh, what do I need the money for?" he asked, kneeling down to embrace Chiave. He moved with far less pain than he had the day before, though he still looked every bit like a mushroom. Looking up at the mansion, he added, "Well, a new roof. That would be nice. You pay for that, and I won't fight you in court."

Sergeant Pepper was more than agreeable to those terms.

Both Chef Zahra and Shakespeare Wikander did quite well at the flower show. The chef won Best Breeding, while the front desk manager won Best Horticultural Technique. (Neither Sloane nor Amelia knew what that was, but Shakespeare Wikander seemed pleased.) They each received $25,000.

Kuneman won Most Elegant Petals, and Baker won Best Color. Each threw the other smug looks as she claimed her trophy, and each seemed convinced that she'd won the better award.

An elderly man no one had actually noticed won Best in Show. Neither Sloane nor Amelia could remember seeing him before. Amelia was convinced that he was actually a ghost.

"I bet he's been trapped in the attic with all of those cursed dolls," she told Sloane as they packed up to leave. "I bet that when the tree branch crashed into the attic roof, it freed his spirit."

Sloane had to admit that she didn't have a better explanation.

Contrary to Mr. Boening-Bradley's worries, all the snooty rich people actually declared this year's competition the best anyone could remember. Or at the very least, the most interesting and exciting. The competitors all unanimously agreed that they'd like next year's competition to take place at Tangle Glen again.

And they wanted Amelia, Sloane, and Shakespeare Wikander back as the entertainment.

Which made Mr. Boening-Bradley decide to step down from being the president of the Ohio Peony Enthusiasts Club.

That, in turn, made both Kuneman and Baker declare that they wanted to replace him.

An election would have to take place. Neither Sloane nor Amelia was sure that either Baker or Kuneman would survive the voting. Not given the way they both held their gardening trowels and glared at each other.

Someone was definitely getting turned into mulch.

Fortunately, that someone wouldn't be either Chef Zahra or Shakespeare Wikander, who were now friends again. They even helped convince the other peony competitors to give Sloane a start of all their flowers for her grannies' garden.

Still very disapproving of what her grannies had done, Sloane wasn't at all sure she wanted to give her grannies those starts . . . until she took a look at Grandma Millie Snyder's Instagram again and saw a picture of Mackenzie Snyder, looking insufferably smug. Below it, she'd typed: *Best granddaughter in the world! #solucky #bestgranddaughter #mygranddaughterisbetterthanyours #donthateme #soblessed #betterthanyou.*

And suddenly, Sloane understood exactly how her grannies had been feeling.

"Help me get these into the van, will you?" she said to Amelia. Together, they picked up the many buckets and stuffed them everywhere they could. On top of the luggage. Between the seats.

On top of various Miller-Poes.

Chef Zahra sent them off with an entire container of thank-you macarons.

Shakespeare Wikander did one last magic trick and produced two bouquets of peonies from up his sleeve.

Sergeant Pepper likewise offered them bouquets of roses, though she didn't pull hers from her sleeve.

Mr. Lindsay said they could stay at Tangle Glen anytime.

Chiave licked their faces and seemed to say the same.

And with that, they were off. Back to Wauseon again.

David Osburn was waiting on the front porch to greet his daughter when the Miller-Poe van screeched to a halt at the curb. There wasn't a single Seife in sight, just him with his hands in his pockets and a broad grin on his face.

That grin wobbled into astonishment when he saw the vases

of peonies they would have to deliver to Granny Kitty and Granny Pearl, but all of that would come later.

First, he wanted to just spend some quality time with his daughter.

"Do you have any idea how big that house is without you?" he asked sadly as they sat down outside at Red Rambler Coffee. David Osburn drank a black coffee, while Sloane had a frozen orange creamsicle Frappuccino. They sat together on one of the patio couches, feet up on a wicker coffee table.

"I dunno," Sloane admitted, chewing on her straw. "Big?"

"Very big." Her dad nodded. "Very, *very* big. It never seemed that way when your mom was alive and you were little. And it's even okay when it's just the two of us. But when it was me on my own . . . it was too big and too empty and too lonely."

"Oh." In her mind, Sloane pictured her dad wandering from room to room, all by himself.

In each one, he seemed smaller and sadder than he had in the one before.

"It's been a long time since I was by myself. I guess I don't really know how to do it anymore. So, I kept inviting Cynthia and her kids over. To fill up the house and make it feel like a home again. It made me feel like you were there, too." Her dad looked down at the paper sleeve around his coffee cup. "I guess that's pretty selfish of me, huh? To need to feel like you're around. I *want* you to go and have fun with your friends, Sloane. I really do. I just . . . don't know how to be only 'David Osburn.' I've been 'David Osburn, Sloane's Dad' for so long, and it's my favorite thing in the world to be."

"I'm glad Cynthia was there for you," Sloane assured him.

She really was, too. Cynthia and her kids had spent the whole weekend, having fun with Sloane's dad so he wouldn't be lonely. It was a nice thing to do, and exactly the sort of thing Maisy Osburn would have done.

Her dad wasn't replacing Sloane.

Because she could never be replaced. Any more than her mom could be.

He was just adding more people with whom to share his life.

Their lives. His and Sloane's.

Just because new people came into your life didn't mean you had to get rid of the old ones.

Caring about people, Sloane realized, was sort of like building a fire.

The more you added, the warmer and cozier you got.

Sometimes, though, it can take a little while to get that fire built. Sometimes, even if you want to build a fire, you don't always know how.

That was the trouble with the Miller-Poes. When they looked at Amelia, they wanted her to be part of their lives. And they wanted to be part of hers, too. However, now that they were no longer bossing her around, they just didn't know what to say or do.

If there was one thing a Miller-Poe hated, it was not knowing what to say or do.

It was like admitting that they weren't the best at something.

"Hey, our latest video is number three in Antigua!" Amelia crowed, checking her phone in the huge, sparkling kitchen of the Miller-Poes' huge, sparkling house right around the same time Sloane was slurping down her frozen orange creamsicle Frappuccino out at the Red Rambler.

"Don't worry!" The Judge clapped her on the shoulder. "I'm sure you'll be number one eventually!"

"Are you sure that's a real place?" Ashley smirked, doing stretches before her run.

"Sounds made up to me," Aiden agreed, downing a protein shake.

"Hush, both of you." Amanda Miller looked pained. Like they were all discussing farts in public.

"All right, that's it!" Amelia cried, jamming her fists onto her hips. "I'll have you know that being number one in Nauru *and* number two in Liechtenstein *and* number three in Antigua in even a category as small as 'Historical mystery YouTube videos made by kids' is pretty impressive! You all spent an entire weekend obsessed with peonies! Peonies! *They're just flowers!* Sloane and I have solved two mysteries that no one else could for years! As of a minute ago, we have 5,280 subscribers on YouTube, and people are contacting Osburn and Miller-Poe Detective Agency from all over to have us solve their mysteries for them. You should be proud of me! Not making fun of me or acting like it's something we shouldn't talk about!"

Panting, she finished her rant and looked around at her family.

Who all looked shockingly ashamed.

And uncertain.

Miller-Poes never looked uncertain.

In a small voice, Ashley admitted, "I'm sorry."

"Not as sorry as I am!" Aiden cut in swiftly. Realizing he was just acting competitively, he choked down a mouthful of protein shake and then admitted, "No really, Amelia, I'm sorry. I just . . . never know what to say. So I end up teasing you about it so I . . . don't feel stupid."

"I've never tried to make you feel stupid!" Amelia protested hotly.

"No, you haven't," the Judge agreed. "It's just that, for the longest time, we had to take care of you. Then, for a long time, we didn't, but we kept on doing it anyhow."

"We're trying to let you be you," her mom added. "But that doesn't mean we've figured out how to be us around you yet."

"How about just saying, 'That's great, Amelia!'" Amelia suggested, arms crossed.

The Miller-Poes all looked at each other uncertainly. Then, they shocked Amelia by enveloping her in a hug and crying, "That's great, Amelia!"

(They shocked her less when they all started to argue about who had said it best.)

"Do you still feel cursed?" Amelia asked Sloane the next day as they helped Granny Kitty and Granny Pearl plant the starts of their new peony bushes in their garden. Millie Snyder and her granddaughter, Mackenzie, watched sourly from a nearby deck.

"Oh, definitely." Sloane nodded her head. But then she grinned. "But you know, Amelia, when you have someone to be cursed with, being cursed isn't such a bad thing."

Afterword

Tangle Glen is not a real place in Toledo, Ohio. However, anyone who is familiar with the city will recognize it as looking very similar to Wildwood Manor. Once a mansion owned by the Secor family, it's now one of the city's most popular parks. However, it doesn't sit anywhere near the Maumee River. Instead, that inspiration came from the Linck Inn building on River Road by the river—it has a smuggling tunnel used by bootleggers in the 1920s and '30s.

Like Tangle Glen, neither Ma Yaklin and her gang, the Jacks, nor Two Thumbs Lundquist and the Digits Gang were real either. However, their rivalry was based on two real Toledo gangsters: Jack Kennedy and Yonnie Licavoli. Much like Tangle Glen, Licavoli's house had a hidden room in the basement. Though he used it to hide himself from the police, rather than his smuggling from rival gangsters.

Bloodhounds really are super sniffers, but it's best to keep them away from peonies. The flowers are fine for sniffing but will make them sick if eaten. And with dogs, you just never know what they'll try to eat. (My sister once had a dog who ate printer cartridges, just like Bunny the librarian dog early in the book. Meiko was fine. But it was still a weird and upsetting thing to do.)

Anyone who was in the University of Toledo's English

department in the early part of this century will recognize many of the last names in this book. I stole those names shamelessly from my professors. Except for Ma Yaklin, who is named after my long-time friend, Sara Yaklin.

Eli is named after Eli Bishko of Eugene, Oregon, for placing the winning bid to name a character in my next book during the Kidlit Against Anti-AAPI Racism Fundraiser.

Finally, the characters of Kuneman and Baker were supposed to be throwaway characters that I added in to make my friends Lindsay Kuneman and Jillian Baker laugh. Sometimes people ask me how I name my characters, and there's the answer: I steal them from anyone I can!

Acknowledgments

Thank you so much to my ever-amazing editor, Kate Prosswimmer, and my equally amazing agent, Hilary Harwell of KT Literary. Additional thanks to Kate's assistant, Nicole Fiorica, and copyeditor, Brenna Franzitta. Final thanks to the spectacularly talented Flavia Sorrentino, who is responsible for the artwork on both this book and *Tangled Up in Luck*.